THREAD THE BONE

M. R. PRITCHARD

Midnight Ledger
Publishing
14391 Spring Hill Dr. Suite 203
Spring Hill, FL 34609
MidnightLedger.com

Third Edition: June 2025
ISBNs: 978-1-957709-69-7 (paperback)

Printed in the United States of America

ABOUT THREAD THE BONE

The gods waged war, and she was the price.

Born in the image of the Creator, she was meant to be eternal—until the war took her life. In his grief, her father shattered her soul, scattering its pieces across time itself. Then, he trapped the children of every god who had a hand in her fate within an endless cycle of rebirth, including her forbidden love.

Now, they are bound to the loop, drawn to each other in every lifetime, only to forget before they can break free. Until one of them remembers.

As the memories unravel, so does the fragile balance of their world. If they can't escape the cycle and stop the Creator's descent into madness, time itself will collapse—taking their world with it.

Fate brought them together.
Love will set them free.
But only if they can remember before it's too late.

"*Thread the Bone by M.R. Pritchard demands your full attention. From the complex world building to the characters, your attention cannot wander for long or you will get lost. But keeping your attention won't be difficult; this book is rich in imagery and vibrant mythology. The story is definitely a bit slow, but enjoy taking your time. The story needs to settle, to age, to solidify into another layer of precious stone, like those in the tower (IYKYK), before it becomes precious.*

Thread the Bone is as beautiful as it is haunting, a must for lovers of Brandon Sanderson, T. Kingfisher and Hanna Whitten." -Reviewer

"*M. R. Pritchard does a great job in telling a dark fantasy novel, I enjoyed the idea of a higher power taking revenge on Old Gods for a lost loved one. This worked really well as a fantasy novel, the characters were what I expected and I enjoyed how good the characters were. It had a unique take on the genre and the fact that everyone had a dark side."* - Reviewer

"*Thread the Bone was such a great read. I really enjoyed how Pritchard was able to weave the story between the past and present and then crash it all together for an epic ending. The four female main characters were written so differently, and I really enjoyed how their differences became their strengths in the end. You could feel Cara's loneliness and Noomii's feeling of freedom. It was what each needed to develop into women who could save their world.*

Through Pritchard's world-building, I was able to envision the Land of Man and all the creatures and beings within that world. I loved the small nods to our under-

standing of the world and how the Land of Man was laid out and developed over time. One of my favorites places was Highrock. I also enjoyed the poems at the beginning of the chapters.

The characters seemed so separated from one another through out most of the book, and I was shocked to see how they culminated in the end. I could not anticipate where the story was going to go. I really appreciate a plot which I don't see coming. Overall, a really awesome read which I highly recommend!" -Reviewer

"She wasn't doing a thing,
I could see, except
standing there leaning
on the balcony railing,
holding the universe
together." —J. D. Salinger

Chapter 1

The Saltpan War

This Creator knew with all his being that he did not belong here. A Creator belongs in the peaks and valleys of the land, in a mausoleum laced with devotions, in a sky surrounded by a billion stars, in a mountain with a grand step-well. Not the battlefield. A golden arrow whizzed by his ear, nearly missing the tentacles that draped from his face, sinking into the warrior behind him. The warrior kept fighting but the Creator knew what damage was done. The warrior was his creation; he threaded those bones, that muscle, the agile brain. His creations were part of his soul, and he felt each injury as if it were his own. The Creator swung around, gripped the arrow, and withdrew it from the warrior's gut with his left hand, his right hand hovered over the wound. Blood poured out of the gash as the golden threads of life went to work. They stifled the blood flow, stitched layers of intestine, muscle, and skin. When the Creator was done, the warrior whispered a prayer of thanks and went on fighting the mindless war.

The Creator's stomach punched as more of his creations were injured. He searched the Saltpan for the worst of them. Running toward a fallen warrior, his daughter beat him there. She crouched, the threads of life flowed from her fingertips; stitching and fixing.

"You shouldn't be here," the Creator warned.

"But I am. I cannot let them die." She looked up, eyes meeting. "You know this."

The Creator nodded, knowing her draw to create life was just as great as his. She was his daughter after all. Cario was more of him than he'd like to admit. The Creator had molded her to be beautiful and strong. She was his greatest creation. Shaped from the finest grains of sand, he'd threaded her bones with a shard of his femur. Threaded her muscle with his own sinew. Her marrow was not far off from his.

Cario nodded, sweat dripping down the sides of her face. "I'm weak." Cario's stomach growled as her hands hovered over an injured woman, stitching together a nicked thighbone.

A loaf of hot bread rolled across the dusty ground. The Creator saw an old woman weaving between the warriors, her figure wavering and transparent. Meddling Celestials.

The Creator kicked the bread. "Steele yourself against the distractions. You will weaken but you will heal. The food will bind you to this land and you'll never leave."

There was a loud thud as a horse fell, crushing the woman riding it. The Creator turned quick and rushed to their side. Threads rose from his palms and moved the horse. He stitched both creatures together until they were well again.

"When will it end?" Cario asked as she helped the injured woman to her feet, the femur healed and the rip in her pants the only hint of injury. "Be well," Cario wished the woman. The woman smiled, reaching into her pocket and dropping a palmstone at Cario's feet in thanks before she rejoined the war. Cario bent, rubbed the smooth palmstone between her fingers, and tucked it in her pocket. She'd examine its layers later; after the war had ended and she had a moment's peace and wasn't under the prying eye of her father. She'd add it to her collection.

Commotion came from the edge of the Saltpan. Figures broke through the sparse forest. The demigods had arrived to join their respective parents in the fighting.

Cario's head turned in their direction.

"Leave them," the Creator warned his daughter. "Now is not the time for friends. They will not help you."

"The sons and daughters of the old Gods are not as terrible as you think," Cario muttered as she moved to another injured soul. "They could end this."

"You are better than them. I made you more than a God. More than a demigod." The Creator lifted the horse, and it galloped away as he began threading together the broken warrior left behind. Smashed bones and leaking blood went back into place. His tentacles wavered as he worked.

"They are not their parents," Cario said.

"Wait and see how they turn out," the Creator warned.

The ground shook with malice. Sand vibrated to the air, choking the warriors.

The Creator and Cario worked the battlefield in tandem, never choosing a side other than life. This is what their kind did; created life, healed and fixed the creatures of this land until they were ready to move on to the next.

Cario stood, quick on her feet as she headed toward a fallen warrior with a severed arm. She kicked at the rising sand of the Saltpan to clear a space for her to work. As she reached out with her palms, the golden threads began to work. Objects whistled through the air, disturbing her dress and hair. She didn't worry. She was a neutral party, never a target on these lands. The man's arm was stitched together, bone to bone, vessels to vessel, muscles and.... Something struck Cario in the chest. The last thing she heard was the cry of her father. She'd never heard the Creator make such a noise.

CHAPTER 2

HIGHROCK

*Mud and bone,
streets of white, buildings of gold.
Your best-dressed, your skin is cold.
Your first love, the Goldlands hold.*

Highrock was a narrow mountain with slick cliff borders; a needle that stood in the middle of the ocean at the edge of the world where the water halted for infinity, lapping against the cold dead of space.

Noomii traveled from the Darkmoors where the sun never breached the clouds, a land heavy with silt and smoke from the opulent fires of the Goldlands. Now she stood on the edge of The Land of Man, her feet sturdy on a rocking dock. She took a deep breath of the briny air and thought it wasn't much different from the taste of the icy chill at the peaks of the seven mountains. The mountain in the distance was definitely taller than any of the mountains she'd climbed.

She turned; there were six mountains now. No one cared about the mountains any longer, but the sea was different. The sea was reserved for the fishermen and the rich and those of the Creator's choosing. If she had been born into a higher caste she might have been baptized in the sea, she might have spent her summers playing in the sand and eating cold shrimp. But Noomii had been born in the muck and that had kept her from ascending. The greater the suffering the greater the peace, her mother had always said. No, she'd never been to the sea before which was why she couldn't take her eyes away from any of it. Sunlight sparkled off the small wave peaks. It was like a dream. The water was a clear blue, so unlike the muck of the Darkmoors.

"You're the one going to Highrock?" a helmsman asked as he approached Noomii, the thin weave of his clothing frayed and worn to the color of straw.

"Is it that obvious?" Noomii asked.

"There's a certain look about the ones who go to Highrock." He motioned for her to follow him with a wave of his hand. "We go by sailboat before the sea becomes angry with the changing of the guard."

Noomii skipped to keep up with the helmsman's quick stride. "The sea cares about that sort of thing?" she asked.

"It's not the sea," he said with a wink, "but the God of the sea. However, those who no longer believe in the Gods will tell you some nonsense about the pull of the moon and the tilt of the earth."

The helmsman led her to a small, sturdy sailboat. The wood was rubbed smooth and the sails weathered white. He took her bags and settled them before turning and offering his hand. His fingers were thick and rough; no doubt his palm would feel warm and firm beneath hers.

Noomii's eyes narrowed. "Do you know what I am?"

"Of course."

The helmsman didn't seem to care that she was a bastard

woman of the Darkmoors. Not even a man bred of her caste would offer a hand, and none had in her entire life. Instead of taking his offer, Noomii steadied herself using the dock post. She stepped onto the boat and wavered for a moment, adjusting to the motion of the wake.

The helmsman told her to sit as he unknotted the line and wound it in a neat coil. She watched his shoulders tense, thick with muscle earned from a lifetime on the water. He seated himself, took ahold of the oars, and paddled smoothly away from the docks. The more she watched him, the more she'd wished she'd taken his hand. But—no, she wouldn't give that burden to a stranger. Noomii shook the thought away and focused on the water.

"We don't get many sea days like this," the helmsman continued as they left the shore. "This might be the swiftest journey I've ever sailed to Highrock." He steered the boat without as much as a glance behind him.

"Do you go there often?"

"Often enough." He stretched his back as he settled the paddles then moved to release the sails. They caught the wind with a smooth jolt. Noomii gripped the sides of the boat to keep herself upright. "This is your first time visiting the sea?" he asked.

Noomii nodded, afraid to open her mouth from the way the rocking of the boat made her stomach pinch.

The helmsman chuckled as he worked and quit with his prying questions. They sailed away from the dock. Noomii turned to get a good look at the aged dock as it became nothing but a speck. She turned her attention back to the clear water, her fingers moving to touch it. Cool and thick, she'd never touched salt water before.

The boat was moving fast, faster than she'd ever moved in her entire life. The wind chapped her cheeks and blew her hair wildly. In the distance, the needle of the mountain was no bigger than Noomii's pinky finger. It grew larger and larger as her head tilted up millimeter by millimeter. Eventually, Noomii had to lean back to appreciate Highrock, though the early morning fog blocked her view of the peak. The water became choppy close to the mountain and Noomii gripped the slick sides of the boat to secure herself.

"We're here," the helmsman said. He grasped a foothold in the pillar and held the boat steady as the chop threatened to bash the hull. He looked at Noomii expectantly. "Now is your time, miss."

Noomii blinked, refocused. She had never been called miss before, it was always *girl* or *barmaid* or *whore*. "How do I get to the top?" she asked.

"I suppose you could fly if you had wings." He looked up. "It's too bad you hadn't been dropped from the heavens atop Highrock on the day you were born."

Noomii fidgeted with the strap of her bag. "What good would that have done?"

"You wouldn't have had to leave everything. You wouldn't have had to leave your life on The Land of Man behind." The helmsman had a solemn way about him, worse now that they'd reached their destination.

She wondered if he'd miss her even though they'd just met. Noomii knew better, no one missed her. She was sure not a soul would recognize that she'd left the Darkmoors.

"What makes you think I left anything behind?" Noomii asked. She didn't think she'd miss her life as a bastard. There had been more than enough years of ridicule on The Land of Man. There were plenty of nights she lay in bed wishing she'd been born a creature of the sea or a beast of the sky. If only life were as simple as eat or be eaten.

"Everyone who comes here has left something behind," the helmsman interrupted her thoughts.

"Not me." Noomii reached forward and ran her fingers across the rough mountain. "I have nothing left." The mountain was lined like the striations of a tree trunk. In the dull light it resembled varying shades of gray.

"Surely you have left behind someone you love?"

"No." Noomii shook her head. "The last person I loved was my mother and I left her in a shallow grave on the outskirts of the moors."

The helmsman folded his arms on the ends of his paddles and narrowed his eyes on her. His gaze was imploring, as though he didn't believe her.

"What?" she snapped.

"Well, at least you know the truth." His eyes traveled up the mountain. "At least now you know with absolute truth that there is a Watchtower at the edge of the world. For some it's worth knowing."

Noomii rubbed her fingertips over a strip of smooth stone that looked out of place. "Some believe there is no Watchtower here. Some think it's a charade; make believe tales to keep them in check."

"Some think the sky is blue because we live in the eye of a giant floating Celestial. Some think the mountains of the Land of Man are nothing more than piles of shit from a galactic moose. Now you might learn the truth." The helmsman pulled on the foothold, righting the boat from drifting away. "I cannot hold on forever. You must go sometime." He tilted his head in suggestion. "Sooner rather than later, please." The helmsman pointed to a rickety rope ladder layered in barnacles and lichen. "Or I could take you back."

It was all coming to a point and Noomii wondered if she'd made the wrong decision. "What if I need food?" Noomii was suddenly worried that she'd starve to death or run out of wood to burn during the winter cold. She'd felt the stabbing pangs of hunger for too long and her toes still ached from the chill of the Darkmoors.

"Send a pigeon to the coast." The helmsman pressed his lips in a tight line. "I'll bring you what you need."

"It doesn't look very safe."

"There is little safe about Highrock." He shrugged. "There

could be dragons on the edge of the world." He opened his palm to the endless sea.

"There are no dragons," Noomii replied sharply.

"You won't know until you climb." The helmsman tilted his chin toward the ladder.

Noomii was close enough to grasp the first rung. She shook it, testing its strength. The rope creaked and the wood clanged against sturdy rock. "Do you leave as soon as I start climbing?" she asked.

"I might. I am afraid of dragons." The helmsman smiled when Noomii turned and gave him a dirty look, which melted away as he held his hand to his chest and said, "On the occasion that you drop into the sea from exhaustion or doom or regret, I will wait here to collect you and return you from where you came."

That was a dire promise if she'd ever heard one. Noomii bent to collect her belongings. She'd been dreaming of this place since she was a child. She'd scaled all the mountain ranges on The Land of Man; a pull from her center drew her to them. This was her last.

"What's your name?" Noomii asked the helmsman before she rose.

He shook his head. "My name is not important."

Noomii had heard the phrase many times. In so many instances throughout her life it had been told to her, and she'd said it to others. The name of an untouchable was never important.

The helmsman stood and offered Noomii the support of his hand once again.

Ignoring him, Noomii gripped the lower rungs of the ladder and rose out of the boat, steeping her feet against the wide base of rock, slippery with algae and crusted with mussel shells. Then, like those before her, she climbed.

Highrock jutted more than four hundred and twenty-three meters into the air; for most the ascent led to exhaustion and possibly death. It was not a modest climb, but Noomii was used to scaling tall mountains and breathing thin air. She'd climbed high mountains of ice with two picks in hand, boot spikes, and no tethering ropes. Climbing the rope ladder was different though. The length between her grip and feet bowed with tension then slack as she climbed each rung, making it difficult to land her feet soundly. Still, she climbed, and as she climbed the low clouds thinned and she began to notice that Highrock was not simply shades of gray stone, but slivered rings of a rainbow; colors of rock she'd only read about, some she'd never seen before in her life.

Noomii didn't have time to inspect each ring of color if she wanted to breach the peak in the daylight. She climbed as her arms and legs ached. The bags on her back became heavier and heavier and sweat dripped down the sides of her face and neck. The hollow clanks of the sailboat rocking against the mountain grew fainter and fainter until, finally, the peak was near.

Noomii gripped rock edge, her fingertips numb and sore from the rough rope ladder. With one last burst of energy, she pulled herself over the top and collapsed on the hard ground. Rolling to her side, she got her first look at her new home. The summit was the size of a pasture and concave in shape. The center held a small pool of clear water, surrounded by vibrant green grass speckled with clusters of boulders. There was a small patch of seagrass and a lighthouse seated on the far side. The house was secured in crags and nooks; the basement carved into the pillar, the westerly wall shielded by pillars nearly two meters thick making the house look like it was birthed of the rock. The Northern edge was an even taller peak that reached into the sky like a knife. Highrock left just enough land for a man to ward off madness by stretching their legs a short bit each day.

The door opened. Caught in the wind, it slapped against the side of the lighthouse. An old woman stepped out. Her hair was long and windblown, bleached by the sun, her clothing coarsened by the harsh sea air.

"It took you long enough," the old woman said as she swung the door closed and walked closer. There was a spring in her step reserved for those much younger. "I've been waiting for half the day." Her face was burnished brown and deeply wrinkled.

"Apologies." Noomii rolled to her feet, leaving her bags on the ground. "I was climbing." She was still out of breath and standing took effort.

The old woman looked over the edge. "The wind was weak today." She licked a finger and held it up. "When I climbed the ladder, the gusts were forty miles per hour. I nearly lost my fingertips trying to hold on." She turned to face Noomii and muttered something that sounded like, "Despina." She held out a hand in greeting. It wasn't an offer like the helmsman, but a formal expectation for the changing of the Watchtower servant.

"Noomii." The woman's hand was warm and calloused. "How long have you been here?" Noomii asked.

Despina waved the question away. "One cannot set their thumb on the tincture of time when living on the summit of Highrock. But now that you're here my time is done."

"Just like that?" Noomii asked. "You just leave?"

Despina tapped her chin. "Oh," she raised a finger, "I nearly forgot." She walked toward the edge and leaned over the side. "Before I can leave, you must mark your beginning." She pulled a mirror from her pocket and tilted it until she recognized a rod sticking from the stone. "There it is." She motioned. "My beginning."

Despina tilted the mirror so Noomii could see. There were more rods pegged into the rock.

"There have been many," Noomii said.

"Of course there have been many. The Creator has chosen a soul to man the tower since the beginning. Now, before I can go, you must denote your arrival." Despina handed her a steel peg and hammer. "Go. Go." She waved impatiently.

Noomii paused to think. "I must stake this below yours."

"Yes," she answered.

"How will I do that?"

"Jump into the sea and climb back up or scale the cliff side like a mountain goat. I'm sure you could figure out a way and not die in the process. The rest of us have."

"How did you do it?" Noomii asked.

"I'll tell you after."

Perhaps, it was a test? Noomii took the steel peg and hammer from Despina and tucked them in her pocket. She went to her bag and pulled out the climbing items she'd brought with her; a few clips and strong ropes were enough to get her to the base quickly.

Noomii first secured her rope around the tethering pin that held the rope ladder in place, then she secured the rope around her waist, tied her knots, and set her locking carabiners. She walked to the edge where the ladder hung, dropped to her knees and twisted, backing up slowly and lowering her body to the ground. She scooted backward until her feet touched air and her thighs rubbed against the cable secured in stone. She gripped the rough rope, her hands sore from the climb up, and took a deep breath. Making her way down was easier this way. Noomii pushed off the rock and dropped to the whisper slick sound of line sliding through the pulley. She slowed herself, her feet firmly pressed on the side of the mountain, taking quick steps before pushing away and dropping again. She was down in a quarter of the time that it took to climb.

The helmsman was sitting patiently in his boat. Watching.

"Why didn't you tell me?" Noomii asked. She settled her ropes before removing the peg and hammer from her pocket.

The helmsman looked amused. "It is not my place."

Noomii glanced over the rock, unsure of where to place her peg.

"At the water line," the helmsman said. "Your time starts where the water stops."

Noomii tipped to the side and positioned her peg with the cold ocean water lapping at her fingertips. Cool and smooth, there was something about the water here;; not quite translucent but not quite murky. She tapped the peg into the rock, hitting it harder and harder until it stuck.

"There." She stood with her hands on her hips as she counted the other pegs. Hers made twenty-eight.

The helmsman nodded as Noomii glanced at him one last time before gripping the ladder and climbing up. Noomii was much slower at the climb this time. Strangely, she had the feeling that she'd completed this climb before. Not the few minutes prior in which Despina sent her back down. But previous to that. In some other time in her life. The way the salt spray caressed her cheek, the way the heavy ropes thwacked against Highrock, the way the setting suns scorched her back. Noomii was sure that she'd been here before. When she reached the peak the suns were ready to set over the flat edge of the earth.

Despina was gazing toward the edge. "This will be my last sunset in this place," she said as she turned to face Noomii. "It took you long enough."

Noomii crawled to her feet. She rubbed her hands and stretched her back as she stood. "You said you would tell me how you did it." She rolled her shoulders to work out the sore muscles of her arms.

"I tapped my peg before I climbed the ladder to take the place of the elder before me." Despina flicked Noomii on the forehead as she walked by, headed for the opposite drop-off.

Noomii scrunched her face, rubbed the sore spot on her head and leaned away. "Will you tell me about the striations before you go? It doesn't look like normal rock to me."

"What do you know about rock, girl?" Despina asked.

"Only what I've taught myself. Only what I've seen on the seven peaks of the Land of Man. Where to stick a spike and what stone crumbles easier than others." Noomii straightened her back proudly. "I've climbed them all."

"So you've seen amazonite, apache tears, malachite, black moonstone, dolomite, gneiss, and the lore of their presence?"

Noomii shook her head.

"Before I arrived I had memorized every one of them. I could identify the stone with one glance." Despina reached into her pocket and pulled out the mirror. She extended the silver telescoping wand and held it over the side. "Layers of eternal stone form an archive of the atmosphere, dust and solids. We measure time by counting the striations and each band tells a story." She pointed to the image in the mirror. "The greenstone is from the iron age, the white from the long winter that lasted five years, the wheat-colored quartz from the decade of drought." Despina skipped over a light purple band. "There's the clear quartz from the floods after the ice caps melted. Ruby fuschite from the pretty princess who escaped to the moon for peace and quiet."

"What about the black?" Noomii leaned forward, her toes dangerously close to the edge.

"Bloodstone. From the dark ages. Plagues and death ruled the lands. If you get close enough you can see the blood mottled throughout." She snapped the mirror closed and tucked it in her pocket. "If you're lucky, you'll be here when the black line comes about again. Away from the death and despair on land." Despina sounded detached from it all.

"What about the purple band?" Noomii asked. "You missed that one." The thin purple band was sandwiched between the bloodstone and white moonstone. Barely visible.

Despina waved her hand. "Amethyst. No one knows." She began walking away. "Whatever it was. The Land of Man has never endured a span of time like it again. It was so long ago and the language of the books were so ancient that I'm sure it was interpreted incorrectly." Despina had walked to the opposite side of the mountain where the blue sky faded to gray and orbiting planets could be seen in the distance.

"I wouldn't focus on the amethyst, there are much more interesting bands of history wrapped around Highrock. There is the band of petrified wood from when the volcanoes erupted and smothered the forests. After that came the band of orthoclase, the books say it is formed from the desiccated skin of man. There were so many deaths after the ash settled that they did not decompose." She pointed across the sea to the edge of land. "If man digs deep enough he'll find a layer of bodies underneath the soil with skin holding in color just the same as when they were alive." She moved away from the edge. "There is the band of yellow feather jasper, from when the flying creatures owned the skies. White moonstone from the years after the ash settled and killed the forests and the men; there was no light then. The soil wasted to taupe under the filtered light of the moon. Do you remember the story of the moonstone?"

Noomii shook her head.

"Ah, one of the most tragic eras. The goddess of the moon and the son of the sea had fallen in love. The Creator, of course, forbade this. His daughter did not belong with a minor God's son," Despina scoffed. "After the Moon Goddess burned the Creators lands, she was banished to the night sky and he was banished to the depths of the sea."

Noomii had heard stories about Highrock and history but none in this detail.

"If you see the ocean jasper, sound the alarm." Despina sounded serious.

"What is ocean jasper?"

Despina sighed. "A green band with eyes of radial quartz and feldspar crystals. When the band of ocean jasper appears, the creatures of the sea have fled for land, watchdogs for the god of the ocean, given eyes to spy on The Land of Man, searching for his goddess." Despina shook her finger. "Nothing good becomes of the years when the gods leave their realms to spy. Chaos always ensues."

"If there's chaos, wars, or another band of black, what do I do?" Noomii knew The Land of Man was changing. She'd spent many days fully convinced that hell was empty and all the devils had swarmed the land. That was why she took to the mountains. Devils didn't climb snowy peaks, or so she'd heard.

"Highrock is a needle that stitches together time. A sacred land of the Creator. You will always be safe here." Despina tipped her head and her wrinkled face wrinkled further. "You took your oath before arriving. You should know this."

"Yes," Noomii nodded, "Yes, I know. It was just so much information. I wanted to be sure."

"Highrock will only grow taller with each band, with each minute that passes. One day it may even scrape a chasm in the moon. One day it may even cleave the moon in half." Despina turned in a slow circle as she gazed up at the sky. "Oh what I would give to see the Moon Goddess pay her respects to the one who chops her moon in two. That will be the day." She turned to look at Noomii, her eyes wide with wonder. "Stranger things have happened."

"What about out there?" Noomii pointed at the abyss of space in the distance. It was unnerving to see it this close. The flatness pressed against space at a ninety-degree angle. It seemed unnatural. It seemed... unfinished.

Despina slapped Noomii's hand down. "There are many who will never see the edge of the earth. Some still think this planet is round. Could you imagine, walking forever in a circle? There is an edge to everything, where the land meets the ocean, where the ocean meets the land, and where the ocean meets the abyss of space."

"What if the ocean spills over?" It had always been a fear of Noomii's. Irrational, her mother had told her. But still, it was there. "What will become of us if we spill over into space?"

"Were you raised as a wild thing, girl, with not a speck of faith in your bones?" Despina's eyes narrowed. "Let the Creator worry about the ocean spilling over. You man the Watchtower. You survey the bands. You sound the alarm if a band of ocean jasper begins forming. You sound the alarm if you recognize a band of lapis lazuli. You sound the alarm if you notice kambamba jasper. You sound the alarm if you notice a boat in the ocean headed toward the edge. You sound the alarm if the waves reach the top of Highrock."

"What if I see something out there?" Noomii pointed to the space beyond the edge where planets were collecting in nocturnal orbit.

"At times you may see the Celestials dance. You may see their fireworks and sparkling dust clouds. You may look upon them in wonder, but take heed, the Celestials will not breach the sea. They are watchers, guiders, that's it." Despina narrowed her eyes on Noomii. "We pledge our lives to the Watchtower. We may be bastards or spinster or untouched, but we were chosen by the Creator for a reason."

"I'm still not convinced that the best way to help the Land of Man is sitting in a tower at the edge of the world." Noomii coiled her climbing ropes, crouched at her bag and tucked them away.

"You want to help?" Despina's face was smooth with shock. "Is that the lie you tell yourself?" She paused to chuckle knowingly. "We all told it. Funny thing is, a bastard doesn't want to help. A bastard wants to watch everything burn in payment for the years of torment. But here we are, for whatever reason. Escape, I think. That's what I've concluded after all these years. I didn't want to burn them by my own hand, I wanted to escape them. We all have our reasons. Maybe you are here for you, not them."

Noomii cleared her throat and her cheeks pinked. "I told them that I wanted to help people. I wanted to go to the tower and keep my fellow man safe."

"You came here to escape The Land of Man." Despina looked Noomii up and down. "Just like the rest of us. Being a bastard isn't the worst of it. They'd never allow someone bred of prestige and legitimacy up here. It's not so bad being like us." Despina made eye contact for the first time. "Something tells me you're feeling the same." She spread her arm wide. Highrock was scenic and grand

and she felt a tiny bit sad for the people back the Land of Man who would never see this. "We get to begin and end our days with this. Not the smog and high rises of the cities that have taken over every speck of land. I bet the Goldland buildings are so tall that you can't see the suns anymore."

Noomii looked away as she nodded. It had been that way since before she was born.

"Bah." Despina waved her hand in disgust. "Don't waste your thoughts on them. If they had treated you differently, you'd never be here."

Noomii knew that Despina was right, but it didn't erase the years of ridicule as a child, it didn't remove the scarlet letter from her sleeve when she grew older, it didn't take back the years of working in bars and cleaning the homes of the rich only to know she'd never have better.

"What about the amethyst?" Noomii pressed. "I should know."

"It is never mentioned in the scrolls." Despina walked toward the edge. "You can look yourself. You'll have plenty of time."

"I suppose I will," Noomii murmured.

Despina pointed in the distance. "There's your house." She pointed across the sea. "There's the edge of the earth." She lowered her arm. "Read the books and the diaries of past Watchtower servants and the scrolls of time."

"You're not going to show me?" Noomii asked.

"You'd be bored to tears all your years up here if I spoil the secrets on your first day." Despina rubbed her hands together as if she were wiping away dirt. She passed Noomii the mirror from her pocket then nodded, sharp and tight, like she'd made up her mind about something. "Good luck," she waved at Noomii as she moved toward the edge. But Despina didn't lower herself down to the rope. Instead, she ran and leaped off the side of Highrock. "Until we meet again in another lifetime," she shouted as she fell.

Chapter 3

Highmount

Cara DiCara stood on the cliff edge of Highmount. Thin mountain air whipped her hair loose from its tight knot. In the distance she could see the peak of High-rock, the flat motion of the sea, the darkness that drew her gaze. Goldland born were already elevated, they would never think to leave the glistening gates. But here she was, halfway to her final destination.

"You are the one going to Highmount?" a man asked. His clothing was thick and padded, his boots sturdy and wide, a hat tied under his chin to prevent the mountain winds from stealing it away.

"How did you know?" Cara asked as she bent to lift her suitcase.

"I can take that for you," the man motioned to the small wooden cart behind him. "The ones who come to Highmount have a certain look about him." He motioned to the sea in the far distance. "Usually it's the view. Most can't appreciate the cold abyss of space. It makes them feel things."

"I have perfect vision, even better in the full sun. Can see a beetle digging in the mud of the Darkmoors from the edge of the Goldland gates," she replied proudly.

Cara set the bag inside the cart and thanked him, noticing the wood was rough and pockmarked.

"From the ice," the cartman said. "Ice gets into the grain and splits the wood." He moved, lifting the arms of the cart and placing the curved handles into leather pockets on each side of his hips.

"You've no mule to drag the cart?" Cara asked as she rubbed heat into her hands.

"Had a mule once, but the Divine Arrow decided I was better off without." His boots dug into loose stone. "Sent a thunderbolt from the clouds and struck it dead." He stepped forward. "We must go before the Arrow becomes agitated with the changing of the guard and sends the night before it is due."

Cara fell in step with the man, following the rugged path and steep incline. "Does the Arrow care about the changing of the guard?"

"Some say," his voice was rough. "Some used to demand this trek to begin at the first spec of dawn, before the Arrow was awake. Shifting day to night is easy magic, made easier by the confusing haze of dusk."

"I climbed as fast as I could." Cara looked away as she walked. She was embarrassed. She wasn't bred for a lifetime of hardship. A working class Goldland born with dreams, being selected to man the peak of Highmount was last on her list of things to do. Now her life was over. She would never walk the street of bone or shield her eyes against the glare of the seven suns shining on the golden towers. She would never play tag with the ghosts of the Goldlands, or run through their cold glimmers while chasing her friends.

Cara DiCara climbed with aching legs and lack of breath. She tilted her head only to be sure that she'd never reach the peak. Glancing at the cartman, she envied his steady breaths and stamina. He untucked a scarf from his padded coat to let the cool air touch his skin.

"One day you will climb the same as me," he promised Cara. "You will pray for the thin air and the cold wind. Nothing else will bring you the same freedom as climbing Highmount."

Cara gulped, her mind scrambling to think of a response, but she could only focus on putting one foot in front of the other. Each step was one further away from everything she'd ever known. It was further from her friends and her mother, both of whom she'd never see again. Tears surged behind her eyes, but Cara blinked them back. She didn't want this stranger to see her crying, and she didn't want to insult the Arrow for choosing her.

As they trekked, the stone beneath their feet changed from dull gray to earthy brown. Colors emerged; pinks, blues, mottled greens, stomped flat to form the trail.

"What is wrong with the dirt?" Cara asked, her words coming out as an ache on thready breath.

The cartman grumbled, "The layers of Highmount hold memories. A history, if you look close enough."

Cara bent to pick up a piece of sparkling stone and held it to the sun. Recognizing the gemstone, she shoved her hand in front of the cartman's face. "This is ocean jasper!" She retracted her arm to inspect the stone again. "My mother had a promise-ring of ocean jasper." Weighing the gem in the palm of her hand she said, "This could buy my freedom back to the Goldlands. I could pay someone else to take my place on top of this rock." She paused for a moment, her eyes searching the crumbling path. "If only I could find a big chunk of rainbow moonstone, I'd be set for life."

"One would need more than a palmstone to fill that wish. And not much escapes the mirrors of the Goldlands." The cartman reached down to his sides and gripped the wooden handles of his cart. "This is the steepest part." He nodded to the road ahead.

Cara tucked the speck of ocean jasper in her pocket and trudged on. It *was* the steepest part and Cara's legs burned. She glanced at the cartman, feeling useless, but he seemed strong enough and never once asked for help. She could barely drag herself up let alone pull a cart that big. They rounded the peak and Cara's new home came into view. A portion of the peak was treed, not much bigger than the Goldland park she grew up playing in. There was a cabin and a cleared grassy area scattered with boulders and rocky paths. The caretaker's cabin was not much more than a two-story shack. Plank wood siding and warped pane windows gave way to a metal roof with thick vent pipes. The design was a stark contrast to the glittering towers of gold she'd grown up in.

The cartman headed for the door and tugged it open. He lifted two logs from near the walkway and brought them inside.

Cara followed, tugging at her clothes that were sticking to the sweat on her skin.

"You're warm now but the night will bring a chill to your bones." The cartman lit a fire in the stove then went outside only to return a few moments later with an armful of wood.

Cara watched him, wide-eyed, taking it all in, her heart beating rapidly. Her skin was now slick with fearsweat.

"Feed the fire." The cartman stacked the wood in an iron basket. "If it burns out, you'll be sorry."

Cara was staring, her mouth slightly open. She was not much more than a child and it showed; she was not ready for this.

The cartman was quick to walk out the door.

Cara followed him, her boot heels clicking hollow on the wooden floor. "Where are you going?"

"This is where I leave you." The cartman handed Cara her belongings. He picked up the handles of his cart. "Half the day has passed. I must make it down the mountain before nightfall."

"Wait." Cara took a few steps toward him. "Who… was here before me? Where did they go?"

He shrugged. "There is always a tower servant, they come and they go. Now, I must go before the night comes."

"I don't want to be here."

The cartman pressed his lips together in understanding. "There have been others before you who lacked excitement in their post."

"What if I just leave? There's not much keeping me here." She waved her hand toward the trail. "I could just try and find my way back. I don't need you."

The cartman placed his hand in the middle of his chest and said, "If you are lost, I will find you and return you to where you belong."

It was nearly the nicest thing a soul had ever said to her. Cara wanted to reach out to him, she wanted to grasp on to someone and not be left alone up here. But a Goldland born did not grip onto a cartman and beg him to stay. No, Cara still had her Goldland pride. "Won't you show me what to do? What did the others do here?"

"The Divine Arrow will show you what to do," the cartman said. "Put your faith in the Arrow. Light your flame when the time comes."

"Then I guess you should just leave." Cara tried to hide her anger.

He nodded before turning to the path.

Cara rubbed her arms as she watched him walk away, and when she could no longer see him, she turned her attention to the skyline. In one direction she could see the Watchtower at the edge of the world and beyond. There were faint glimmers as the Celestials began their nightly devotions. Most could barely see the edge and the lights, but Cara had the perfect perch and the night vision of a nocturnal raptor. The darkness enveloped her, the only light coming from the distance and the crackling fire in the hearth. As Cara bent and settled her knees on the rough ground, she waited for the moon to slip away from the clouds and hover overhead. Cara pulled the gemstone out of her pocket and held it to the moonlight so the radial quartz and feldspar crystals glittered becomingly.

The Goldlands glitter with the sins of the dead. That's what her mother always said. Ocean jasper was worth a highrise on the east bank with a sea-facing window so you would notice when the creatures of the sea came crawling back, spying with their crystal eyes. The gem would bring freedom but it would also bring chaos. Everyone would want a piece.

Cara shoved the gemstone in her pocket and stood. She shivered as the northwinds blew in. Turning away from the view, she headed for the steps to her new home. She swung the door closed to the house and fumbled searching for the lock but there was none. She doubted anyone would come up here but pushed a chair against the door just in case.

After adding a few logs to the fire, Cara lifted her suitcase from the floor and opened it on the small dining table. She set a few linens next to the sink, draped a blanket over the wooden rocking chair near the fire stove, and unwrapped a carving of the Divine Arrow and placed it on the windowsill over the sink. People of the Goldlands didn't follow a deity; gold ruled, gold was worshipped, but her mother thought the statue might bring her luck atop Highmount. She climbed the stairs, bringing the suitcase with her to inspect the second floor. There was a ladder that led to a small attic space with a tower. A simple loft with a bed and dresser, there was a desk that overlooked the balcony to the first floor and stacks of journals. Cara walked closer and picked one up, flipped it open to find pages and pages of handwritten stories. She set the journal down, her legs tired and eyes heavy. There wasn't anything else for her to do so she collapsed on the bed and fell asleep.

27

Chapter 4

Highrock

Noomii ran to the edge, dropped to her knees, gripped the side of the mountain and watched as Despina spread her arms wide like an eagle in flight. Her loose clothing billowed behind her, refusing gravity's pull in desperation. She hit the water below with a loud *crack*.

The helmsman heaved his boat away from the rock and rowed to where Despina had hit. The waves from her impact jostled his boat as he searched the water and dipped his paddle where some bubbles surfaced.

Noomii didn't wait to see if the helmsman found Despina. She stepped away from the cliffside, her gut feeling as if there were a load of rocks churning inside. She'd been warned about what years of solitude could do to a person and Noomii was certain she wouldn't choose the same ending as Despina. After all, Noomii had spent plenty of time alone climbing mountaintops, traveling to her mountaineering destinations. She'd been alone while cleaning the bar after last-call, washing the glasses slick with liquor and spit, going home to her one bedroom apartment, eating dinner at a corner table. Noomii shook her head and tried to ignore the fact that she'd spent much of her life alone. Manning

Highrock would be a piece of cake. At least there were no assholes to deal with up here.

Noomii collected her bags and headed for the house. She'd never had a full house to herself before with closets and a full mattress. She'd always lived in slums and ghettos, single-room coffins that she could barely stretch her arms out in, never able to upgrade to something more. Her mother could have written anyone's name down. No one had come forward. Noomii would prefer any name to the blank space that had dictated her life. She reached for the door and took in the peeling paint, wondering if the helmsman would bring her back a few buckets of stain to spruce up the place. She opened the door and stepped inside. The house was dark, the ceilings low with thick beams. There was simple wooden furniture and a loft for sleeping. Noomii set her bags down on the table and began unpacking. She put her clothes in the loft and hung her climbing gear near the door. She found her figurine of Highrock wrapped in brown paper and set it on the windowsill over the sink. Her mother had given it to her as a child and Noomii felt it was appropriate to bring Highrock to Highrock since her childhood consisted of tales and lore that rarely anyone believed anymore. These days they all believed the superstitions but not the faith. The gift from her mother would never find another home except in the trash.

Her first night at Highrock was uneventful. Noomii dusted and rearranged. She opened all the windows and let the salt-sea air bristle away what was left of Despina. She changed the sheets and oiled the cracked wood of the bedframe. She moved piles of books in the study and found hundreds of journals from past Watchtower servants. Noomii didn't take offense to the term; she'd been nothing more than a servant for all her life. At least here it was for a good cause. As she searched the drawers of the desk that was pushed against an alcove of windows, Noomii found pencils and old scraps of papers, bits of gemstones and a dusting of fine sand, and she also found a spyglass.

The Moon Goddess had blessed her with a full moon tonight. Noomii thanked her as she opened the window over the desk, climbed up on the desktop to sit and looked toward The Land of Man. She could see everything with a few twists of the spyglass; the Goldlands, the Darkmoors, the shadows of the Seven Peaks. She looked toward the beach and saw the Helmsman tie his boat to the docks before lifting a body wrapped in cloth. He'd found Despina's corpse after she jumped, just as he promised he would hers. The Helmsman had wrapped Despina in fine silk, celestial blue dotted with golden embroidered stars. As he walked across the docks, other men milled about, glancing at him uneasily. It wasn't until he reached the boardwalk that an elderly man acknowledged the Helmsman and dropped to a knee, bowing his head as the Helmsman passed with Despina's body. He continued on as Noomii dropped the spyglass in disappointment. So many had forgotten the old ways, they had forgotten the old Gods. There was a time when the changing of the Watchtower servant was an event to behold. People would line the streets to pay their respects. When her time was done she'd ask the helmsman to drop her body at the edge, by that time she was sure there would be no more believers left.

The wind was mild on the edge but the sea was not. Noomii had read that waves a hundred meters high or more slapped at the base of Highrock in winter, the old God of the sea was forever trying to topple it when he became bored.

Noomii walked to the edge and used the telescoping mirror to check the striations of rock. Nothing new had formed under her pin. Noomii read the diaries of previous servants and found that sometimes the rock stretched every day, sometimes not for years. And then, Noomii was unable to read the oldest diaries. The script became strange, there were odd dashes and dots of ink and there were words she did not know. After a while, Noomii gave up without learning as much as she'd hoped. She started a log of her own and so far, each entry began with "No difference in Highrock today." It was beginning to make her worry. Each day she checked and the rock never budged from the water line, her peg stuck out like a broken mop handle. Brazenly useless.

The helmsman would visit every few weeks with a bag of supplies; fresh food from the Land of Man and household items.

"Where are the pigeons?" Noomii asked.

"Pigeons?" The helmsman glanced at the peak.

"You said that I could send a pigeon if I needed something."

"You've no pigeons up there?" he asked.

Noomii shook her head. "I've been there for months and never have I seen one."

The helmsman scratched his chin. "I'll bring you more."

Two months later he arrived with a sack of supplies and a wooden cage of cooing birds. For the first time since Despina had launched herself into the sea, Noomii was not alone on the top of Highrock. She had a small flock of pigeons. She fed and watered them each day, she woke to the lull of their gentle cooing, and when she opened their cage to give them time to spread their dappled wings, they all flew away. Noomii watched them with the spyglass as they glided toward the Land of Man and settled on the docks to peck sea bugs.

The helmsman arrived not long after. "I received your pigeons but there were no notes."

"I didn't send them." Noomii waved in disappointment. "They escaped."

The helmsman frowned. "I'll bring more or maybe something else. Pigeons don't suit you. Perhaps a Tanager or a goose." He tapped his chin as he thought. "A magpie could work. Or an ibis. Or a hawk. Hm. I'll have to think on it," he said as he passed her a sack. "Be careful with that, it's filled with golden plums and spotted goose eggs."

Noomii palpated the sack. "Those foods are only for the Goldlands. You could go to jail for bringing them to me."

"Times are changing on the Land of Man." He sat and tested a knot, securing his sail before pushing away from the rocks.

Noomii climbed the rope ladder, doing her best not to jostle the pack too hard. She wondered what he meant. She went inside the house and set the pack down before heading to the study to get the spyglass. Noomii looked at The Land of Man. The Darkmoors were the same, shadows and grit. The Goldlands sparkled exceptionally. The people didn't seem much different at first glance. They went about their business; working, purchasing goods, chasing children.

Noomii left the house, extended her mirror over the ledge of Highrock and checked the striations. Nothing had changed. There was no colorful stone emerging for her to interpret. There were just her peg and the sea and more disappointment.

Noomii had an idea. The gemstones of the Watchtower weren't so different from the layers of rock that formed the Seven Peaks. She'd had her face sprayed with rock after an errant hack of the rock pick, she'd seen the secrets the slate held, fossils of creatures long dead and sparkling specs that looked like stars. Noomii collected a few items before descending the rope ladder.

The Celestials began a nightly battle of fireworks and shooting stars and dust plumes. Noomii's eyes roamed to the edge. Sometimes she thought the water lapping looked strange, other nights it was still as glass.

"What are you doing down here?" the Helmsman asked as he hopped from his boat.

Noomii had just finished chiseling off a piece of pink and black layer. "Hm." She rolled the stone between her fingers before using the spyglass to study it closer in the moonlight. She took a few notes in her journal.

"It looks like rhodonite," the Helmsman said as he leaned close enough for Noomii to smell the fresh-pressed vanilla bean of the Goldlands on him. "I've been told those were years of love and darkness." His finger pointed out the bold black streak mottled throughout the pink stone. "It was the time of the Sultans. Each had thirty-six wives and while the Sultans were happy the wives became jealous. Many of them were murdered and the land turned black with hate as the Sultan's blood tinted the waters pink."

"That makes perfect sense." Noomii took note of his story, writing it in her book. Then she set the gem in a pouch where she'd collected the other layers of Highrock that she'd chipped off.

"I've brought you something." The helmsman bent and raised a small cage from his boat. Inside were small birds with black caps and gray backs. "I thought about it and the chickadee suits you much better than the rest." He passed her the cage.

"These aren't birds of the sea." Noomii took the cage with hesitation. She'd seen chickadees many times as she climbed the mountains on The Land of Man. "I'm afraid they'll die out here." She glanced to the shore. "They'll never make it to land. They're too small."

The helmsman smiled. "You shouldn't underestimate creations of the Creator. No matter how small."

"Take them back," Noomii said. "They are not meant for this space."

The helmsman left the food and the birds, his oars gliding whisper smooth through the dark water. Noomii spent her months watching for change that never occurred. She released a chickadee when she needed supplies. With each visit she tried rare foods that the helmsman brought her. Each time she warned him that she was not Goldland born and he reminded her that the Land of Man was different than when she last left it. When she asked how he did not elaborate and she could not see much of a difference from her spyglass. The helmsman brought her more chickadees but their chirps quieted the more time they spent on the mountain. Their cheerful charm had changed; they were gloomy and withdrawn, depressed even. Noomii couldn't help but think it was her fault. The way people had treated her, the way the birds changed. Was it her? Noomii set them free and told him to stop bringing them. Life on Highrock was singular it seemed. She was the only living creature at the peak. The helmsman never approached the ladder, the seagulls never landed, and the crustaceans never climbed higher than the bottom quarter of the rope ladder. It made for quiet sunrises and even quieter sunsets.

Noomii studied her chipped pieces of rock. Some she'd rubbed smooth and others she'd begun carving. It only seemed right that history had a shape; something more than a simple layer in Highrock. If she could give them shape, their meaning might last, those of the Land of Man might not be so easy to forget.

Noomii carved the piece of yellow feather jasper into the shape of a bird, she took care to fleck its smooth back to create wide wings then she carved a grand beak with a sharp curve. It was a creature of the sky whose flocks blocked out the sun and the statue should resemble such. She whittled the stone away to reveal feathers embedded within and smoothed them over the carving as though it were a real creature. Noomii thought that if she could breathe life into it, the bird just might fly. She set the statue on her desk and moved on.

Noomii chiseled away more layers. She spent her days rappelling down the side of Highrock and her evenings climbing back up until her muscles were strong and her fingers calloused. Until one day, when she decided to make an improvement upon the mountain. She chiseled and chipped the current layer she was inspecting into the shape of a step. Just wide enough for her foot. Noomii returned to the layers she'd already inspected and chipped away at those until she was well on her way to creating a winding staircase. With each step she created, she examined a new layer, she memorized the descriptions in the journals, and she carved a statue to always remember. By the time Noomii reached halfway to the peak, she no longer needed the journals to find answers, which was good because she'd reached the old ones that she couldn't read. With a bit of examination, sometimes with the spyglass, Noomii could see what had occurred all those years ago. She couldn't tell the fine details; but she could see that there was death, there were strange creatures, there was darkness, and there was light. She even came across a band of Ocean Jasper. Noomii carved it into an elaborate octopus with feldspar crystal eyes and suckers. The tentacles sparkled with radial quartz. She polished it smooth and set it on the windowsill next to the others. She sat back and took in her carvings. There were creatures of the sky, of the ocean; there were bones, and plenty of reasons for her mother's faith to have been so strong, especially with broken hearts of rhodonite and such.

"You're building a stairway?" the Helmsman asked as he passed a bag to Noomii one morning.

"Is that not allowed?" Noomii peered in the bag. There was a bottle of elderberry wine, candied goat cerebrum, dried ramen, and fresh bread. "From the Goldlands again?"

The Helmsman nodded. "I don't think the Creator would mind an improvement to the Watchtower." He pointed. "That ladder is eons old."

"I guess it was time for a stairway then." Noomii shuddered at the thought of rope so aged, glad it hadn't broken in all the times she climbed it.

"It seems change has come for many. The mountain, the land. I'm sure the sea will be next." He passed her another bag. "The black chocolates have probably melted." He used his sleeve to wipe sweat from his brow. "The suns are punishing today." He blinked as he focused on her. "Perhaps a stepwell more than a stairwell."

"It does lead to water." Noomii took a breath. "I never thought I'd say this, but I could go for a boar's rump boiled in pilsner or mash with green onion and salt." She could taste the bitter meat and savory potatoes on her tongue. She always craved something more and never thought she'd miss the food of her homeland.

"Ah, you said you'd left nothing behind on the Land of Man and you did not leave your taste for Darkmoor cuisine." He tipped his chin and settled his hand over his heart. "I will return with them." He waved as he returned to the shore.

Noomii sat on the edge of the rock facing the horizon as the suns dipped. She chipped the staircase into formation and transcribed the past. For days and months and years the horizon looked the same. Until one night, it didn't.

The suns were halfway down when Noomii noticed something strange on the skyline. She stood with her toes on the edge of the mountain, her eyes squinting as she focused on the distance. It was there. A bump. A lump. Something at the edge of the earth where there should be nothing. Noomii paced. She rubbed her face and gripped her temples and racked her mind for what to do. It could be a ship. It could be a Celestial invading earth. It could be the God of the sea. She wasn't sure what to do. Should she light the alarm? Should she wait calmly to see what comes next? Or she could check the striations and see what Highrock had to tell her. Noomii went to the other edge of the mountain, opened the telescoping mirror and found her peg. There was no movement. No new striations had formed for her to interpret. Noomii closed the mirror and put it in her pocket. She rubbed her eyes and looked again, across the sea at the edge of the world, but by now the sun was down and the light was fading. The bump looked like it could be a rogue wave in this light. She blinked a few times, her eyes feeling dry. It could be her eyesight or a figment of her imagination. Noomii knew she'd been waiting for something exciting to happen for months. This could be nothing but the madness of desire.

She focused in the distance but the darkness came and the Moon Goddess did not gift her with a full moon, just a sliver of light that did nothing to illuminate the bump that may or may not be threatening the edge of the earth.

Noomii decided it was best to sleep on it and see what happened in the morning.

The bump was still there when the sun rose and the tide was

low. When Noomii checked the striations she noticed the sea no longer lapped at the height of her peg instead it was a good distance below. Noomii climbed down the rope ladder to get a closer look.

The base of Highrock was dry. Noomii could walk a full circle around the mountain now uninhibited by steep cliff and rock and water, there was just dry land.

Something felt off about it all. She climbed to the peak again to get a look at the horizon.

Noomii stared in the distance as she drank her morning tea. She stared as she ate a sandwich. She stared as the sun was setting; making it abundantly clear that there was definitely something on the horizon: an artifact, an object, a *thing*. It didn't seem threatening at the moment, but Noomii swore it looked larger than the night before. She held up her pinky finger, closed her left eye and measured it against the length of her knuckles. The bump was about a third of the length of her pinky. When the suns set, the moon didn't even give her a sliver of light. Tonight it was all darkness. A brooding cloak. A blackened heat. An endless hole. When she looked to the sky her whole being flooded with a sinking feeling that maybe the edge of the world was always up and never out. Maybe Despina was wrong.

Before bed Noomii climbed to the tower to check her supplies. There were stacks of candles coated in dust and boxes of matches still smelling of phosphorus and chlorate. She cleaned the sea spray off the glass with a damp cloth in case she needed to light the alarm. She wanted the Creator to easily see. Those on the Land of Man would see the alarm as well. Noomii paused as she gazed in the direction of the land she'd left so many years ago. There was no one to taunt her on Highrock, no one to spill ale on her shoes or tip her with pennies, no one to remind her of her caste and bastard status. For a moment, Noomii wondered if it would be best not to light the alarm. Perhaps allowing whatever danger was lurking at the horizon to take its wrath out on everyone born above the mud of the moors was the perfect revenge for all the years of torment.

The next morning, the tide was lower than ever. There were no new striations.

Noomii held her pinky finger up to the bump on the horizon. It had grown in the night, now it was nearly the length of her entire finger. She paced the peak of Highrock deciding what to do.

"Ahoy!" She heard a shout from below. It sounded like the helmsman. Noomii ran to the edge and waved. He held up a sack. "I brought peanut pastries and liversugars," he shouted proudly.

Noomii climbed down the mountain to greet him, quicker than ever with her new steps.

"Aren't you worried?" she asked as the helmsman passed her the sack. "The tide is so low now. I had to walk five minutes to reach your boat."

"It is a bit strange," he said as he inspected the island now surrounding Highrock's base.

"Should I light the alarm?" Noomii asked.

"That's not for me to decide." The helmsman glanced toward the edge. "That is for you to decide."

Noomii pressed her lips together in agitation. "There is something on the horizon." She pointed to the edge of the earth. "It's getting bigger. I've been measuring it." She held up her finger. "Kind of."

The helmsman was far too calm for her liking. "And what are you going to do about it?" he asked.

"Well, I could light the alarms and let the Creator know that something is amiss." She itched her scalp where she'd been worrying a strand of hair so hard it had come right out. "But I don't know." She turned to the helmsman. "Have you ever seen the tide this low before?"

He shrugged. "Once, maybe."

"Maybe?" Noomii was annoyed.

"It was a very long time ago. I was young. You know how the

memories fade." He was gazing in the distance at the bump and two wrinkles began to crease his forehead.

As they spoke the sea receded more, until the helmsman's boat was settled on sharp rock. Fish flopped on the edges of the island, unable to seek safety as the tide flushed further out.

Noomii set the sack of supplies near the base of the peak then returned to the boat. "Take me out there." She pointed.

"Out there? To the edge of the earth?" The helmsman asked as he dragged his boat back into the water. "It is forbidden."

"Forbidden by the Creator?" Noomii was climbing into the sailboat. "The Creator who chose me to man the Watchtower? Take me out there, now.

CHAPTER 5

HIGHMOUNT

Highmount was a lonesome place. There were not even spirits to watch, no flickering ghastly faces to take the chill of loneliness away. In the Goldlands the ghosts were ignored in public, but Cara always had a hard time overlooking the ones that would drift through the walls of her home. There was none of that here. The only thing floating in the air was the mist that hovered below the peak on early mornings and dreary days. The only chill came from the ice crusted windows when the sun went down. She missed the gleam of the Goldlands, the heat from being so close to the seven suns, the tap of her shoes on hollow bone streets.

Cara searched for something to relieve her boredom, she wandered the small house until she found herself standing in the loft, amongst the stacks of journals. She ran her finger along the spines, top to bottom. Stopping closer to the bottom she pulled one out, opened the journal, and read the first entry.

There was once a sultan with thirty-six wives, each of a different age and spirit. On the day of the Sultan's death, he was afraid to pass to the underworld alone and asked his fourth wife to come with him. The fourth was his favorite; he'd draped her in silks and rubies, he never asked her body to become thick with child, but he did ask her to go with him to the underworld so their souls could live on together, forever. The fourth wife agreed but only on the condition that the Sultan delayed his last breath until all thirty-six wives could say goodbye individually. The Sultan did his best as his room filled with women of varying age. The women chattered like buzzing bees and the Sultan did his best to make out what they were saying. Words of jealousy, anger, love; they all flitted from the women's mouths. The Sultan cried out for number four, fearing he could not hold onto his last breath for much longer. She took his hand and pulled him from the bed, and the other women helped carry the old man to the river. As they settled his frail body in the cool water, each wife pulled a gleaming ruby knife from their robes. The Sultan's eyes widened as he shouted, but the women had their own plan for his passing. The river ran red that day and the jealous women turned on each other after setting the Sultan's soul free. Red rivers do not nourish plants or creatures of the Land of Man, and the land turned black with disgust, the trees wilted with envy.

Cara closed the journal and set it on her thighs, fingertips tapped on the cover. She bent her fingers so the nails clacked on the tough leather beneath them. She closed her eyes. *Tap, tap, tap.* It nearly sounded like she was walking on the Goldland streets once more.

The cartman came the next day. He brought salted coffee, steamed clams, and candied hearts for the cupboards. "I can't stay long," he said as he brought the packages inside and set them on the table.

Cara held up one of the journals. "Have you ever read these stories?" she asked.

The cartman squinted. "Ah, journals of history. Not stories." He tipped the cover gently and let the pages fall open. "There should be more."

"There are stacks." Cara began storing the goods in the cupboards. She opened the bag of candied hearts and ate a few before setting the teapot on the stove.

"You'd do good to read them all."

"I've a Goldland education," Cara said. "Learned plenty of history."

The cartman clucked his tongue. "You've learned a Goldland history. This is different. This is a history of the Land of Man. The Goldland glitters with tales that have never breached their gilded gates. Did you ever wonder why you never learned about the Darkmoors or the Gulf shores? I'm certain they never told you the stories of the Creator, the old Gods, the needle of Highrock that stitches together time."

Cara stared blankly at him. "I know of the Darkmoors."

"There's a difference between what you know and what these books will tell you." He flipped a few pages, his eyes bright with anticipation. "Ah, here it is." He began reading.

There was once a prince who lived on the edge of the moors. A curious boy with rosy cheeks and dark hair that drew the eyes of his people whenever he passed. Such a darling child, the townspeople would say after his mother. The light always shone in place of his shadow. In contrast, the moors were draped in shadow and often stank of sulfur, gases released from eons of decay. While some couldn't stand the downwind stench, the people of the moors knew better to build upwind. The soil of the moors was rich; it could grow an acre of rice with just two seeds. There was something about the land; an aura of sorrow and thrill twining in helix. It was hard to deny a young boy the pull of the thrill. More than once the prince had gone missing, and his mother threatened that one day the moors would swallow him up whole and their people would weep for his memory. The prince would laugh because every young boy thinks they are invincible, and the world is theirs to explore and conquer. One day after breakfast, the queen sent her son to wash his face and dress for the day. Only, as she made her way to the parlor room, the prince snuck out the kitchen door. He ran across the country garden and leapt onto the wooden swing that hung from a giant oak. The moors called for him. The mud ached for his footprints, the bugs chirped, the birds sang a hypnotizing melody. The prince jumped off his swing and ran for the path. Thick with mud and dark magic, flanked with tall reed, the path twisted and turned until the prince couldn't remember his way out. The queen knew the moors swallowed creatures whole, it swallowed men whole, it was the curse of the land. That afternoon every man in town set out for the moors to search for the prince. But the moors had tugged him deeper and deeper, swallowed him whole, encased him in darkness. Only a third of the men returned. This was the day the Darkmoors were born and the queen's screams were heard as far as the flats of the Saltpan.

The cartman closed the book. He closed his eyes and took a deep breath.

"I'm not sure I liked that story." Cara dried her hands and leaned against the table. "I feel so sad now. So empty."

"But now you know where the naming of the Darkmoors came from. They used to simply be known as the moors. Before the dark magic came and willed so many souls to sink below the murky surface of the moors."

"That's wonderful. Magic has been outlawed for a long time now." Cara let out a sigh. "So what am I supposed to do here? I read all these stories and what?"

"You could write a few of your own." The cartman slid the journal her way. "The Divine Arrow expects you to watch over the Land of Man and light the warning if you see danger. It's an important job."

Cara crossed her arms. "I had other dreams. I'm not even sure how I was forced to come here. The Goldlands worship gold, not deity."

The cartman tipped his finger before turning on his heel and walking out the door.

"Wait!" Cara started after him. "Don't go."

"I must leave before the night comes." He was growing impatient. His gaze flicked to the edge.

"Why do you have to go so quickly? Can't you stay for another story? Or I could cook some food and we could watch the sunset? You could watch the Celestials light the sky." She spanned her arm over the horizon.

The cartman shook his head. "I must go." He picked up the handles of his cart and headed down the rocky path.

Cara made dinner and ate alone, sitting on the stoop of her new home. She watched the cottony clouds drift between the seven mountains of the Land of Man, the seven suns set in unison and as the din settled for the night, the sunset glinted off the gates of the Goldlands. They weren't that far away; she could see the buildings in the distance, the winding road. Her vision sharpened as the night came, and she could see Goldland born walking the streets; wisps here and there, the garden center near the bluffs. Cara wanted so badly to go back. She tore her gaze away, looked to Highrock in the distance and turned to look over the empty Saltpan. She could see in all directions from this peak—she actually looked down upon the Goldlands from here. The palmstone in her pocket might buy her a penthouse in the highest tower, but here she was higher.

Cara grabbed wood and stoked the fire, she cleaned up and then readied herself for bed. As she walked up to the loft she was torn between the bed and the desk. There was an empty journal and the cartman's words echoed in her ears. Maybe she could write a story. She'd never tried before but she could start. Cara sat at the desk and pulled a pen from the drawer. She opened the journal and pressed the tip of the pen. She wrote: *There once was a girl*. She stopped, closed the journal and went to bed instead.

Over time, Cara read more of the journals-half a stack at least. She stood on her perch and observed the Land of Man. Time passed differently at the peak; the land below seemed to pass in fast motion. Her eyes wandered to envy the Goldlands and the life she would never return to. Every so often, she would notice her mother standing at the Goldland gates and staring in her direction. At least her mother hadn't forgotten her. Cara waved, knowing that her mother couldn't see her.

She found her curiosity of the Darkmoors growing. Each evening she watched the moors, searching for specs of the magic mentioned in the story the cartman had read her. Many times she saw men suddenly veer to the moors and disappear below the mud and could only guess at what drew them. Maybe it was the same draw that brought souls to the Goldlands?

Cara's mother stopped showing up at the Goldland gates in the evenings and she could only assume it was because her time had come to an end. "Pray the Shadowline doesn't keep your soul," Cara murmured and blessed herself. She blew a kiss across the valley, from Highmount to the Goldlands. Not wanting to disappoint the Arrow, she held her tears. Cara's heart grew more hollow now that she was truly alone in this world. She felt empty on the inside. Vast as the sea and the night sky. Now that her mother was gone, the feeling ate at her.

When the cartman visited again he brought firewood, sun oats, pickled dates, and shrimp from the gulf. Cara helped him unload the cart; it seemed like too much for one man to drag up the mountain by himself.

"Did you lack faith in the Arrow?" Cara asked. "Is that why he struck your donkey down?"

"There have been times when I have lacked faith." The cartman nodded. "I think he did it to show me I didn't need to rely on a beast. I tell myself the Arrow knows me better than I know myself." He picked up a heavy chord of wood and set it by the stoop. He reached in his pocket and pulled out a paper wrapped package. "This is for you."

Cara took the package. She hadn't received a gift since her graduation; it was a melancholy event in which she unwrapped a handful of gifts from her mother only to be greeted with her orders to Highmount. She had to leave everything behind. Ripping the brown paper revealed a telescoping mirror. The guards at the Goldland gates used them to check under seats and heavy skirts to make sure there were no tagalongs or hidden items. Cara ran her fingers over the thick brass handle. "It's a strange thing to give me," she murmured.

"A useful gift." The cartman held his hand out to take the mirror from her. He walked to the edge of Highmount, extended the handle by a good three feet and tilted the mirror over the ledge. "Things you might not have seen." He tipped his head.

Cara moved closer to see the side of Highmount, there were trees and animals and some people, digging and climbing. "How long have they been there?"

"There are always people from the Land of Man milling about. It would be best to watch out for the creatures of the sea and creatures of the Saltpan and creatures from the abyss of space from all angles."

"And if I see any of those?" Cara took the handle of the mirror.

"That's easy, Cara DiCara, Goldland born, Highmount watch. You light the flame and warn the Arrow and he will strike them down."

Cara retracted the mirror and tucked it in her pocket. "Thank you." She nodded. "How can you be sure he will strike them?"

The cartman paused. "It is the way."

Chapter 6

Highrock

The helmsman grumbled as he rowed the boat away from the rocky shore of Highrock. He steered them toward the edge. The wind was strong and blowing in the opposite direction from where they were headed. After fighting with the sails, the helmsman tied them down and took to the paddles.

They paddled in unison, the helmsman with hesitation and Noomii with an everlasting need to know. The sun stroked them with heated rays and the constant rowing brought blisters to the palms of their hands. With each moment they drew closer to the thing on the horizon.

Noomii was preparing herself for being so close to the edge of the world. She'd read that looking directly into the abyss of space could drive a person crazy, that it could suck your soul out into the greedy vacuum of darkness, that no one ever came back from the edge the same and that was why it was forbidden.

"What is it?" the helmsman asked.

Noomii blinked and squinted her eyes. "It's rounded. Perhaps... a creature of the ocean?" She shook her head. "The thing could be an egg, or a new mountain protruding from the sea." She doubted her words. "Heck, it could be the God of the sea making a grand and drawn-out entrance so everyone on the Land of Man sees. We must get closer."

They rowed until they were close enough to touch it.

"It appears to be made of stone," the helmsman said as he settled his oars.

The sea shifted and the thing grew.

"Oh my," Noomii said as she took note that it was not an egg or a simple mountain, it was a carving of the head of a man, the head of a man that had thick strands of seaweed for a beard. And as the sea drained, the statue grew and the neck and shoulders became visible.

Noomii looked behind them at Highrock in the distance. "It hasn't grown an inch since I've been there," she thought out loud. "Highrock hasn't moved but this thing has." Noomii turned again to face the helmsman. "The Land of Man forced me to halt deep thoughts of things that were no business of my own. But there is something wrong here. Highrock hasn't grown an inch but this thing is growing by meters in minutes."

Noomii had been expected to interpret the striations of Highrock, but this stone beast growing from the sea was not made of ocean jasper or lapis lazuli or opal. This was carved of something new. Noomii reached out and touched a rounded shoulder. The surface was smooth and hard, as black as midnight in the Darkmoors.

"It's onyx," the helmsman said.

"For someone who couldn't remember the last time the tide was this low you can recall a rare stone quite quickly." Noomii glided her fingers down the slippery carving. The stone was so polished she could see her reflection.

"It's just... so familiar." His face pinched as he started rowing past the statue. "The edge was right here. For ages it's been right here."

Noomii focused on the sea. From where they sat in the boat it extended for hundreds of yards. She was sure the edge should have been right there. From where they floated, both should have been able to gaze into the abyss of space all while feeling their guts drop from visualizing the sheared edge of the earth with nothing below.

"There's so much more," the helmsman said as he paddled.

Noomii picked up her oars and assisted him. "Keep going," she urged.

They paddled for hours, until the suns set in a blaze of unsteady lies at the horizon. Thankfully the moonlight gifted them with a night bright with sepia light.

"It doesn't end," Noomii finally said as she turned and glanced toward the Land of Man, recognizing from this distance that the ocean curved just slightly.

"After all of this time," the helmsman paled as he realized there was no end to the earth and that sea didn't halt for infinity nor lapped at the cold abyss of space.

"We could go on forever," Noomii said as she realized it was all a lie.

"I fear my arms have become as heavy as the mud of the Dark-moors." The helmsman settled his oars. "We should return or we'll be adrift out here all night." Noomii nodded in agreement as the helmsman loosened the sails.

They passed the statue rising from the sea and noticed much of its waist was now visible. Carvings stood out in the light of the moon. A thick belt was engraved with the hilt of a sword protruding from the water.

"Who do you think that is?" Noomii asked.

The helmsman shook his head. "I'm not sure. It could be the Creator. Or a lesser God."

"Why would he be birthed of the sea?" Noomii asked. "This doesn't make sense."

The helmsman was scowling as he glanced to the night sky. "Maybe the Celestial's son."

"Maybe the sea was never his?" Noomii wondered.

There was much more land surrounding Highrock now. The helmsman secured the boat to a rock crag.

"Will you return?" Noomii asked.

"I fear the docks are not the same as when I left them." He looked in the direction of the Land of Man. "I've witnessed the chaos of man, the danger and riots that change brings. I fear if I go back I may never return."

"Stay here," Noomii offered. She didn't want to be alone in this time of uncertainty. She knew something was coming and she worried that if he left, she might never see him again.

The helmsman stood and exited the boat. He held his hand out, an offering to steady Noomii as she stepped onto the rocky land.

Noomii knew she was a bastard of the Darkmoors, not to be touched by any. She hesitated for a moment, thinking to refuse his help as she had many times in the past, but this time Noomii gripped his palm firmly and didn't let go until he said, "No." The helmsman looked toward the Land of Man. "It is my duty to row from the land to Highrock, and Highrock to the land. I must go." He let go of her hand now that she was steady on the rocks and got back into the boat. He shoved off, away from the shoreline, and headed toward the docks. "I will return tomorrow," he promised.

Noomii climbed Highrock. She ran across the peak and grabbed the spyglass off her desk. She focused out the window until she found the helmsman. He was walking toward the docks, over sand and rocks as he left his small boat at the edge of the water. Other boats were run aground, listed to the side while still tethered to the docks. And on the docks, others were waiting for him. Men and women from the Land of Man their faces red with anger and worry. They raised their fists and shouted at the helmsman. They'd seen him sail to Highrock; they'd seen him bring back Despina's body. They knew he was somehow involved. And now that they couldn't fish and their boats were stuck, they were sure it was the helmsman's fault. Noomii watched in horror as the helmsman walked fearlessly toward the crowd.

"No," Noomii shouted, knowing well that he couldn't hear her.

The people on the docks engulfed him in a wave. They stripped away his tattered clothing to reveal a body she somehow recognized. She had the same feeling of remembrance, similar to the one she had as she climbed Highrock that first time.

"No," Noomii said as she watched, her heart heavy. "Noooooo," she screamed, decades of anger and grief welled inside her released. She screamed until she was short of breath. Unaware of the wave headed toward the docks. It splashed before reaching the people. Rivulets of ocean water trickled to the dock footings for the first time in weeks. They barely noticed what they'd awakened in the sea.

She set the spyglass down and wiped her eyes. Noomii had never cried for anyone before, not even her mother. That is the way of the Darkmoors. It's depressing enough in those lands without the spilling of tears. But now, with the helmsman gone she was completely alone and trapped at Highrock. The carvings caught her eye and Noomii picked up the octopus made of ocean jasper. If only she could breathe life into the carvings and send them to the land. Perhaps the Creator would stop this; perhaps he would bring peace again or even bring the helmsman back. Her desk was lined with bones, birds of prey, cauldrons of bubbling blood, monsters her mother had warned her about. If only those on land would remember the books, if only they'd seek peace then there might be fewer carvings of death and destruction. She picked up a disk of amethyst. She pinched it between her fingers. The layer was so thin she couldn't carve a single thing from it. She pressed the spyglass to the disk for the hundredth time, trying to see what had happened those years, but nothing stuck out. There were no bones, no feathers or scales, no rotting skin, no flourishing berries or flowers pressed within the stone. She tucked the disk in her pocket before heading downstairs.

Noomii ate the peanut pastries and liversugars from the sack. She made tea from lilac leaves the helmsman had previously delivered and as she sipped the fragrant infusion Noomii realized this was the last time she'd eat Goldland foods. Maybe that was why they'd killed him. They'd found him sneaking her delicacies reserved for the high crust. She'd warned him it was prohibited for an outcast of the Darkmoors, it didn't matter if she'd been chosen to serve the Highrock, but he wouldn't listen. *Times are changing on the Land of Man*, he'd said. Noomii was disgusted with the Land of Man. They'd killed the only man who had ever shown her kindness. Maybe Despina was right. Maybe Noomii did want to watch them burn.

As she prepared herself for bed, Noomii took one last look at the docks with the spyglass. There was nothing but dark streaks staining the wood, and in the moonlight she could see a crumpled figure in the sand. She recognized the helmsman's worn clothing. She crossed the room and looked toward the edge. The figure was still there, the circle of moonlight reflecting on his forehead. Noomii held up her finger, pleased to see that it hadn't grown again.

In times such as this, one shouldn't be able to sleep soundly; but being born of the Darkmoors had prepared Noomii to find rest during times of mourning and stress because that was every day in the Darkmoors. That was survival. If you'd gotten a liter of ale dumped down your back, you still slept at night. If Goldland children exploring the ditches for the day had spat on you, you still slept at night. And if you'd watched your mother suffer from the black lung for three long years before finally passing because the doctors refused to treat an untouchable, you still slept at night.

The morning brought a great fog over the sea and the land. Noomii could barely see a thing with her spyglass. The sound of a hollow clank at the shoreline was enough to get her moving. She left the house to see what the noise was only to find the helmsman's boat had returned, empty of course. The sea had brought his boat back to her. Noomii collected a few items, including her carvings, before walking down her newly chiseled staircase to the shore. She made her way over rocks and shallow tide pools, nearly slipping on the damp algae. She found the boat in the pale mist and settled her belongings before climbing in. The helmsman had made it look easy when he shoved the boat away from the rocks and rowed in smooth strokes. Noomii found it quite challenging; there was splashing and clanks from the hull as it scraped against rock. Now that there was significantly less sea, the travel to the Land of Man was quick. Thankfully, the God of the sea was silent and the water calm as glass except for a few small bubbles that came to the surface. She paused, swore she could hear a voice erupt from the popping bubbles. She tipped her head in curiosity, but the bubbles stopped and she kept going.

Noomii saw no others as she made her way. She dragged the boat onto the rocks and headed for the docks. She'd brought a large piece of cloth, had intended on using it to sew herself new clothing but there was another need now.

People started collecting as she got nearer. Word must have spread that she had left the Watchtower. The last time she stood on the docks the sun was bright and the air clean and crisp. Now, it all looked so gray under the cast of the fog like she was part of a dream. One thing was clear: it had all aged. But Noomii had aged differently than these people; those who saw her arrive at the start of her term saw her no different now. Time was different on the top of the Watchtower, barely moving. Time was different for the helmsman. Perhaps that's why they killed him. Now, they shied away from her and Noomii wondered if it was because she was a Watchtower servant and before that untouchable. She was certain none of the servants before her ever returned to the land alive. They'd all lived to the end of their years and expired on the peak, or below it.

Noomii didn't head for the docks; instead she made her way to the dry sand below and the crumpled pile that had been the helmsman.

She dropped to her knees, removed the cloth from her bag and laid it out flat. She pushed the weathered clothing aside to reveal bones dried and hollow from the harsh sun, preserved from the salt of the sea. She moved them gently from the sand to the cloth before rolling the fabric together and tying it securely. She placed the bundle in her bag and stood, walking to the boardwalk and avoiding the crowd.

When the Helmsman had brought Despina's body back to the Land of Man, there was one single old man who acknowledged the importance of it. Noomii was sure that old man was long dead by now. She searched the storefronts of the boardwalk; some of them had been shuttered closed for years. Her eyes landed on a pub, a roughly carved sign for The Rye House. There was something she had learned from her time in the Darkmoors, the bartender knows all.

Chapter 7

Highsandplateau

Shadowline, shadowline dark and free
Touch the shadowline and it will never set you free
Souls of monsters and beasts roam here
Pass the Shadowline,
the Saltpan is now your home

There is a tower on the back ledge of the Land of Man, unseen by many eyes. To the far east, past the seven mountains that would become flat and past the shadowline of the towering Goldlands, laid a Saltpan that stretched for eternity. Dry and desolate, it is a forgotten place of the Land of Man. The skies reflected off the crisp Saltpan like it was still water. If one stood at the edge of the shadowline, held their hand shading their eyes, and focused, a tower could be seen in the distance. It resembled a pillar of sand, hammered down from the desperate peak it once was. This was Highsandplateau. Rarely seen and long forgotten, a broken tower eons old, it held a creature the Land of

Man had not encountered in a very long time. Not since the days this watchtower mirrored the others in height.

Io stood in the ribcage of a creature long ago deceased. Thin skin stretched between the rib bones, loose pieces fluttered in the wind. It wasn't a castle, but it was a home to Io. Her island of packed sand and coarse salt rested in the middle of a crystal clear pond atop Highsandplateau. She wasn't sure how she got there or how long she'd been there, but as far back as she could remember this had been her home. There was a time when the dead creature's fascia stretched to the ground and provided a barrier against the harsh winds. Now, tattered and blanched gray; it was losing its once protective properties.

Io stood and walked to the edge of her island. Pale eyes, bleached from the seven suns reflecting off the glass of the Saltpan, searched the horizon. There was a shadow in the distance; it wavered like a flame, black against the sand. Io watched with interest. She knew better than to venture out into that wilderness. She'd tried many times and knew that shade or cool water would be gifts to any errant soul who tried to cross the Saltpan. It seemed this fool had neither.

The third sun was straight overhead and Io knew that it was time for her to turn her attention elsewhere. She scanned her eyes past the edge, where the land ended in an abrupt edge.

Io returned to the ribcage and sat cross-legged on the ground. Bone-white hair poured down to her waist, covering her bare breasts. The only clothing she wore was a strip of angled leather around her pelvis. And some days that was too much for the heat of the Saltpan. She meditated, eyes closed, sweat dripping down the concave middle of her spine. There wasn't much to do on the island, and Io was clearing her mind for the next step she'd take. She would leave the island, eventually. But first, the shadow in the distance needed to arrive.

Pale eyes opened.

The fool was coming closer with each minute that passed. Io was in disbelief. She'd seen men blister and fade to dust out there. But not this one. No, this one took step after step until he reached her pond as though he were driven by something other than his own stupidity.

He stood on the edge of the pond, clothing frayed and ragged. He waved but Io simply stared. He stepped forward, his feet immersed in the pond. There were once creatures in there that Io had outlived, creatures with teeth and scales and hunger that was never satisfied. But this fool had come at the perfect time. All of those creatures were gone, and nothing stopped his trespassing. The water reached to his ribcage, he held a bag of belongings over his head so they didn't get wet. Within a few minutes he was walking up her beach.

Io stood.

"I saw floating rocks out there." Concern wrinkled his forehead.

"Who are you?" she asked.

The man hesitated before replying, "What a strange greeting. I'm Gail."

Io's right hand shot forward, her free hand gripped her right forearm as she rotated her hand in a circle, stopping with her palm open.

"Ah," Gail nodded, "the greeting of the old ways." Gail paused before mimicking her, their fingertips barely touching. "Why?" he asked.

"I could have had a bone shank behind my back. This way you know that I don't." She moved from the greeting, flashing both palms at him. "Now that I know you don't. Why are you here?" Io asked. "No one from the Land of Man has visited here, ever." Io's features were cold, uninviting. She was on the verge of telling him to leave. Having him on her island felt unnatural. This was her land; she'd been here since forever, alone.

Gail began to open his bag and placed wrapped items in the shade of her dwelling. "I've brought you some things."

Io picked up one of the packages and ripped the paper. "What is this?"

"Food." He lifted a smaller pack. "Chestnut snails roasted in palm oil."

Io hissed, dropped the package and kicked it into the pond. "How dare you!" Io's pale eyes were wide with rage.

Gail back-stepped, dropping the package of chestnut snails. Io kicked it and the shells scattered across sand. Glistening shades of brown promised a savory snack and if it were Io's early years her mouth might have watered, but she knew better.

"How dare you bring that to me. Are you crazy? Anchor my gut to that land." Io gripped her thin stomach and waved past the shadowline. "I will never eat. And I will never eat that." She kicked another one of the packages, sending it skipping across the pond until it sank.

Gail paled as he repacked his bag and stood. "I didn't know."

"You didn't?" Io advanced on him, threatening. "How could you not? Did you come here to kill me?"

Gail shook his head. "No. Never."

Io reached for him, her fingers turned pinschers as she raked at his face, but her hands simply went right through him. Io hissed again, this time harder. "You are something!" She screeched. "Get out of here! Go away!" She fled to the bones and picked up a tool off the ground. She picked up a handful of sand and threw it at him. "Go! You are a *ghost*!"

Gail backed away. "I came to help you," he said. "It is my mission."

"Damn your mission." Io kicked more sand. "Your mission is not wanted or needed here." Io advanced, forcing Gail to back into the pond. "You better watch yourself in my waters," she warned. "Your head might dip under the surface and you might find yourself in a different time. You might remember all the old ways." Io closed her eyes and thought to summon a vortex back to the old days. She couldn't though, she needed more time. A vortex like that took a day's meditation.

Gail's forehead creased in confusion as he continued to walk away, across the pond and to the other side.

"Stay there!" Io shouted as she pointed to the greenery of the Land of Man in the distance.

Gail turned and ran away.

Io sat calmly. She crossed her legs and rested her thin wrists on bony knees. She had to prepare her mind. She needed to meet someone. She meditated for hours before she was ready and stood again.

The Saltpan was once a gulf and the pond was littered with coral, long dead and salt-bleached. Io stepped forward, her toes touching the water, and she transformed in a heartbeat. Her slender form changing into that of a crab. Crusted legs tapped down with a crunch and shards of coral turned to dust with each step. She scurried along the bottom of the pond, pausing until the vortexes appeared. This water was a conduit to the past and present. Io could travel through time. She chose a vortex and, emerging on the other side, her eyestalks twisted to note her island was still there. It was, but it looked different; hazy and wavering like a dream. It always did when she left. It made her wonder if her island was a dream. Maybe this life was a dream; it often felt like a mirror waiting to be shattered.

Io scuttled across the Saltpan, her ventral eyes closed to the sharp sparkle of the crystals below. Today she had one plan: to find the children playing by the edge of the Shadowline.

As she scuttled, tall clouds towered in the sky. The Saltpan had no obstructions to the view. She passed two columns of rock that appeared to have once been an arch; giant boulders hovered in the air, shards of rock and gems alike, vibrating in lament, never falling to the ground nor rising to the sky. An old Moongate. A shiver passed through her shell. Some memory of dark magic existed here. All this time she'd avoided exploring it, but Io knew one day that broken Moongate would need to be addressed.

Io kept going. As she got closer to the Goldlands she'd pause and hover near large rocks, steady and still so as to blend in. She was very close when she heard the children shouting and inched forward. Antenna-eyes rotated and focused on the group of children; one stood out, the one she had come searching for. The group moved closer to the Shadowline, and Io inched forward finding solace in the darkness that separated their two worlds.

One child stepped forward, drawn to Io just as Io was drawn to her.

"Don't do it, Cara!" a little girl shouted. But it was too late; Cara was reaching out across the Shadowline, her fingertips stretching to touch the giant crab.

"What's that inside it?" a boy shouted.

Io didn't know that in her crab form her carapace was clear and her body shivered in the fetal position for all to see. Morbid and mesmerizing. If eyes ever fell on her in this form, it was hard for them to ever turn away.

The children moved closer, curious. One moved closer than the others, her toes nearly touching the Shadowline.

"Cara, no!" another child shouted. "It will eat you. It's a monster!"

Cara didn't stop at the warning of her friends. The tip of her shoe passed the Shadowline as her hand reached out, drawn to the giant crab as a Goldland man was drawn to coins.

"The Shadowline will keep your soul," a boy whispered.

Io lifted her chitinous front leg and touched it to Cara's fingertip and the movement was stop-motion, an ethereal hesitation. Yes, this was the one. There was something about the child named Cara, something pure and unadulterated, something *familiar*. A Goldland gem. Some innocence that used to be a part of her. Io was tempted to grab Cara and run off, back to the island with Goldland child in tow. It might be the best option; it might save her. Io knew all gemstones break down to sand in the end and so she broke contact with Cara. No, Io decided to leave her. Now that she'd found Cara and made the connection it would make her task that much easier in the future. She'd been marked. She'd be easy to find.

Io scuttled away from the children, hiding still in the Shadowline. She searched for witnesses wanting to remain unseen. She knew the Land of Man was superstitious; a strange creature would incite violence and fear. She'd seen it. She'd seen the Gods push fear into the minds of man so that they killed anything and anyone that threatened their land. Even when men forgot about their Gods, the fear stuck. The manipulation lasted for eons.

The Shadowline was clear. Io scurried from shadow to shadow. She hid behind rocks with each noise that echoed across the barren land until she noticed a figure standing on the boundary of the Goldlands and the valley.

Io recognized Gail. He had a face that was hard to forget because Io never forgot the face of those who tried to kill her. She found him standing on the edge, perched, unsteady, his eyes vacant, his mind somewhere far away. He was looking as though he were about to jump into a vat of brine but didn't really want to.

Io tapped one pinscher against a grain of sand, making the slightest noise.

Gail caught her movement and turned his head to focus.

Io raised her pinschers and gestured something particularly rude for a crab. Something that only another crustacean might have understood but from the look on Gail's face she determined that he understood. With that, Io scrambled away.

She ran across the Saltpan, and the moon chased her all the way. The sand had cooled in the night, and she was glad to splash her pinschers in the warm water of the pond. Io dipped under the still surface and found the vortex that would take her home.

Io rose from the water in human form. Thin as a rail, water

trickled down her pale form of angles and planes. It had been so long since she'd enjoyed the taste of food or drink, but Io knew better. Food and drink would tether her here and she'd never be able to escape, she'd never be able to be whole again. Io crawled into her shelter, rested her head on folded hands, and replayed her plan in her head.

Chapter 8

Highrock

Noomii pushed open a rotting wood door and the commotion in the pub quieted for an instant. Yes, times had changed. There were women and men alike; their clothing was different but Noomii could still discern the castes. And she was sure they could tell what hers was. She stopped at the bar top and hailed the bartender.

"Your kind isn't welcome here," the bartender said as he stood in front of her. "Nothing from beyond the sea has been welcomed since the recession. Not a fish, not a mollusk, not a shrimp. And definitely not a woman. I'll serve you, but you should know once you leave these walls they'll come for you."

Noomii cleared her throat. "I'll have rye."

The bartender swiped the counter, looking bored. "And how will you pay for that?"

Noomii never had much money to herself. Enough for a half-cot and one meal a day. Being a Watchtower servant didn't exactly pay. But, Noomii did have something. She dug in her bag, pulled out the octopus of ocean jasper and slid it across the bar. "It's all I have."

The bartender's eyes grew large. "A gem like this could buy you a home amongst the clouds in the Goldlands." He picked up the carving and tested its weight, glancing at his guests.

"How about a drink and a quiet room for the night?" She shifted her bag, careful not to knock the other carvings.

The bartender waved her to the end of the bar. She retreated to the shadows, became invisible as a creature of darkness on a pitch-black night.

The stir of the pub went on and Noomii was glad she no longer held their attention. She sipped the drink slowly until the pub emptied and the bartender went to lock up. As the door closed, Noomii said, "I'm looking for any sanctuaries of the Creator."

The bartender went rigid. "Don't speak of the Creator or the old Gods." He pressed his hand against the door. "The Watchtower was lit years ago and they never came. They never saved these people." The bartender tipped his chin. "What do you need of a sanctuary?"

"I have a task," she replied.

He glanced at her bag. "I saw you collect those bones from under the docks."

"And now I must bury them," Noomii interrupted. It was the least she could do for the helmsman after all he had done for her.

He nodded, as if he agreed to rot on the beach was never a good way to leave this world.

The bartender showed Noomii to a large room with a lock and a view of the ocean. Rough-hewn wood lined the walls. There was a clean bed, simple furniture. Not much different from her home.

"I need a change of clothing and safe transport," Noomii said as she stood by the window.

The bartender was silent.

"I've paid you well," Noomii said.

"Where will you go?" he asked.

"I think one of the mountains." It was the closest thing to a sanctuary she could think of.

"The mountains are gone." The bartender said solemnly.

"Why?" she asked.

"Blasted away to build the Goldlands higher." He raised his arm above his head.

Noomii thought for a moment. "Then I will travel to the Darkmoors."

He nodded. "You might be the last soul to pass through those lands. Those of the Darkmoors were culled to deconstruct the mountains and shoulder large rocks for building."

Noomii blinked. "If there is no longer faith in the Creator or the old Gods, then why build?"

"Oh, but they worship the gold." The bartender tipped his head as he began closing the door.

"And what do you worship?" she asked.

"The rye." He winked and the corner of his mouth tipped in a playful smile. The door closed with a click.

He was nice enough, but Noomii slid the dresser in front of the door. She'd read enough layers of eternal stone to know what terrors the night could bring, either God or human-created. She didn't know this place.

In the morning there was a knock. "I bring clothing and a guide," the bartender's voice sounded.

Noomii moved the dresser and cracked the door. The bartender passed her a thick cloak lined with beaver hide. "The Darkmoors are wet this time of the year."

"Thank you." Noomii nodded. "But this is—"

"Worth much less than what you paid me." He cleared his throat. "There is an errand boy with a carriage waiting outside. He has been paid well for his silence."

Noomii closed the door to dress. She opened her bag and removed a few of the carvings, tucking them into her pockets and waistband to easily access in case she needed to buy her freedom. She left the room and made her way down the stairs. Finding a back door, she left the pub and found the carriage and boy.

"Are you the one who is going to the Darkmoors?" The boy wasn't that young, perhaps a year before adulthood. Noomii nodded and the boy held the door open. "The mud is thick from heavy rains."

"It usually is." Noomii seated herself in the middle of the carriage, worried the bartender was right and that they would come for her.

The boy climbed into the carriage seat and clicked his tongue; a black horse took off at a moderate pace. Noomii watched the landscape pass from the window; it had changed. The roads looked different than when she walked them so many years ago. Trees had died and the fog drifted forever over the road. There had been birds chirping and flying across the plains, now there was not a living creature in sight.

As the carriage rocked over the road marred with deep tracks, the bones of the helmsman clanked a hollow sound from her bag.

Noomii could smell the Darkmoors before they arrived, sulfur and ammonia thick in the air. They were in the shadow of the Goldlands now and the closer they got, the darker it became.

"Would you like a light?" the boy asked.

Noomii didn't want the boy to stop the carriage, so she said no and thanked him. Her eyes adjusted as they always had. Some of the streetlamps were still lit, but the streets lay empty. They passed the pub where she'd worked and the coffin-apartments where she'd lived.

"Would you like me to stop?" the boy asked.

Noomii leaned closer to the window. "Take me to the graveyard on the edge of town."

The boy clicked his tongue and the horses' hoof beats upped their pace.

There was nothing here for Noomii, just memories of who she once was.

The carriage stopped at an overgrown graveyard. The people of the Darkmoors had enough sense to bury their dead on high ground and today it was the only land that wasn't saturated with mud. Noomii opened the door and the boy was there, one hand holding the door, the other in his pocket. She grabbed onto the frame of the carriage as she climbed down.

"Do you have a spade?" she asked.

"Yes, miss."

The title didn't surprise her as it once had. The helmsman had rid her of that. "Bring it," she told the boy.

Noomii walked through the middle of the graveyard. She knew where she was going; she'd chosen the plot herself. She'd dug the hole and lowered her mother's frail body down since there were no undertakers in the Darkmoors who would bury an untouchable, especially one who'd died of the black lung. Noomii stopped at a tall patch of grass and pressed the blades away with her foot to reveal a small statue of Highrock, identical to the one she'd brought with her when she left the Land of Man. It must've broken off a headstone long ago.

"The spade," Noomii requested. The boy passed it to her and she dug. If memory served her right, the grave was shallow and not wanting to disrupt the corpse of her mother, she didn't dig deep. The soft silty soil of the moors only caved in on itself and she didn't have the tools to dig a proper grave. She stopped to open her bag and remove the cloth containing the helmsman's bones. She set the cloth-covered bones in the dirt and stood.

Noomii wasn't sure what to say to honor the helmsman, she wasn't sure what the helmsman had said to Despina when he'd buried her. She threw a shovelful of dirt and repeated her mother's words, "The greater the suffering, the greater the peace." She paused, knowing the helmsman deserved more but all she had to offer him was his own simple promise. "I will collect you and return you from where you came."

"Did this soul mean much to you?" the boy asked.

"Yes." Noomii took a carving from her waistband and set it in the dirt as an offering. "He was the last person to show me kindness." She covered the hole with the rest of the dirt before passing the boy the spade. "The only person, really."

"Grave robbers will find that," the boy warned, and his eye twitched nervously.

Noomii settled a corner of dirt under her foot. "Would that grave robber be you?"

The boy cleared his throat.

Noomii pulled another carving from her cloak. "I suppose you know I come from the sea." She passed the carving to the boy. "This is your payment to ensure grave robbers such as yourself do not disturb this plot."

The boy took the statue. "Yes, miss," he promised. Noomii looked twice as he took it, she swore she saw a shadow of a tendril slide out from his coat sleeve. She blinked to make sure her vision was clear.

As she returned to the carriage, Noomii pulled her spyglass out and glanced in the direction of the mountains. The bartender had been truthful. There were no peaks in the distance; the land was as flat as the ocean once was.

"Where have all the wild creatures gone?" Noomii asked the boy.

He shrugged. "I've never seen any in all my life. Only pictures of them," the boy said as he opened the door to the carriage. He did not offer a hand to steady her, Noomii took note.

"Where will you go now? To the Goldlands?" He seemed hopeful. "They might have creatures there."

"I don't belong there," she replied. A strange feeling overcame her, one telling her that she did not belong and needed to leave. "Bring me to the docks, quickly."

The boy returned to the head of the carriage, climbed into his seat and clicked his tongue. The Darkmoors passed in a blur, the plains as well. The rough road jerked the carriage and Noomii had to hold on tightly to the window frame.

The carriage came to a stop at the docks. The crowd was three times the size it was when she arrived the day before. The people were pointing in the distance and shouting. Noomii exited the carriage and made her way across the boardwalk as the commotion grew.

"There's a man coming!"

"He's walking faster."

"Call the army."

"The army only serves the Goldlands now."

"There will be no Goldlands if that arrives." A finger pointed.

"What is it?"

"A creature of the sea!"

Noomii walked under the docks, sneaking toward her boat.

"It's a man of the sea."

"It's a God of the sea! He'll kill us all," a woman's voice screeched.

The people were shouting at each other. She whispered a prayer to bring darkness in which she would not be seen. The warning from the bartender was strong with the crowd as riled up as they were. Noomii waited until the sun was setting before she ran to the boat. Noomii was blessed with a sliver of a crescent, just enough light to see where she was going. The water had receded more in the night and the scraping sound of Noomii moving the boat drew attention.

"What's that?" a man shouted.

"The woman from the sea!" a woman screamed. "Kill her! Kill her just like the other one. She brought that monster to us!"

Noomii ran. She shoved the boat as hard as she could, running into the water as rocks splashed around her. One thudded off her shoulder, another off the side of her head. Noomii kept going, until the water was too high for her to move easily. She leaned against the side of the boat and rolled inside. Her hands gripped the paddles as the mob moved from the moorings to the water, picking up smooth rocks to throw at her. Noomii was too far out now. She paddled faster toward the shadow of Highrock, and when the boat scraped to a stop, Noomii leaped from it and ran up the stairs to her home.

She'd never thought of Highrock truly as home, but it was the only place that had ever brought her safety and comfort. Noomii checked the candles in the tower before making herself something to eat and then, she went to sleep.

Noomii woke with a dizzy feeling. Her head felt full of cotton. The pressure and confusion reminded her of the time she slipped and fell behind the bar, hitting her head on sturdy wood or the time she'd reached the highest peak when climbing the mountains on the Land of Man where the air was thin and barely breathable. She sat up and looked out the window only to find that things weren't where they should have been.

Highrock had grown in the night, that was how she knew she was dreaming. Noomii ran out of the house, telescoping mirror in hand, and she stopped at the ledge. Her peg had moved. Caught in the reflection of the mirror, she got a glimpse of the full moon over her shoulder, much larger than she ever remembered it being. She turned and looked toward the night sky. Noomii watched in horror as the raised northern edge of Highrock began to cut through the moon the way a glacier cuts through the land, slow and steady. She held on to the nearby jutting rock, sure her house would fall or crumble or become damaged. But it didn't. Instead, as the moon orbited, Highrock cleaved it in two. And then the strangest thing happened. Half of the moon fell like a large bite of a soft-boiled goose egg dropped out of the jowls of a greedy fat man.

Noomii felt a pinch deep within her heart.

Highrock was an ax, a punishment to the Moon Goddess. The God of the sea had tried to rise to fight for her once again. This time the goddess did not shy away and recede into her orbit. She fell. The God of the sea caught her in his waves as a mother cradles a child. The Celestials lit the heavens with falling stars, fireworks of nebulas and lightning as half of the moon settled behind the onyx beast.

Noomii ran inside to check the alarm candles.

She looked out the window on her way through the house.

In the fading moonlight the onyx stone glimmered. Noomii could see that the giant man was exquisitely carved, muscle and sinew, with a belt and sword and boots that tied to his knees. The one who had risen from the sea was a warrior. She raised her spyglass to its face and the giant blinked.

"It's alive!" Noomii said to herself as she stomped up the stairs to the tower. She shoved the door open. "It's alive," she shouted at the candles, which were nearly burned to their bases. The Creator had not come. There was no message as to what to do, after all this time. No guidance. She took another look at the giant's face. It was still as stone. Unmoving.

Noomii blew out the candles as an aging adult might a birthday cake, with disappointment and trepidation to the future.

When Noomii peered over the edge she could see the water was starting to rise again. She looked to where half of the moon had fallen. There was only one thing to do. Noomii collected her things and climbed down the mountain.

She rowed to the onyx statue, which the sea was beginning to cover again. Only the head was visible by the time she got close. She stopped paddling and set her hand on a giant seaweed strand of beard.

"What have you done?" she asked the giant. "You've ruined everything."

There was silence as the gemstone of a man blinked once.

Noomii sucked in a breath and took her hand away.

"So this is the bastard woman born of the Darkmoors." The giant's voice rumbled smoothly in her mind and it reminded her of the helmsman's.

Noomii gripped the paddles. She could feel the salt spray from the waves on her face and it all seemed too real to be a dream. "I am."

"The one who has climbed the seven peaks of the Land of Man?"

"Yes." Noomii nodded.

"The one who forced her squire to row to the edge of the earth and face fate?"

"I did." Noomii had been holding her breath for so long that her heart beat in furor. She inhaled sharply. "I was born of the mud of the Darkmoors, an untouchable, that is all that I have known. I was born of mud and I will return to mud when my time here is complete."

"But you have been touched. You lost much to the Land of Man but that is not what sealed your fate to the peak of Highrock. You have lost just as much as I have. You've lost your home. Everything you knew is gone. You are no longer what you once were. We are the same, dust of creation, beings to be worshipped." The onyx man paused. "He is lost. You need to find him again. He has wandered for infinity."

Noomii was silent. There was truth to his words. She tipped herself to the side to stare into the giant orbs of his eyes, each a black hole with a speck of iris that resembled a twinkling star.

"You were not born of the mud, you were born of the stars. You were born humbled in the dirt only to transform into a burst of firelight. Awake your soul." The giant's iris burst from a star to purple cloud. "While others reached for the sky you journeyed to the edge. When has a soul from the Goldlands or Darkmoors had the courage to climb even one of the seven peaks of the Land of Man? When have they ever offered to escape their petty lives and serve the Creator or the old Gods? When was the last time they studied the books? When was the last time they worshipped the goddess of the moon?"

She knew, it was fresh in her memory now. Her mother had

told her and she'd witnessed it. "Decades," she said. "Maybe longer."

He blinked slowly and it was as though he were tipping his head in understanding. "You should see what the Moon Goddess has sacrificed. What you have sacrificed." With that, the water slowly rose over his head as he slinked back into the ocean and the sea returned to its normal level.

There was an edge to everything, Despina once said, but Noomii couldn't see the edge anymore. She couldn't see where the ocean halted for infinity, lapping against the cold dead of space. What Noomii could see was that there was a soft curved edge to the island of moonstone. She paddled until she was close enough to reach the shore. Noomii lifted the small anchor and threw it up on the land. She climbed out of the boat. The island was welcoming, warm and peaceful. She knelt and pressed her hands into the soft moonstone. The texture wasn't much more than firm clay, she pulled out a ball in her fist. For so many years she carved creatures from the pieces of Highrock, she couldn't stop herself now. There was no history to read in the white mass, just a milky clean slate. Noomii formed a flock of small birds, then lizards, she shaped tiny creatures and large until she came upon a tall mound, nearly taller than her head. She moved her hands over the mound, applying pressure here and there until a shape began to take form. There were feet. Bare, slender toes with soft skin that had never walked the streets of the Goldlands or sank in the mud of the Darkmoors or been slivered by the docks. She paused to think of how to bring her newly cast creatures to life. What would the Creator have done? Shock them with lightning, bleed into their veins, or give them her breath? She focused on her current work and found she'd been carving the helmsman's likeness; the point of his chin, his slender hands. She used her calloused fingertips to pattern a soft suit that would make any man of the Goldlands jealous.

When the sun began to set, Noomii pressed her hands into the ground and pushed down and away. She parted the soft moonstone, molded a sunken bed and a thin blanket. The Celestials lit the sky in purples and blues and reds. Noomii settled for the night only to rise with the sun. She ate from the foods she'd brought. She moved and felt the disk of amethyst in her pocket.

Noomii thought for a moment, perhaps it was interpreted correctly. Perhaps nothing really was as it was revealed in the books. Perhaps the Creator twisted the truth, and no one ever investigated the past, they simply ignored and forgot it. She stood and pulled the disk out of her pocket, broke off a small piece, and pressed it into the man's chest. Nothing happened. Noomii's heart sank. She hesitated for a moment before she touched the gentle curve of the helmsman's cheek. "But I carved you from moonstone," she whispered. "I gave you a heart of amethyst. Come back."

There was only silence. Noomii was tempted to pray to the old Gods, tempted to pray to the Creator. But what she'd done felt wrong, it felt... forbidden. She was a Darkmoor creature. Creation was not her forte. Surviving was, or at least it had been. She'd survived her life in the Darkmoors and was happy to escape. But time on the top of Highrock had changed her. All that time had passed carving creatures, and now Noomii was embarrassed that she attempted to create a man.

The man stood still, an empty silhouette, tidy in his moonstone suit and unfrayed pants. Noomii was sure his hands would never callous with life. Life was singular on the peak of Highrock. Life was singular in the Darkmoors. And now it seemed life was singular on the island of moonstone. Noomii decided she no longer wanted to be by herself. She missed the company of the helmsman, and in this loneliness she could see how Despina had chosen her ending. Her time was over. She walked to the edge of the island and stood on the ledge, her toes curled around the soft moonstone. She wondered if she should run and jump like

Despina had, if she should feel the wind sucking at her clothing, if she should relish the weight of gravity. She decided to drop like a rock, arms raised in worship, the last believer of the Creator and old Gods. She lifted one foot, and then the other, and plunged.

CHAPTER 9

HIGHMOUNT

Cara's time was empty. She knew that her hair had become windblown, and her cheeks chapped from the evening breeze, but she couldn't stop watching them all. She stood like a statue on the ledge, many days and nights. One evening she was watching the Darkmoors, the dark magic drew her eyes as it drew souls to the mire. She saw a small girl walking with her mother across mud-stained planks. Their clothes were worn, their cheeks narrow, but both smiled as they clung tightly to each other's arm until they reached a door. She followed their progression by the lights that were lit, up two sets of stairs before a light turned on in a narrow apartment. The window was opened to let fresh air in from the opposite side of the moors. Cara could see one bed, a small table and a tiny kitchen. The mother made a quick meal of porridge and berries and the two sat at the table and spoke quietly over their evening meal. After, they cleaned the dishes and got ready for bed. The mother lay down and pulled her child to the bed, embracing her and singing a soft lullaby. Cara couldn't look away; the interaction reminded her so much of her own mother.

Each day Cara watched them. The child grew taller and the mother more wrinkled. Cara watched the girl develop into an adult and the mother turned ill. The girl ran out of the apartment, doing her best to drag the doctors back to her door but they always stopped in the street and refused. Eventually she died and the girl was alone. It appeared the children of the Darkmoors didn't have the opportunities as the Goldland children did. This girl never had a valediction party, she wore the same faded clothing each day, she worked from sunup until the moon was straight overhead and then collapsed in her bed for a few hours before starting it all over again. The hard work must've paid off because one day the girl brought home a package. Cara moved to the edge of the cliff to watch her open it and reveal a pair of heavy boots. The girl began a collection of old ropes and rusted metal pieces. One day, instead of walking to work, she hailed a cart and set off in the opposite direction. Cara watched her for as long as she could, and sometimes she'd lose the trail since it was hard to see through thick forests and the other six mountains of the Land of Man. But when she did find the girl again, she was climbing a mountain. The girl did this for many weeks; she'd work long hours and on her day off escape to the mountains.

One day, she arrived at Highmount.

Cara grabbed her telescoping mirror and watched below the cliffside. The girl started at the base. She knotted ropes and rubbed her hands with drying powder and began to climb.

The girl was climbing, her arms tremored with exhaustion, but she kept going. When she got very close, Cara pulled her mirror back. She paced the peak, eager to have the girl reach the top. Cara hadn't had any human interaction except for the cartman. Cara ran into her house and checked her reflection in the mirror. She opened her cupboard doors to see if there was food to offer her. There was–of course there was; the cartman brought more than enough food for Cara to survive.

Cara went back outside, sat on her stoop, and watched the ledge in anticipation.

A hand reached up and over the cliff. It grasped for purchase, finding it in a jutting rock. The girl pulled herself over the edge and up on Cara's mountain. She dragged herself a few feet, her arms slick with sweat, and rolled to sit, facing away. She crossed her legs, settled her elbows on her knees, and simply stared as she took deep breaths. Cara didn't say a word. The girl was still so close to the edge, and she didn't want to startle her.

Remembering the small, dirt covered child of years ago, up close Cara could see how much she'd grown. She carried a cloud though; it was a sense that was hard to ignore. There was something about this girl whose dark lingered near the surface. She finally stood and turned around.

"Oh," her eyes went wide. "Forgive me. I didn't realize someone lived up here." The wind caught her dark hair, swiping it against sunburnt skin.

Cara smiled. "It's okay." She hesitated and Cara remembered the ways of the Land of Man. This girl was born of the Darkmoors, Cara was born of the Goldlands, and she had to remember the rules of their castes. Cara simply waved as a greeting.

The girl's brown eyes narrowed as she took in Cara's tattered skirts and jacket. "I won't be here long. I just need to catch my breath."

"I didn't realize people climbed this far up with only rope and a few bits of metal."

The girl toyed with the thick ropes that were wrapped around her pelvis and knotted tightly. "It's safe. I promise."

Cara wanted to offer water or food, but she knew she wasn't supposed to. She ran her fingers over the smooth edges of the stone in her pocket.

"How many of the mountains have you climbed?" Cara asked.

"This is my seventh. The furthest from home. Probably my last."

Cara nodded. She knew.

The girl turned and looked over the Land of Man. "There's

just something about standing up here in the wind, away from all the bullshit. The freedom from it all. I'll miss it."

"You won't climb anymore?"

"I've conquered the seven mountains of the Land of Man. Now I must find something new to climb."

It was inspiring. Climbing, alone. Traveling to all these places. Most people from the Darkmoors never saw more than the dank mud of the moors until their souls passed to the Goldlands after they'd breathed their last breath. Breaking that chain was enough to impress Cara.

Cara decided to break a rule. "What's your name?"

The girl's face pinched in confusion. "Noomii," the girl said. She didn't ask what her name was.

"I'd like to offer you something, but I know I'm not supposed to. If someone were watching..."

Noomii waved her away. "I'm leaving soon." She paced the edge of the cliff before crouching down and securing a pin, threading it with rope. "I'm surprised. This isn't a Goldland mountain." She side-eyed Cara.

Cara let out a breath. "It's hard to break these rules we've been raised with."

Noomii nodded. "Thank you for letting me climb your mountain."

"Oh, it's not mine. I'm just... here." She made an awkward gesture with her hand. "Do you want to walk down?" Cara asked as she motioned to the winding trail that she and the cartman used. "It might be easier."

Noomii smiled. "Nope. Going down is the best part." She secured her ropes and metal bits before leaning back over the expanse. "It was nice to meet you." And then, Noomii moved a metal bracket and swooped down the mountainside like an eagle diving for prey.

Cara moved to the edge and opened her mirror. She watched Noomii slide down on her ropes in less than a quarter of the time that it took for her to climb. Once she reached the bottom, Noomii packed up her belongings and headed home.

There was something very Darkmoor about Noomii. Cara watched her return to the apartment before she turned her focus to the ocean, the Watchtower above Highrock, her eyes spanned the cliffs of the Goldlands, the twinkling gates, roved to the shadowlands in the east, the desolate Saltpan. She saw nothing perplexing, nothing that might cause her to need to light the waxy wick in her attic.

Cara wandered the plot of land she now called home. Rocks came lose under her feet, she bent and picked up a stone. A deep blue transparency, Cara recognized the gem as Kyanite. She flexed her fingers around the stone, glanced to the Darkmoors and sensed Noomii's frustration even from this distance. "This is your history," Cara murmured to herself. She slipped the gem in her pocket before sitting on the stoop and watching the night take over. The Celestials lit the horizon in vibrant hues. When they were done, Cara went inside. Less hallow by the measure of a grain of sand, she had more purpose now than ever before. She sat at the desk in the loft, pulled out the journal she had begun writing in so many moons ago, uncapped a pen, and began to write.

There once was a girl of the Darkmoors. Born of the magical peat, her creation was something she could never escape. The dark draw of chaos would always consume her.

Cara stared out the window as she focused her thoughts of Noomii. And for a moment her sight didn't end. She saw past the moors and the beaches and the sea, she saw the Watchtower of Highrock, a dark shadow looming beneath the surface of the ocean. She followed the cold abyss of space and kept going until she fell off the edge... but she didn't fall, no, she wrapped herself around the bottom and saw dark things under the land, her vision kept progressing until she came to Highmount again and then it was all a blur as time warped and her vision sped. Following the elliptical tunneled path, she saw mountains fall and the Goldlands rise, she saw the light of the Highrock, she saw Noomii in the future.

It happened so fast, Cara held her breath until her vision returned to nothing more than the room she sat in, and she sucked in a deep breath.

"You had a visitor," the cartman said as he settled his cart on the ground.

Cara was sitting cross-legged on the edge of the cliff, watching. She turned as he spoke, retracted her mirror, and slipped it into her pocket discreetly. "I did." She stood and brushed her hands off on skirts that were once deep burgundy and lined with lace. The peak of Highmount and the stretch of time had turned her skirts threadbare and faded. "It was unexpected. For us both, I think."

The cartman began removing bags from the cart. He motioned to the door of Cara's house. "I have supplies. Some food and wood and bone pens."

"I'll help you." Cara made way for the pile and lifted a bag before following the cartman into her home. She set the bag on the table and paused. "How long have I been up here?" she asked.

The cartman stopped, his hand on the door. "Time is only relative, to the Arrow, to the Land of Man, to the peaks of the Watchtowers, to the old Gods and perhaps the Creator. I cannot tell you how time has passed because I do not know."

"How long have you been here?" she asked.

"I'm not ever really here." The cartman opened the door and headed out to gather more bags. "But I am there." He pointed to the curving path that led to the base of Highmount. "Forever it seems I am there. And other peaks. Highmount, Highrock, High-sandplateau." The cartman paused. "You seem different."

"I've seen something," Cara replied.

"On the horizon?" the cartman turned and focused in the distance.

"You won't be able to see it. It's far ahead. Far into the future."

"You saw into the future?" The cartman's interest seemed piqued more than ever. "None of the Watchtower servants have been able to see into the future. Or none that I can remember."

Cara rolled the Kyanite in her pocket. "I'll write it in the journals."

The cartman nodded in agreement.

"I'll light the tower eventually." She looked away from him, afraid of just what her eyes might see. "Just so you know." Cara toyed with the frayed hem of her sleeve. "Would you like to stay? For dinner or sunset?"

Today the angst of loneliness was worse than ever. And she'd seen him in the future. She just didn't know how to warn him or what do say. How do you tell a man they're a wisp? That every footstep is a black shadow, a curse that haunts him?

"You know I cannot." He went to his cart and lifted the rough handles, settling them in the leather pockets at his hips. "Until next time." He waved and began his trek down the mountain.

Cara watched until he went past the first bend and then she ran after him.

"Wait!"

But he didn't. The cartman carried on just like a wisp of the Goldlands, forever passing through time, rarely acknowledged or acknowledging. She wondered if he was even solid or if he'd pass through a wall just as easily as a spirit.

Cara's feet skidded to a halt, unease filled her belly. There was something strange about leaving her post, something strange about *trying* to leave her post. Cara wanted to leave, she wanted to go back in time and not open the door when her invitation to

Highmount came; she wanted to stay with her mother and the spirits that frequented her home. She could barely remember the sounds of her solid boot heels on hollow bone, the feel of her mother's palm on her cheek, the icy chill of a wisp entering the room. Cara kicked the dirt, sent rock and gemstones flying over the cliff edge. She tried to move but the feeling in her belly worsened and her vision blurred. Cara backstepped until it stopped.

"Damn you," she murmured.

Chapter 10

The Eternal Bartender

The Rye House had always been at the center of the boardwalk. It didn't matter how high or low the tide was, how warm or chilled the air became. Since the years of the koi fish, since the times of ruby fuschite, the Rye House had endured in some capacity. Whether it be a butcher house, an ale house, a soup kitchen, or empty building; the Rye House stood strong for the people of the gulf and beyond.

Drax reached for a clean mug. The water at the pub never got the glass quite clean and a milky film remained. The patrons didn't seem to mind, the rye looked the same, tasted the same, got them drunk the same. Some quicker than others. They all came from near and far; the boats, the moors, the Goldlands, and lesser mountains on the Land of Man. Drax had never received a patron from past the Shadowline though. He expected one day someone would show up from the Saltpan, but none did. Word was that it was still stark desert out there and none were brave enough to inhabit those lands.

"Do you think the world is going to cave in?" A tall woman with red hair pinned to the back of her head revealing a porcelain neck and fine face asked from the corner of the bar.

Drax paused from filling the mug. "The world is perpetually caving in, my dear. Flat as it is, there is nowhere to go but inward." He cleared his throat, finished filling the mug before sliding it down to the opposite end of the bar. "What can I get you?" he asked the woman.

"House special," she replied.

Drax filled a mug, taking the time to find a cleaner cloth from behind the bar and shine the mug as best as he could. He filled her mug to the top before walking it to her. A few strands of dark hair fell lose from their knot and Drax suddenly wished he'd taken the time to shave this morning.

"No slide?" she asked as the corner of her mouth tilted up.

"Not for a lady." Drax set the full mug down, folded his arms and leaned in. "And what brings a fine specimen like yourself to this hole in the wall?"

"The famous Rye House?" She made it apparent that she was looking around the establishment, taking in the paintings on the walls, the booths, the scraped floors. "Looks to be more than a hole in the wall."

Drax waited.

"I came exploring," she finally said.

"Exploring." Drax's interest was piqued. "Who came with you? Your husband, must be." He tilted to the side and scanned the room, looking for a man who was looking for this woman.

She laughed. "Bless the Creator and old Gods, no." She shook her head. "There is no husband. I don't need a travel companion."

"Brave woman." He glanced at her fingers. There were no rings.

She shrugged and took a drink. "Duty calls, sir." She pointed to a young fisherman who had been trying to get Drax's attention.

Drax threw the bar towel across his shoulder and went back to work. He kept her mug full and brought her order of house stew out when she ordered it. He did his best to impress this lonely traveler. He had hired a musician for the week and folk music played throughout the night. The up-tempo rhythms brought in more people from the boardwalk and as the moon rose, the pub filled to the brim.

Soon the band started playing a song that everyone in the bar recognized. The woman turned to dance and clap with the rest of the room. Drax tried not to stare. He busied himself with rinsing glasses and plates. He raised his head more than a handful of times to find her looking in his direction.

The night went on and after Drax shouted for last call, the woman hailed him to her end of the bar. Her pale skin was flushed, and her words slow.

"I've heard you rent rooms. I would like one for the week, please."

Drax smiled. "If you needed a room, you could have asked sooner rather than listen to this treacherous noise for half the night."

She watched his lips, her eyes half-lidded and sparkling. "If I'd gotten a room sooner, I wouldn't have been able to watch the show all night."

Drax laughed. "They are a good group of musicians." He tipped his head to the group as they packed up their instruments.

"Not them." The woman drank the last of her rye and slid the mug toward Drax.

Drax caught the mug, pausing as her words sank in. "Alright then. You must've had plenty to drink for a comment like that." He set the mug in the sink under the counter and walked to the wall where the room keys hung. A few were already occupied, but the corner room was open. That was the nicest one with a view of the Watchtower and the sea. Drax grabbed the key and went back to the woman.

"You should dance with me," the woman said, her eyes scanning him from boots to collar bone.

Drax dragged a heel for the noise. "Sadly, there's no music."

He dangled the key in front of her. "Before I give you this, I must have your name."

She smiled wide. "Is this for business or pleasure?"

Drax leaned in. "If you must know, it's for the room ledger." He winked.

"Pina," she said, grabbing the key out of his hand.

"It's very nice to meet you, Pina." Drax smirked and watched her sway as she stood. "Would you like me to show you to your room? Or would you prefer to try that key in all the rooms above until you find the one it works in?"

"Oh, what a gentleman you are." Pina held her hand out as though she were a royal and he a pheasant.

Drax rounded the bar and snapped the key from her hand. "Follow me, drunkard woman."

He showed her to room five, held the door as she walked through. He fought the urge to reach out and steady her, to settle her in bed, kiss her forehead as she fell asleep, and he left the room. Drax shook his head, chasing away the thoughts.

"This is nice," Pina said as she kicked her boots off and sat on the bed. She rubbed the heavy quilt.

Drax tossed the key next to her on the bed. "Nicest room at the inn. I'll be downstairs if you need anything." He locked the doorhandle from the inside before closing the door. Drax stood outside her room and exhaled a deep breath. The bed creaked as Pina shifted her weight and got comfortable. He stood there, a moment too long, before heading down to the pub to clean up.

CHAPTER 11

SeaBottom

At the bottom of the sea
At the bottom of the sea
The God of the sea lies at the bottom of the sea
Cross his ways or piss in his sea
The Celestials will curse and old Gods will banish you,
to the bottom of the sea.

Cira was a wild rose of the valley. Her people had searched for years since they found out she was missing and her husband disappeared on an inky black night. They hailed help from the Goldlands but none came. The people of the valley would collect hematite and offer it up to the moon, trying to gaze upon her beauty. Cira never dropped down to collect their offerings. She would never walk their dirt packed streets nor shop at their valley market ever again.

Because her people were wrong, the lore twisted; misread and mistold.

Cira was never on the moon. Cira was at the bottom of the sea.

Encased in iron, holes cut into the coffin so she could see the light of the seven suns passing over the sea each day.

It took exactly one day for her to come back to life and die all over again. Cira's eyes opened as the sun lit the water. She gasped, lungs filling with saltwater. She screamed, tiny bubbles of her last breath rising to the break. Cira beat the sides of the coffin. She kicked until her toes broke against the heavy iron. She gasped only to take in more water, tears mixing with saltwater, throat burning, muscles aching from lack of oxygen. Cira pounded on the iron until her arms were numb. Her hands were waterlogged, deep wrinkles distorting her fingertips.

Cira lived only to die within a few minutes, every day for a thousand years. But in those first few moments, she remembered what he had done and prayed that someone would find her. Someone, anyone. She'd even forgive Divine if he'd swim to the bottom of the sea to save her. But she knew better. Demigods are rarely an improvement upon their parents. Cira ached for an end.

Chapter 12

HIGHROCK

She woke up.

Noomii sat up in bed, her chest heaved with sweat and her nightshirt stuck to her back. She moved to the edge of the bed and settled her feet on the floor. She scrambled to the window. It all looked the same. Highrock had not moved as in her dream. She used her spyglass to get a glimpse of the docks. The helmsman's body was gone. She'd buried him with respect, an ending Noomii was sure she would not endure. Especially after last night.

Noomii turned her glass toward the Goldlands. She tipped her chin up so she could focus above the gray clouds. The tall buildings sparkled gold. The sun glinted off domed roofs, and toothpick scaffolding revealed just how much more they were building. The towers of the Goldlands lumbered higher than any mountain or cathedral on the Land of Man. Gold ruled. With rubies and jewels chaos always ensues.

Noomii returned to the stairwell, tools in hand, and chipped away at a layer of sage stone forming a step like the one below it. She saved a chunk to examine later. Next came a layer of light brown and contrasting striations, Herringbone Sequoia. It was a thick layer of petrified wood, opalized into Highrock from a time when the forests were so thick man could not pass through them. The trees grew tall and wide and pushed man to the edge of the land, before man became skilled with an ax and fire and ended the age of the trees. Now the trees stayed rooted in fear of ax and fire. They feared man.

As Noomii worked, she glanced in the distance to see the statue. In her dream the sea had covered him again, but her eyes were now open, and he stood tall and dark in the distance. Imposing. Looming like a dark memory.

Noomii continued working into the night. She watched the base of Highrock, expecting the helmsman to row close and deliver a bag of food. Her stomach grumbled. She was feeling dizzy and weightless. Noomii knew that she'd need to return to the Land of Man or starve on top of Highrock.

She chipped at a layer of mottled green epidote and pink orthoclase. She held a large chunk up to the light to see what secrets the unakite gem held. It took her a few moments to focus and see. There were dragons. Pink and scaled, flying over lands lush with greenery.

Noomii decided that was enough for this day. She returned to the top of Highrock and walked to the pond in the center of the peak to bathe. The Celestials lit the night sky with lazy trails of shooting stars and pulsating nebulas. She'd definitely seen better projections and wondered if they needed inspiration. Noomii glanced to the darkness at the edge of the earth. Knowing now that there was more than meets the eye stole some of the dread. Noomii had pledged her life to the Watchtower; she stood upon the needle that stitched together time, and she couldn't help but feel that there was something more she should be doing, something more she should be searching for. Where had all the creatures she'd discovered in the striations of the Watchtower gone? It seemed unbelievable to her that they would simply disappear. She wondered how differently her time here would have been if the

Helmsman had brought her a dragon instead of silly birds. She missed him. As she floated, watching the Celestials dance, she thought thoughts she'd been instructed to never think. Suddenly the Celestials started moving faster. The few shooting stars were replaced with hundreds. The plumes of dust burst over and over again in oranges and reds and blues. Noomii moved out of the water and collected her things, wary as her thoughts wandered, becoming darker and the night sky eruptions became bolder.

A warm speck started in her gut, spreading with each thought of *what if*. What if she climbed down and rowed away to the edge like in her dream? What if she returned to the Darkmoors and dug up the Helmsman's bones and told them to live? What if she climbed to the Goldland gates and unleashed... something?

Noomii closed the door to the house, her arms and legs now prickling with heat. The Celestial display lighted the windows as she ate the last of her spotted goose eggs and lavender tea. She searched the cupboards only to find a few boxes of crackers. Noomii glanced at her cloak. She knew she was bred of the muck. She knew the Darkmoors were barren. She knew the coast was a melting pot of hate. She knew there was a Watchtower at the edge of the world. She knew the Land of Man had lost their faith. She also knew the helmsman had kept something from her.

Noomii twisted her hair in plaits like she'd seen the women of the Goldlands do. She sewed a dress from white bedsheet that was nothing more than a few proper snips, and darts, and pleats. No one would tell the haste in which it had been made with the fancy cloak the bartender had brought her. She collected more of the gemstone carvings. She carved the unakite into a fine pink dragon with a mottled green back. She carved the herringbone sequoia into a firm, wide tree trunk with little buds at the tip of its branches ready for leaves to sprout. She packed these with the others. And she took the disk of amethyst. The lights outside her bedroom window became brighter.

Noomii paddled to the docks in silence, the oars whispering

with drops of water as they worked. They cleaved through a cluster of bubbles. She ignored the voice, figuring it was a ghost of the sea haunting her. She trusted nothing out here at this point.

The people who had previously thrown rocks and chased her away were nowhere to be seen at this hour. The moon goddess left a sliver of light in the sky to both hide her and provide the smallest amount of light by which to see.

Noomii crossed the dry rocks light-footed. The shadows of the Goldlands hid the Celestials fireworks. She slipped off her shoes to cross the sandy beach without sinking, replacing them again when she reached the boardwalk. She went to the tavern. It must have been all those years in the Darkmoors spent working in the pub for this one to bring her such comfort. Smoke and rich fermented rye rose and rushed for the door when she opened it. The gentle murmur of patrons barely hushed as she walked in.

The bartender's eyes darkened when he saw her. Noomii approached.

"What can I get you?" he asked.

"Dark amber." She nodded as she sat at the end of the bar, out of earshot.

The bartender filled a thick glass to the brim, foam dripping down the side. He wiped it away with a towel and set it before her. "You're back." He said, his voice soft so the others wouldn't hear. "You're different."

"A heavy stone to the back of the skull will do that to a person." Noomii took a sip, enjoying the rush of ease that encased her. She didn't point out that he was different as well, that time had rushed ahead while she was gone and now his eyes were lined with crow's feet and the corners of his mouth draped in fine lines. Still, he hadn't aged like those around him.

"You met none on your way back?" He absently swiped at the counter. "It's been a while. I'm sure they've forgotten."

Noomii plucked through her bag to pay him. "I am not a true

creature of the sea, but I was able to slither in the shadows unnoticed."

The bartender set his palm on her forearm. "You've paid me well enough already." He tipped his head. "What do you need?"

"A room for the night. Goldland shoes." She swallowed hard. "And safe passage to the Goldland gates."

His eyes narrowed. "Everybody out!" he hollered.

The others stood, threw coin down on the tables, and drained their mugs before heading to the door. Noomii stood, confused. The bartender followed the line and didn't acknowledge Noomii as she was the last. He said goodbyes and thank yous and closed the door just before she reached him. His thick arm blocked her path.

"You stay." He turned the lock on the door then began swiping tables clean and collecting mugs.

Feeling at home and familiar, Noomii helped. She collected a handful of mugs and carried them to the bar just as she'd done many years before during her time as a barmaid.

"The Goldlands you say?" The bartender was running water into the sink. He pushed the handle off and metal squealed. "Last time it was the Darkmoors. Now the Goldlands." He scoffed. "The Land of Man is smaller than you think. Word will carry."

Annoyed and tired, Noomii raised her chin. "I don't care what anyone will think."

"Why must you go to the Goldlands?"

"For answers."

"Answers you haven't learned from the peak of Highrock? No one has ever come back from there alive. No one besides that haunted Helmsman and he's dead now."

Noomii was still at the mentioning of the Helmsman. "Did you know him?" she asked.

"Not well."

"Did you know where he went during the hours between his trips to Highrock?"

"The bar. The whorehouse. I didn't keep track of him." The

bartender waved dismissively. "My father and my father's father said he never aged." He tipped his chin. "Like you."

Noomii's back straightened. "I've aged." Noomii thought of all the things she'd learned, of all the years she spent at the peak. She might not have the wrinkles to prove it, but she'd grown. She'd had thoughts that had made the Celestials revel. She was no longer meek and obedient. She'd washed the mud from her skin.

"And you?" she asked. She would have been blind to dismiss his aging. He should be gray and stooped at the shoulders, but instead the bartender stood tall and strong and had only aged in his eyes and his stained clothing.

"Did you know his name?" Noomii never thought to ask the Helmsman his name, but now that she was learning others, it seemed appropriate.

"Some said he was called Gail."

"Gail," Noomii whispered to herself. There were so many times she could have called him such instead of just the Helmsman. Noomii was beginning to understand why an untouchable from the Darkmoors was not called by name, now that she knew his it made him so much more real. More than just a squire.

"Fine then." He waved her to follow. "I'll show you the room."

Noomii followed him up the back stairs to the rental quarters. It was the same room she'd stayed in before.

The bartender bid her goodnight but before he left Noomii asked, "How long?"

"In the morning."

The door closed and Noomii locked it before returning to the window. She gazed out over the sea. The thoughts returned. Thoughts she'd never had before. Thoughts that made the sky in the distance light up. When she stopped they went away and Noomii wondered if perhaps she were controlling the Celestials?

CHAPTER 13

LandbeforeitwasGold

A wife, a wife, a wonderful wife
draped in white and sweet as cake
A wife, a wife, will a sacrifice make.

Cira was flat on her back, there were blue skies painted on the ceiling above, and a boulder resting firmly in the pit of her stomach. No day had ever felt like this, Cira thought. But no day had ever been such as this. Today she was to marry the son of the Arrow.

She blinked three times, then four more, a habit of compulsion. Seven blinks for good luck. Cira was unsure if luck could help her now. Some would call her lucky, but where is the luck in being removed from your mother's home and sent off to marry someone you've never met? She had a hard time finding the luck in this situation. The son of the Arrow was a fearsome creature. Half man, half beast. He had antlers with eight points jutting from the sides of his head. His face angled to that of a buck, with the features of man. Some thought he was desirable and unique, but

Cira knew better; she'd seen a painting of him and he was... disgusting. But she'd been promised. A sacrifice. The only girl in the valley without a father to say otherwise. Her mother had cried for weeks before they took her away.

Cira sat up and moved to her feet. The walls were papered in rich golden swirls with a backdrop of pristine white. The style was very different from the cabins of the valley, which were usually decorated with wood and glass and animal hides. She walked to the heavy wooden door and placed her hand on the smooth, lacquered surface. She pushed as hard as she could, used her shoulder to try and force it open but they'd locked her in the tower so she wouldn't run away.

There was a sharp knock on the door.

Cira backed up.

"Any more of that and you'll have your shoulders all bruised up before we know it." A servant entered the room carrying a gown of white lace. "Your dress is ready. And it's like nothing the Land of Man has ever seen before." She hung the dress on a hook and straightened the fabric. "You're very lucky." The woman busied herself around the room drawing a bath, setting out a brush and flowers for her hair. "Let's get you ready."

Cira crossed her arms and backed against the wall. It was bad enough she'd been forced to come to this place where the altitude made her head dizzy, she wasn't going to participate so easily. As Cira watched the woman note her unease and instead bustle about the room to tidy it and tell her small quips of encouragement. Something in Cira started to melt, and she slid down the wall until she was crouched on the floor and buried her face in her hands.

The old woman shushed her, a gentle hand on her arm reminded Cira of her mother. "We'll have none of that. There's not much time." The old woman touched Cira's hair, inspected her fingertips, touched the feathers of her clothing. "This must go," the woman said. "Come now." She motioned to the tub and helped Cira stand with a gentle tug on her arms.

Cira nodded in agreement. A bath would be nice, she thought. Her face felt tight with the dried salt of her tears, and she couldn't stop smelling the horse that had brought her here. Cira shed her cloak of moss and short dress of mottled-brown turkey feathers and stepped into the tub.

"This thing..." the servant threw the cloak out the window. "It belongs in the forest, not on a creature such as you." The woman picked up a cloth and a bar of soft soap. "Here, rub this between your hands."

Cira took the soap and did what the woman said. She was rewarded with the scent of wildflowers. Cira held it close to her nose. Scented soaps were rare in the valley. Reserved for the solstice and weddings. The people of the valley used unscented soaps on regular days, so they didn't disrupt the natural scents of the forest and scare away the wildlife. Still, this soap reminded her of the valley; lavender and marigolds, field orchids, and fresh grass. Tears burned her eyes. Cira missed home more than anything right now. Her heart ached for her mother. Being alone in this foreign land was a bit too much to handle.

"Hush now," the old woman said as she dipped a cloth in the warm water and washed Cira's face. "There. No more tears. You don't want your eyes all red for the ceremony." The woman helped Cira wash her hair and scrubbed her back until her skin glowed pale pink.

"What's your name?" Cira asked.

The woman tsked. "Now, I know you are not born of the Goldlands and the valley is a bit more free, but here the upper castes do not ask the names of servants. I've already spoken too much to you and if one of the Goldland-born heard me I'm sure I'd be sent to pasture by tomorrow." She inhaled a deep breath. "While you're in the Goldlands you keep your chin up, you don't ask names, and you don't touch a lesser caste."

"But you've helped me bathe?" Cira's face twisted in confusion.

"This is a bit different. The rules don't all make sense but one day they might. This is a new land, after all."

When she was clean, and all remnants of the valley had been washed away, the servant helped her out of the tub and into a towel. She combed Cira's hair and sectioned the front pieces into tiny braids. She twisted the hair into little nests and pulled a handful of gems from her pocket. "You must honor the past on this day." The old woman scrambled the gems in her palm before holding it out to Cira. "Choose three."

Cira knew the gems were precious. She'd seen men come through her valley and purchase livestock or women or weapons with them. But she'd never held a gemstone between her own fingers before. She selected a pink one marbled with black.

"Rhodonite," the old woman said as she pressed it into Cira's hair.

Cira selected two more, one was white as bone, the other black as pitch.

"Selenite and... onyx." She pressed each gem into her hair before turning Cira's shoulders so she could see herself in the mirror. "Interesting choices, my dear." She patted Cira's bare arm. "The son of the Arrow will be pleased with all three." The woman refused to meet Cira's eyes as she helped her into a heavy dress of spun gold. She tied the back laces and brushed out the skirt fabric. "You are the most beautiful thing the Land of Man has ever seen. No wonder you were chosen for him." She glanced down. "Barefoot will be good. It's an innocent gesture." The woman pinched Cira's chin and cheeks. "And don't you look innocent."

Cira blinked a handful of times to calm her heavy beating heart. Outside the window she could hear voices and the savory smell of roasting meat and the sweetness of cakes drifted in the room.

"Ah, I'm sure they are ready for you." The woman clapped her hands and headed for the door. "Come now."

Cira followed the woman down the thousand steps of the

tower, across great empty halls with walls coated in gold, and outside. Cira shielded her eyes as they walked down the stone steps; the goldshine from the surrounding buildings hurt her eyes. The valley never shone as bright as this place; there were too many trees and the only glare came from the still river water.

They walked across garden paths of bone. Cira's footsteps gave an empty echo as Goldland-born watched them from the grassy areas. They went silent, and their mouths opened in shock. Cira didn't see the son of the Arrow anywhere. Dread was a flower blooming in her chest with each step she took. They followed the path through a small park of trees that opened to a clearing and a peak. Cira could smell the salty air from below. She'd never been to the beach, but she could recognize the change in the air. It wasn't stale like the air in the tower or the steep climb to the gates of the Goldlands. This was pure. She turned her face to the sun and closed her eyes.

"Wait here," the woman said. "There are wisps, ghosts of lost souls that wander this place. Ignore them." Her footsteps echoed further and further away. "It's better if you pretend you don't see them."

Cira was alone at the peak. All was quiet but every so often she thought she could see a flutter of smoke out of the corner of her eye. The valley was filled with forest spirits, trees and leaves that spoke in the wind—more in the winter wind. Cira straightened her spine and inhaled deeply.

"I am Divine," a rough voice whispered in her ear. "That's my name." His breath was warm on her ear and it sent a chill down her spine.

Cira froze, afraid to turn and face this beast of a man who would be her husband.

Divine pointed out to the sea. Cira took note of a human-looking hand, the dark hair covering his arm but no fur, no hooves for fingers.

Thank the Creator, Cira breathed out. He had real hands.

"Can you see the eyes?" he asked. "The God of the sea has sent his blessing. That's rare." He pointed to the rock peak in the middle of the water. "That's the Creator's tower, the lesser Gods have been given towers here on the Land of Man. Not that you would ever see one, they rarely come about. I'm not sure if they remember that in the valley."

Cira nodded. She was raised on the tales of the Gods and their evil deeds. The valley took an apprehensive approach to the Gods. They worshipped the land but never forgot. Gods bred with the humans and produced ghastly offspring. Every decade a daughter was offered up to the few who survived to ensure the crops would grow and the forest would provide.

He kept talking. "And then there are Demigods, just a few scattered, out there. And here. Those of us who are lucky enough to survive. Most don't make it past birth. Others have defects and mutations. I got lucky."

He turned her after that last bit and Cira got a good look at Divine up close.

"Oh, you are a sacrifice," Divine muttered, as he looked her up and down. From the top of her head to the tips of her toes, his eyes lingered over every curve of her body.

Cira's eyes were wide with panic seeing him in person. He wasn't lucky. Divine's antlers were bony and rough, the deep fissures reminded her of the cracks in the valley tree trunks. The tips shone white, but the base held flecks of green. She couldn't see where the antlers connected to his head as there was a mop of black hair. His face was slanted but it was not nearly as prominent as in the pictures she'd seen. He had a wide nose, flesh colored and not black like the deer she'd seen in the woods, eyes greener than the spring grass, and lips just as pink as a rosebud. No, he didn't look too much like a beast.

But then he made a snorting noise and his foot pawed the ground.

Cira took a step back. She stood on the edge of what would be known as the Goldland peak. She had a vision that she was falling, her stomach rising to her throat and her hands clawing the air. Rock crumbled under her heels.

Divine reached out and grabbed her wrist, pulling her to him, chest to chest. He wrapped his arms around her. Cira was surrounded by warmth, and for a moment she thought maybe this half-man half-god-beast wasn't so bad. She felt quite comfortable and safe in his arms. Her hands spread across his chest and she could feel flesh underneath his shirt. Maybe he wasn't so different from the men of the valley.

"See, I'm not so bad," Divine murmured.

Cira tilted her head up to look at him. Butterflies lit up Cira's stomach. She'd never kissed a man before.

Divine tilted his head down. His lips moved closer; they moved just like that of her neighbor's horse as it reached for a fresh apple. Wiggling and reaching and completely obnoxious.

Cira fainted.

CHAPTER 14

A CREATION OF THE CREATOR

Cario had never lived in infant form. She'd been made as a child and grew into adulthood. The Creator didn't have the time to sacrifice to infant child rearing. He longed for friendship and an addition to his team. For as long as the Creator had known, he'd been alone. Lingering between worlds, following the old Gods to mold and perfect the creatures they'd wished for. But it was always the same outcome. The old Gods warred. The creatures went extinct. All the Creator's hard work was for null. Except this one. Except Cario. Finally, the Creator had someone to call his own. A partner, a true friend, a child of his own. He'd seen the demigods falter along the same path as the old Gods and his child would be different. She would be pure, she would be strong, he'd teach her to be better. He'd never worked harder than he did on her creation. Many nights were spent in deep concentration. He'd collected handfuls of dust as it fell from the Celestials nightly displays–only the deepest shades of blue and purple, the brightest shimmers of stardust that mesmerized the Land of Man each night. He'd molded her from piles of dust and fine grains of sand. He'd sacrificed his own body to thread hers. Sinew and bone, heart and mind, everything except the tentacles that hung from his face like octopus legs. Cario began to take shape on the table of his workshop, her small frame lay lifeless in perfection. The Creator didn't give her a mother, no, but he did give her breath.

❧

"Cario?" the Creator called as heavy footsteps searched the house.

Small hands snatched at the collection of gemstones on the floor and hid the pile under the nearby bed. The stones rolled on old wooden floor making a subtle hollow sound. It was the sound of little boys emptying their pockets at night, the sound of a squirrel dropping a mouthful of foraged nuts, the sound of a hurried action so no one else would see the treasures. She plucked one palmstone from the pile and hid it in her pocket.

"Cario?" the voice called again.

"In here," Cario replied as she stood, tugged at her dress to unwrinkled and adjusted the white bedding so he wouldn't see the gems. It wasn't that it would make him mad but would bring on a stream of stories of how the gemstones did nothing but record the old Gods' failures, stories of all the creatures the Creator had tried to fix. Eventually the conversation would turn to her friends and his distaste for Cario spending time with them.

Cario set the sheet with a firm tug and tried her best not to look startled when the door opened.

"Ah, there you are." The Creator waved. "I have something to show you. Come, we must practice."

Cario nodded and followed him.

The Creator was calmly excited, his hands animated as he spoke. "Today is the day." He nodded.

"Oh?"

"I've found the perfect creature for you to practice on."

Cario sighed. "I don't want to do that anymore." She tugged at her hair as she walked, pulling it into knot at the base of her neck.

She knew trying to talk her way out of these situations was worthless.

"You're almost there." The Creator clapped. "I can feel it. This won't be like last time."

Cario cringed. She'd rather not remember last time. Last time he'd tried to make her reanimate a giant horse from the valley. It didn't end well. She wasn't strong enough. The threads of life that emitted from her fingertips couldn't pierce the thick hide, nor the strong skeleton. Instead of helping her, the Creator let the creature die in the valley prairie. He made her watch from the forest edge as a young boy found the carcass and screamed for his parents. *This hurts me as much as it hurts you*, the Creator had said. Cario knew he took pride in creating and fixing. One day, she would too.

They walked to the workshop and as the Creator opened the door Cario heard the small squeaks of pain. A tentacle from the back of his head, glossy and black, beckoned her closer. On the table was a small creature. A small rodent from the rock ledges near Highmount. She knew this creature well. She'd created it in secret.

"You thought I wouldn't find out?" the Creator asked. The appendages on his face began waving in angst. "Make it better. Claws to grip the rock ledges. Fat pads to protect the vital organs from falls." He motioned to the creature. "Fix it."

The blood ran from Cario's face, she paled as her stomach lurched. She should have known better. She should have known he'd find it.

"Fix it," he urged again. "Before it's too late."

Cario held her hands out, her fingers tingling as the threads of life appeared. She started with the internal injuries. The threads sewed together broken blood vessels.

"I want to try something different," Cario said as she worked, her brow beading with sweat. Her eyes flicked hesitantly to the Creator.

"Thread the bone," the Creator reminded her. "There are

memories in the marrow. It will learn to heal and next time rodent is injured, it will repair itself."

"I want to use the stones."

The Creator stared hard. "I've told you no. The stones won't make a difference."

"You used strange elements on me," she reminded him, staring at his face.

"This is different." He shook his head.

"But I watched the Moon Goddess create from moonstone."

"I said no!" the Creator yelled. "Remember this," the Creator said, "Your friends can make creatures, but they are rudimentary, hollowed, empty. You craft them, you fix them, you make them *live*. This is what we do. You are not the same as the children of the old Gods. You are more than a demigod playing with sand."

Cario nodded as the corners of her eyes filled with tears. The palmstone in her pocket was suddenly a heavy weight against her leg. If he left the room, she'd try it. She knew it could work. But her father would never leave her alone. Especially now that he'd found something she'd created in secret.

"Finish it," the Creator prompted.

CHAPTER 15

HIGHROCK

The next day, the bartender brought a large box. "Goldland shoes," he said, opening the lid and setting a pair of ankle boots on the floor before her. Pale as a fawn's coat with a real platinum zipper and rhinestone heels, Noomii was afraid to touch them. The bartender bowed as he unzipped one shoe and held it out. "These are Chestnut foal skin. Last season's so not to draw too much attention." She slipped her foot inside, feeling like an imposter. He helped with the other before reaching for a bag.

"I only asked for the shoes and passage," Noomii reminded him.

"But they won't let you past the gates if you arrive wearing an old bedsheet."

Noomii gripped her dress in embarrassment.

"You might have slipped past unnoticed ages ago but not these days." He opened the brown paper package, revealing a velvet black suit trimmed with satin. "This will pair nicely with the cape and the shoes. It will keep you warm. The air is thin and chilled in the Goldlands these days."

Noomii washed and dressed in the bathroom and when she

was finished she still felt like a Darkmoor untouchable, only in costume. She replaced her cloak and checked the pockets for her carvings. She counted them, ensuring they were each there and whole.

The bartender had changed as well. He was wearing a twill suit with a cerulean blue shirt and smooth leather boots.

"Why are you dressed like that?" Noomii asked. "I didn't ask you to go, if that's what you're intending."

The bartender smiled. "A lady of the Goldlands does not travel alone, especially to the sea and back again. You need answers and I need organic rye. We go together." He pointed back and forth. "You need me and I need you. And you should know my name."

Noomii wasn't sure she cared. She never knew the Helmsman's name and she was sure no one besides her mother and Despina had known hers. And, most recently, she had learned to know a name changes a person; it could change the person standing in front of you. They'd no longer be an empty soul, they'd have meaning, a memory.

"It's Drax." His back straightened proudly.

"Drax the bartender." Noomii nodded in acknowledgment.

"And yours?"

She was silent.

"I can't very well arrive at the gates calling you *lady from the sea*. What is your name?" he pressed.

"Noomii."

"Good." He nodded. "Let's go, Noomii. We are wasting daylight."

Noomii followed Drax down the stairwell and out the front door. She paused as he locked the front door to the bar and read the sign he'd hung in the window.

A wedding and a funeral. Wish me luck.

. . .

"I hope you're not the one getting married," Noomii muttered. "Or buried."

"Never." Drax pushed the key into his overcoat and took her elbow. "But, it's a nice distraction and won't raise many questions for either of us. It will keep the gossip strong."

"Am I included in the wedding or the funeral?" Noomii asked.

Drax shrugged as he tucked his keys into his jacket. "Maybe both if we are unlucky."

The boy who had brought Noomii to the Darkmoors weeks before was waiting at the road. But he was no longer a boy. A few weeks had not aged her, but the boy was now a young man. Instead of being shrouded in brown capes to travel to the Darkmoors he was now dressed in velvet and leather and looking every bit a Goldlander. He looked twice as Noomii stepped up into the carriage and settled herself across from Drax.

"Pay no mind to the boy," Drax said as he entered the carriage.

"I'm not sure I trust him."

"You should."

"He has a darkness."

"Says the women of the moors." He teased with a wink. "That giant is still out in the sea."

"Of course." Noomii held on to the window frame.

"What is it?" Drax leaned against the back of the bench seat and gazed out the window at the sea as they traveled further and further away.

"I've been out there. It seems to be nothing more than a carved man made of onyx."

Drax leaned forward. "Onyx, you say?" His thick brows rose in interest. "Onyx is the most precious of stones. The Goldlands haven't seen a speck of onyx in eons. Not since the God of the Southern Mountain's daughter chopped off his third finger and sold it."

Noomii's eyes widened. "How do you know that?"

"Churches of devotion may be gone but the stories are too good to ignore." He winked. "But a giant built of onyx. Hmm." He touched his chin in interest. "A giant built of onyx brings forth stories long forgotten. Books dug out from old family attics. Charred hardcovers of faith that have been tugged from the rubble. Demigods still roam these lands and spread stories and lies."

"There's more," Noomii said. "So many stories of a warped history."

"Tell me," Drax pressed.

Noomii slid her fingers along the golden thread. "A history of red rivers, flying monsters, the Land of Man being smothered by ash, trees that squashed out the sunlight." Noomii took a deep breath as she searched her memories, bringing forth the least absurd histories from the layers of Highrock. "Sea creatures that grew legs and ate man..." Noomii trailed off, ignoring Drax's rapt attention.

"Do you care to elaborate?" Drax asked.

Noomii shook her head. "I don't think I will."

The carriage began climbing the incline to the Goldlands. It was a false mountain that stretched to the sky; she would only acknowledge it as such. Noomii felt her ears pop as the pressure changed.

"Why did you climb the mountains?" Drax asked. "That's a lot of work, climbing a stepwell without water on the summit nor base."

"I'm not sure. I guess I was always searching for silence and a different view that might answer my questions. There is something revealing about standing on the edge of a rock and searching the horizon."

Drax laughed. "Not for me."

"I suppose it's not for everyone." Noomii felt hollow inside, not seeing the mountains in the distance. Noomii had left her climbing gear at the Watchtower. She felt naked and unprepared without it nearby. This would be the first mountain she'd ascend without it.

It was strange to climb without the muscle aches and sweat dripping from her brow, but Noomii kept alert. Her muscles twitched with each heave of the carriage. Of course, it was much harder to gaze over the land in study. The horses moved much faster than she ever did while climbing. She leaned toward the window and could still see the line where the Land of Man turned to water and the Watchtower was nothing but a needle in the distance.

CHAPTER 16

HIGHMOUNT

Highmount shook and a boom echoed throughout the valley below. Cara launched herself out of bed and stepped into her shoes. She dragged a shawl across her shoulders before running out into the early morning chill. Highmount shook again, and the booming was a blast. Rocks rolled on the far side of the mountain. The sound of boulders falling echoed as they crushed the trees below under their weight. Cara rounded the back of her house and followed the sounds. Past a few tall pines and boulders, she noticed deep cracks in the peak. She moved to the edge and opened her mirror, extending it. At the base of the mountain she could see men and women alike with pickaxes and carts, they tapped away at her mountain, taking pieces across the valley to the Goldlands. They lit dynamite and blasted away giant chunks. More people arrived with carts and began loading the pieces of the mountain. The large chunks sparkled with feldspar crystal and lucite, zurite, higher up they dug out quartz and dioptase and took it all to the Goldland peak.

At the gates, the Goldland guards inspected the carts. Their mirrors poked under wheels and beasts' bellies inspecting for anything peculiar. Cara felt sick. She was sent to man Highmount from dangers beyond, but what if the dangers were right here?

Another blast went off, this one taking a few feet worth of the ledge. She backed up, then steadied herself on the thin trunk of a sappy pine for a moment before running back to her house.

Cara's hands shook as she opened a kitchen drawer to find matches. She ran up the staircase and then climbed to the tiny tower above her bedroom. She blew dust from the lamp and wiped grime off the window then she lit the wick with a long match. The wick took to flame and burned bright.

"Divine Arrow, if you were to ever answer the flame, answer this one," Cara whispered before blowing out her match.

She climbed down from the tower, grabbed her journal and pen and made her way outside. She sat on the stoop, afraid to get too close to the edge. She watched the line of workers, the trail of horse drawn carts winding through the forests. Her eyes drifted to the Darkmoors. Noomii was working at the bar today. Cara watched her through the windows. She saw the way the travelers treated Noomii, the pennies they left for tips, the ale they spilled for fun. Noomii kept a straight face through it all, she always did. But Cara knew that if she looked into Noomii's heart, she'd see the pain it caused. Time passed, and Noomii was called to Highrock. Cara watched her pack a few items and leave the only home she'd ever known. She walked away from the Darkmoors, stopping when her feet rested on a rocking dock of the gulf.

Knowing it would take the men below a long time to collapse this mountain, she uncapped her pen and began to write.

The Darkmoor girl had grown only to watch her mother whither. She'd seen the unjust ways Goldland travelers treated her, the way her Darkmoor caste kept her treading water, never able to fully release herself from the beckoning clay of the moors.

. . .

The blasts continued on the far side of Highmount. Cara sat on the stoop and alternated between writing and watching until she heard the familiar squeak of the cartman's cart.

Cara stood as he rounded the corner and made his way to her.

"It seems you've some trouble," he said as he settled the cart.

"How did you make it up the mountain when they are blowing it down?"

"They're on the far side still," he said, nonchalant. He began to unload the bags he'd brought.

Cara watched him, her mouth hung open in bewilderment. He didn't seem the least bit concerned that they were blowing down the mountain.

"A light load today," he said as he stacked a few chords of wood.

Highmount groaned as another blast went off.

"They are blowing up the mountain." Cara's voice trembled. "What are you doing?"

The cartman paused before he lifted his cart and began to walk away.

"Don't leave me," Cara begged, moving toward him. "I can't stay up here while the mountain crumbles around me."

"You've lit the light. The Arrow will decide what happens next."

"No." Cara rounded him and stood in front of him. "You can't leave me here. You must help me get down. You... you .... Whatever is your name and why have you not told it to me?"

"My name is Gail." Worry settled over the cartman's face. "I cannot help you with that." Gail... like the gale winds that blew in sea storms, Gail like... he had a name now.

"You do everything else? You bring me food and firewood, you literally brought me to this forsaken place and now you'll just walk away and let me tumble down like the rocks?" Cara's heart was beating fast, her hands shook, and her arms felt heavy. Panic was setting in.

"I will not." He took a step forward but Cara didn't move out of his way. "I must go before the night comes. The suns set fast these days."

"No." Cara was defiant. She backed up, closer to the turn in the path until the sick feeling took over her stomach. "Gail, you have to help me."

The cartman settled his cart, lifted both of his hands and settled them on her arms. It was the first he'd ever touched her, his palms firm and cold. Ice cold, like warm blood had never pumped through his veins. There were rules for touching, caste structures that were to be followed. She was Goldland born and he was... he was whatever he was. Familiar, but not Goldland born. She wiggled out of his reach, but this caused her to back up and nearly cross the invisible threshold that kept agitating her nerve endings.

"I must leave now." The sun dipped and the blasts and vibrations in the mountain finally stopped for the day. "I must go now." Gail reached for the handles of his cart, missing twice before grasping them.

Cara noticed he wouldn't look in her direction. "I said, *help me*," she walked closer to him.

In the moonlight she caught a glance of blackness in his eyes. She grabbed his face, shirking all rules. He flinched but let her turn his cheek so she could see.

His eyes had turned completely black. The more she stared into them the further she could see. Tiny specs of stars. She glanced away to the edge of the world, looking back at him she realized the same was mimicked in his eyes. Jet orbs, each a black hole with a speck of iris that resembled a twinkling star. Cara could pop them out and sell them in the Goldlands for a life of luxury. She could get her life back and leave the wretched cold mountain.

"This is what the Arrow does when he is disobeyed." Gail blinked but the black did not clear. "I should have left before the suns set. I am on untethered ground of an old God. I cannot stay here."

Cara sucked in a breath. "I'm so sorry. I'm sorry." She reached out and grasped his coat. "I didn't know." She was shaking her head. "What can I do? How..."

The cartman chuckled, he sounded exhausted and defeated; his shoulders slumped, and his eyes moved to the distance, mimicking the movements of a wisp. "I've walked this path so many times, I should know it like the back of my hand." Cara released his jacket and he lifted the handles of his cart and settled them in the pockets on his hips. "Until next time."

The cartman walked away, his back straight and proud. Blinded, he didn't miss the turn of the trail, or the large rock to the left or the dip in the pebbles. Cara went after him, stopping when her body would no longer let her go any further. She turned her head and listed to the grinding wheels of his cart turn as he descended.

Cara spun sharply to see her light was still dancing in the tower. So the Arrow had time for punishments but not to answer her call.

Highmount shuddered once again and the sound of falling rocks echoed through the Land of Man.

"It's not about that," Cara shouted at the sky. "It's not just about the mountain, it's about *her* too!" Cara glared at the blue sky as she thrust her finger toward the Darkmoors. "Why would you bother to bring me here if not to listen?"

The Divine Arrow never answered her call in that moment. It left Cara bubbling with uncertainty, so she went inside and made some tea. She had a gem in her pocket. It was white, scaled with orange dots and milky throughout. Cara sipped her tea and held the gem close to her eye. She did the only thing that she found soothing anymore. Interpret the histories. Get lost in time. She studied the rock until the story came to her.

The oceans were ruled by the Koi Fish. Giant creatures, mottled with orange and white. Their size was greater than any ship built by the Land of Man. The air was so humid it parted as men and women walked down the streets, so thick the Koi Fish could draw oxygen from it and float through the air as though it were water. A time of grayness, there were no defined laws of physics when it came to water and air and things like gravity. The Land of Man was in flux, but man didn't seem to mind. They went on working, sleeping and spawning. All as the Koi swam around them, above them and next to them. It was not uncommon to so be sitting at the dinner table and have a Koi swim through the open window, mosey around the living space, nibble on the salad or nudge that back of a child's head. A visit from a Koi was considered good luck in those times.

Cara wrote the history in her book.

The Arrow will strike down those closest, the cartman had warned her. The longer time passed without a visit from Gail, the more she feared she'd caused his demise. There was no one closer to her since her mother had died. No one else that Cara knew. Only Gail. Guilt was a hot iron in the pit of her stomach. She'd caused him to travel blind. He could have fallen off a ledge. Nearly half the mountain was gone now. Cara knew that soon she'd fall to her death with the blasting of Highmount.

Cara stood at the trail that led down to the Land of Man, she tried to see but her apprehension wouldn't let her. So, she started walking. Her stomach went queasy just like all the other times she'd tried to walk away. This time she braced herself and walked right through it. Her head ached and her eardrums felt like they were underwater. Cara passed the first bend and walked faster. Her eyes scanned the path for a crumpled body or wasted cart. She moved quickly, taking deep breaths. The air was heavy below the peak, air she hadn't breathed in years and suddenly wondered how she had ever breathed it for all her years before Highmount.

Cara walked, her hands trembling, her body sweating as the heat of the Land of Man enveloped her. Accustomed to the chill of Highmount, she shrugged off her shawl and wrapped it around her waist. After some time, her ears popped and her head felt foggy. Cara paused to rest against a boulder. Rocks shuddered as blasts continued to take down the mountain. Her vision blurred. Cara blinked in rapid succession trying to focus but it didn't work. She began walking again, the dense air heavy in her lungs. She rubbed her eyes as her vision worsened, the rocky path turned mottled, trees and plants were no longer defined but blots of green or red. Cara knew it would be hard to find Gail like this. She sat for a moment to catch her breath. She looked off in the distance toward the Goldland gates but could see nothing. She turned her head to look toward the edge but could see no further than a few feet. Cara blinked, she blinked and blinked and blinked until ... it all went black.

"No!" Cara shouted. She rubbed her eyes as she stood. Panic flooded her body, Cara's arms shot out straight to balance herself, she shuffled her feet along the path trying to go slow.

"I'm sorry," she shouted. "Divine Arrow! I beg you." Tears streamed down Cara's face. This was not the future she'd wanted; this was nothing like she'd hoped for. All her dreams of escaping Highmount and returning to the Goldlands were gone now. She knew she'd never make it far. She stumbled down the mountain, rocks tumbling down with her as man blew it to pieces.

There was a strange noise, the snort of a beast. Cara froze. While she was blinded, for an instant an image appeared, a giant stag with golden antlers that had twisted into a halo above its head. Cara sucked in a breath. It was treacherous; the way she could see its skeleton glowing gold through its hide, hair and skin the color of moonlight. The creature cried horribly before rearing up on its hind legs.

Cara screamed and ran. While she could see the beast for a moment, she could see nothing else, and she stumbled and tore her hands on the rocky path. The bits of Feldspar Crystal and Pearly Orthoclase cut like a knife. Cara scrambled to her feet, tried to remember the trail curved but while moving fast she lost her way, one step her foot hit solid ground but the next she hit air and fell. Cara screamed into the darkness that was now her reality. She screamed for her mountain toppling, for the beast she'd met on the trail, for Gail, for Noomii's future. Her legs kicked and her arms flailed, but only for an instant.

Someone gripped her, forearm to forearm, a hand wrapped tightly around her elbow. "If you are lost, I will find you and return you to where you belong," a gravelly voice whispered in her ear.

Cara knew it wouldn't be enough, those words weren't meant for her. The mountain was coming down and she had real doubt that they'd survive it.

"You must show her kindness," Cara whispered, knowing these would be her last words as the explosions began again. "You must tell her those words."

The mountain crumbled. Heavy rock and glittering crystals tumbled around them.

CHAPTER 17

LANDBEFOREITWASGOLD

Opening her eyes, Cira found herself laying at the edge of the park. She pushed up on her elbows and looked around. She didn't see Divine anywhere. She sat up and brushed the grass and leaves off her dress. She could hear the celebrations from her wedding party from beyond the trees. They were celebrating without her. Cira had never felt more alone than in this moment.

"He thought he killed you," the familiar voice of the servant said. "But I could see you breathing still and told him it was okay to continue."

Cira stood as the woman walked out from under the shade of the trees.

"Oh?" Cira's fingers touched her lips, remembering. "I think I fainted. It's all a little much for me right now." She looked away still feeling a bit weak and made her way to a park bench.

"He is special," the woman said as she sat and took Cira's hand. She hesitated at first. "He is special but so are you." The woman tipped her head knowingly.

"I don't know what you mean." Cira pulled her hand back. Her face turned red with anger. "I should have never come here. I should have run away the night before like mother begged me to do."

The servant pinched Cira's chin and tipped her head up. Inspecting her eyes, her ears, her mouth and neck, she finally said, "Maybe it's too early to tell." She dropped her arms and faced the sea. "At least the God of the sea has given his blessing. That never happens." She raised her eyes to the Watchtower. "And from the Creator, nothing." Her eyes flicked to her periphery. "Divine is back." She walked away, disappearing into the small park forest.

Divine walked through the park with the quiet strength of a wild buck.

Cira couldn't tell where he was coming from until his horns broke through the shadows. She stood, her legs feeling weak and stomach uneasy. She opened her mouth to apologize. "I'm so—"

Divine smiled awkwardly. "You don't have to say anything." He raised his palm to quiet her. "I'm sorry. I guess I came on a little strong. It's a problem I have." He made an awkward gesture.

"Okay." Cira nodded. "I'm a bit nervous."

"Why are you nervous?" Divine asked. "You're getting to experience the formation of the Goldlands. You're traveling. You're marrying a demigod." There was excitement in his voice.

"Yes." Cira nodded. "All of that is.... It's just nothing like the valley."

"Oh." Divine paused before moving to the bench and beckoning her to join him. "Come. Sit."

She followed, her eyes glued to the grass even though she could tell that Divine's were glued to her.

"You are very desirable," Divine said before clearing his throat.

"Thank you."

Divine was silent until Cira finally raised her gaze.

"And what do you think of me?" he asked.

Cira's eyes widened. "I—you're better than the paintings I saw in the tower."

Divine laughed. "Oh, thank the Arrow. I knew my father

wasted his time on that painter. I've always hated those portraits. They are a bit, impressionistic."

"I guess." Cira fidgeted with the gold ribbon on the seam of her dress.

"You thought I'd be an animal? A giant beast?"

"Kind of. But, I'm glad you're not."

Divine reached out, he took her hand and brought it to his face. "I've always wondered if people actually liked the way I looked or if I disgusted them."

"You're not," Cira swallowed hard, "you're different, but very nice to look at." She smiled as her eyes met his. "I'm glad."

"I don't want you to be afraid of me." Divine looked away this time, his hand leaving hers. "Like the others were."

Cira held her breath. She didn't know that there had been others. She should have known better though. "What happened?"

"I wouldn't know." Divine shrugged. "They all killed themselves rather than be sacrificed to me." Sadness echoed off him as his shoulders slumped.

"Oh."

"It's one extreme or the other. They throw themselves at me or..." He shook his head.

Cira moved her hand to touch him; her fingers hovered over his dark forearm corded with muscle and thick veins. She wished she were as comforting as her mother could be. A warm touch, a gentle hug to anyone who needed it. Giving comfort to others had always been difficult for her. She closed her eyes and settled a single finger on his skin. "I'm sorry." She offered.

Divine made a grunting noise as his arm tensed under her touch.

He stood quickly and moved away from her. "This is hard for me. Especially with you looking like that." He paced away for a moment. "Let's return to the celebration."

"Did I do something wrong?" She stiffened.

"No. But I might if I spend one more moment in the dark with you." He turned sharply and headed for the trees. "Come."

Cira stood and followed what little she could see of his silhouette in the darkness until she came to the clearing. The park was lit with tiny lights. The tables were dressed with pristine white linens, embroidered with a single thread of gold. The tables were topped with candied apple-grapes, pink gulf shrimp, a whole pig that had been glazed in clear sugar. There was more food than Cira had ever seen in the valley. More than any of the Goldland born who were in attendance would ever eat.

Cira followed Divine as he moved through the crowd. He stopped to speak with men in fancy Goldland suits. He introduced her and she shook dozens of hands, but the day was exhausting before this celebration and Cira couldn't recall a single name. She nodded quietly to the women and sipped on her fermented tea.

"They make that special." A man whispered across her shoulder. "It's brewed from corn-tea hybrid grown in the mud of the Darkmoors."

The drink paused at Cira's lips and she swallowed against a dry throat instead.

The man laughed. "It's quite good." He toasted against her glass. "Long live the wife of Divine." He tipped his head back and drank the contents of his glass.

Cira turned, eager to flee the strangers who'd surrounded her and found Divine was no longer at her side. There were more people here than she ever encountered in the valley. From the corner of her eye she saw a flash of white. Cira turned to look and the Goldland-born near her had stopped their conversations and stared. A wave passed through Cira's stomach. The silvery figure moved again, this time wavering in front of her face. Cira focused, and it looked like her mother. She reached out.

The old woman who had been guiding her through the day suddenly appeared and took her hand. "Come now, dear," she was talking loudly. "It's time to get you some rest." She wrapped an arm around Cira's shoulder and guided her away from the crowd. "I warned you about the wisps," she whispered to Cira.

"I thought—that was my mother." Cira tried to turn but the woman dragged her along.

"Don't look. Remember." The old woman's voice was soothing.

"Where's Divine?" Cira's heart was racing and her hands shook.

"He'll come along." The woman patted her shoulder as they walked, the Goldland-born buzzing like bees in their hive as the Celebration continued without Cira.

The woman led Cira through the opulent halls and up the thousand stairs to the tower where she had waited for days.

"Goldland-born do not allow adults to acknowledge the wisps." She locked the door. "They'll come for you if they see you do it again."

"What does it matter?" Cira moved to the window.

"It crosses a boundary. The veil between worlds is thin. The veil between gods and monsters and magic is even thinner." The old woman winked. "Goodnight."

Cira woke in her wedding gown. The room was empty. Quiet. She moved to get out of bed and noticed a shadow from under the door.

She opened the door to find Divine sleeping on the floor.

"Oh no." She bent and shook him awake. "What are you doing out here? Are you sick?"

Divine rolled to his back and one eye peeked open. "You locked me out."

Cira's hands flew to her mouth. "No."

"Yes." He smiled.

"No. I don't even know how."

"Well, someone did." Divine moved up off the floor. He towered over her. "You're still wearing the dress."

"Ah, yes." Cira smoothed her hands over it.

Divine touched her arm. "I could help you out of it."

Cira stiffened and Divine noticed. "I, ah, I don't think I'm ready for that."

"Of course." He motioned to the door. "You should change for the day."

Cira stepped back into the room. "What about you?"

"I'll go back to my quarters and get ready."

Cira waited for a moment until Divine was halfway down the hall before she closed the door. She locked it herself this time and glanced around the room. She didn't bring any belongings and didn't have any more clothing.

A wisp crossed the room.

Cira stared straight ahead and tried her best to ignore it. But the silvery figure hovered near an armoire. Cira crossed the room and opened it. Inside were clothes and shoes. Cira chose a few items before closing the door. When she did a wisp was wavering right next to her. She stifled a scream and couldn't help but stare. "Please, leave me alone," she whispered. "This is hard enough." With those words it disappeared.

Cira got ready. The clothing was unfamiliar from what she usually wore in the valley, but she did her best. She missed the feathers and skins and soft moss that she used to wear.

She left the room to find Divine and some breakfast.

Cira explored the tower. She couldn't smell food, but she could smell something earthly. Pine needles and smoke. She followed the smell down the hall, down a small set of stairs until she came to a large wooden door. Cira stood in the hallway, unsure of what to do. Should she knock or just open the door, or turn around and run?

Something scraped across the floor. The door handle moved.

Cira stepped back as the door swung open.

Divine took up the doorway, he ducked as he stepped out so as not to catch his antler. "There you are." He smiled, dressed in blue slacks and a white shirt with buttons, loafers of dark leather on his feet. His clothes were flattering to his tall, muscular stature. Cira tried not to stare. "Ready to get something to eat?"

Cira nodded.

Divine reached for her hand and Cira didn't shy away. She could hold hands, that was simple enough.

Divine led her down winding stairways, talking the entire time. He spoke of the history of the Goldlands, the history of the tower they lived in, the important Goldland-born who had attended their wedding. Cira was overwhelmed with it all. There was too much information.

When they finally reached the ground level, Divine led her down a long hallway, decorated with drapes of various scenes of the Goldland rising, to a dining area.

"This is the best part," he said as he pushed the door open.

Cira's eyes went wide. Food was spread out on a buffet; candied bacon and fruit, pancakes, and hardboiled quail eggs. More food than she'd ever seen in her life.

"I hope you're hungry." Divine dropped her hand and picked up a plate and handed her one, piling his high with so much food she could barely believe a person could eat it all. But he wasn't a human, she reminded herself. No, he was a demigod.

Cira took a plate and selected food that she recognized; fruits and simple meats. Something mild to settle the ache in her stomach. They sat across from each other at an obnoxiously long table. There were ten chairs between them. It was strange.

Divine began shoveling food into his mouth but Cira hesitated. She'd seen movement out of the corner of her eye. The wisp was following her now.

"Leave her alone," Divine said on a low breath. The wisp disappeared in an instant. He picked up his plate and moved closer, sitting in the chair to her right. "This is better." He flashed a smile and studied her face for a moment. "Are you going to be ok?"

"I think so." Cira stabbed a blueberry with her fork before placing it in her mouth. "The wisps." She glanced to each corner of the room. "I think they're following me."

Divine laughed around a mouthful of food, swallowing before he said, "They tend to flock to newcomers. They'll lose interest."

Cira nodded. "Okay. But. The one looked like my mother."

Divine set his fork down. "It could be her."

The door to the dining room slammed open and a tall man walked through. He wore a blue suit spun of satin, interlaced with gold fibers. Each finger had a gold ring, each earlobe a gold hoop, and gold-rimmed glasses rested on his nose. "Sir!" he interrupted. "My apologies but we have a situation."

Divine wiped his mouth with a cloth napkin before tossing it down on the table. He stood. "Right. My duties never sleep." He bent to kiss Cira on the cheek. "I'll be back later. Make yourself at home," he whispered in Cira's ear. She flushed at the closeness and as she watched Divine walk away, she caught the man studying her. Cira waved. He didn't wave back.

Cira's life was much different from the Valley. Divine was present for half of breakfast and half of dinner, otherwise he was whisked away by the man in the blue suit to do whatever a demigod does in a growing city. Cira fled to the gardens, she went to the bluffs in the town center where they were wed, the wisps following her. The Goldland-born watched her every movement. Cira wished she could close her eyes as she walked.

There were so many she couldn't look away from them all. They were too hard to ignore.

Cira sat at the bluffs, tall oaks and willows at her back, the benches lined with wisps who were sitting quietly next to her. She heard a snap. The sound of footsteps echoed over the sea. Cira turned and recognized the old woman stepping out of the cluster of trees.

"Hello," the old woman greeted her. "Still so innocent."

Cira smiled a greeting back and as the old woman walked closer, she waved away the wisps that were clustered around the same bench as Cira. They scattered as she sat. "How are you?"

Cira shrugged. "I don't know."

"You look lost."

"I feel lost most days. I wish the buildings were trees and this hollow bone road was packed dirt." She turned to look at the old woman. "The wisps won't leave me alone. Any moment I could look in the wrong direction."

"And your husband?"

Cira looked to her hands, pressed them across her thighs. "He's fine."

"Treating you well?"

"Yes."

"Are you treating him well?"

Cira's head snapped to the woman. "I'm not sure what you mean by that."

The old woman smiled softly. "Men have needs. Demigods even more so. They can't help it. I see how hard he's trying to hold himself together."

Cira sighed. "I'm just not ready for much more."

There was silence as the two women watched over the sea. Gulls and plovers flitted around the bluffs and pecked in the sand below. At this time, the Goldlands were the same height as the Watchtower in the distance. They were equals in height, the same distance to the suns. As Cira sat, she wondered why she couldn't have been sacrificed to a life at Highrock or Highmount. Instead she'd been sentenced to this.

"A life of solitude is not what you want," the old woman interrupted her thoughts.

"How could you know?"

"That is not the way of the valley." The old woman crossed a leg and turned closer to Cira. "You've always craved the closeness of another. It's the way you are. The way you've always been."

Cira mimicked the woman's movement, crossing her leg and moving in. "How could you know that about me?"

The woman waved to the sky. "It's written in the stars, my dear."

The two women sat on the bench, surrounded by the wisps for some time. The seven suns rotated through the afternoon sky.

"Who are you?" Cira finally asked.

"I'm kind of a wisp myself." The old woman stood and walked away, disappearing into the trees.

The wisps surrounding Cira pulsed in silence as the old woman got further and further way, her footsteps fading on the hallow ground.

Something felt off. It felt very wrong to be here.

Cira stood and made her way back to the tower. She pushed open the golden-gilded door and ran up the steps to her room. Out of breath, she circled her room until her heart slowed. Glancing out the windows she could see Goldland-born looking up at her. She flung open the armoire that contained her clothes and looked around for a bag to pack them in. She turned to find the room filled with wisps. Panic set in. They moved closer and one reached out, its hand hovering over her chest. Their mouths were moving but Cira couldn't hear them. They moved closer. Cira pressed herself to the wall, the closest wisp's hand held over her, it's mouth open in silent chant. She couldn't escape them.

Cira screamed. Tears streaked down her face as the wisps continued.

There was commotion outside her door. Heavy footsteps. A thud, a scrape. The door flung open and Divine ran into the room. The wisps vanished but he saw. He ran across the room and scooped her up. "Goddamn things," he muttered as he carried her out of the room.

Cira pressed her face to his chest, soaking his shirt with tears. She heard him kick open a door and then kick it closed. Cira recognized the smell: they were in his room.

"They won't come in here," Divine said as he sat down and positioned her on his lap. He rubbed her back, his fingers massaging. Cira gripped his shirt and held on tight until her sobs slowed and finally stopped.

"I'm sorry," she whispered against his chest. "I didn't know what to do."

"It's okay." Divine shifted her on his lap.

Cira felt something firm against her thigh and remembered the old woman's words. She let go of his shirt and moved, sliding off his legs and stepping away. She focused her eyes on his face and avoided the bulge in his pants.

"I'm sorry," Cira repeated. "I've never been out of the valley and all of this is so different. I don't fit this puzzle."

"I know it's very different here." Divine was watching her closely. "You miss the valley?" he asked.

"Yes."

Divine stood and held out his hand. "Come with me."

Cira hesitated.

"Come. We will go back. I haven't been to the valley since before the second mountain crumbled." He glanced toward the window. "I can tell you secrets now that we're together. Every mountain that comes down has been a minor God falling." He wagged his finger. "There's a war for power right under our noses. It will be nice to escape it." He pinched his shirt. "And these tight clothes."

Cira put her hand in his and the familiar warmth encased her hand as he led her out of the room, down the stairs, and to the dining area. "Pack our things," he said to the man in the blue suit. "We're leaving in ten minutes."

The man's eyes went wide.

"Go!" Divine let out a small shout and grunt.

Cira could tell he was balancing the beast and the human, just like the old woman had warned.

"Are you sure?" Cira asked Divine. "Are you sure you want to leave this place for me?"

"I've wanted to leave this place for decades."

The suns were setting, and they lit the golden buildings in hues of red and orange. Cira had never seen anything like it. This place looked as though it were built by fire.

Divine led her to a horse drawn cart. There was no canopy to cover them and Cira wondered if it was because of his large rack of antlers? He lent a hand as she stepped up into the cart and sat down, then he followed. "To the valley!" he shouted to the man holding the horse's reins.

The ride home felt longer than the ride leaving. Maybe it was because Cira was so anxious to return, excited to see her mother again and feel the comfort of home. She was happy to never see another wisp again. The cart rolled through tree covered roads and empty meadows. Divine was eager to point out every living creature and explain their making by the Creator. "My father said everything in the Land of Man was created for a reason. Everything is intertwined."

Cira nodded. She knew that the fields grew the flowers, and the bees drank the nectar before making the honey that people harvested and drenched their roasts in each Sunday. But she nodded as Divine repeated it all to her.

"You know much about the Creator," Cira said.

"He and my father are close. The old Gods and the Creator have been perfecting this place since the beginning of time."

"That's a long time," Cira replied.

Finally, they arrived and the cart came to a halt.

Divine stepped down and took a deep breath. "Ah, it smells so fresh down here." He rubbed his chest. "It's so freeing." He shook his head and arched his neck. "I like it here. Introduce me to your mother. Show me your home."

The people of her village seemed happy to see her at first, a few moved closer like they were going to welcome her back, but when they saw Divine at her side they kept their distance, stepping away in haste. They'd never seen a demigod.

"I like this place." Divine nodded as they walked down the dusty road. "Is that house yours?" he pointed at the large cabin owned by the local farmer. The surrounding fields were full of corn stalks and wheat and the sound of geese honking echoed.

"No." Cira laughed. "Women without husbands and children without fathers don't live in houses like that." Feeling bold, Cira took his hand and led him further down the road. "Come on. It's just a bit further." She picked up her pace, but it wasn't enough to match Divine's long-legged stride.

He waved to the people of the valley, a little too excited and a bit dimwitted. They watched from the road, from far back in their yards, from behind thick tree trunks. Divine was not a man by any sorts, he was like nothing the people of the valley had ever seen. Half human and half beast, she worried that they'd rather shoot him than make friends. The valley was known for hunting and trapping, after all.

Cira walked to the edge of the village. It had been at least a mile since they'd seen another house. She turned down an overgrown path. Dandelions and Black-eyed Susans lined the walkway to the front door. Cira knocked twice. "Mother!" she shouted. "Mother, I'm home." She turned the dented brass door handle and went inside. Divine ducked and twisted as he stepped inside, the door-frame not tall enough for his antlers.

"Mother?" Cira let go of Divine's hand and ran through the house. She checked the kitchen, the bedrooms, the small bathroom in the hall. The air brushing her face felt stagnant, dry. There was no lingering scent of her mother's lavender lotion. Cira noted the thick dust, the dirt pocked windows. The cabin was empty—had been for some time now. Tears welled behind her eyes and her chin trembled. She realized, the wisp that had been following her in the Goldlands was her mother.

Divine was looking through the cupboards when Cira made it back to the living room.

"Did you—" Divine paused. "What's wrong?"

"She's gone..." Cira couldn't hold back the tears any longer. She buried her face in her hands and began to cry.

Heavy footsteps crossed the room and he wrapped his arms around her small frame. "It's okay. It's okay." His large hands rubbed her back. "I'll take care of you."

It sounded like such a blessed promise. Cira moved her hands and looked up at him. She couldn't see the movement of his lips through her bleary eyes, but she could see his face moving closer. His antlers didn't seem so threatening as they blurred with her vision.

"I will take care of you," he promised as he kissed her. Gently, his lips soft and firm, she tasted fresh grass and roses. What caused her to faint on their wedding day now caused her belly to ignite in flames. She reached up and circled his neck with her arms and held on as his lips explored hers. It wasn't nearly as bad of a kiss as she'd feared—it was quite nice.

Divine lifted Cira in his arms and swung her in a circle. She buried her head in his neck, holding on tight. He smelled like the deep forest, earthy; pinecones and sap and the smoke of summer fire. He squeezed her tighter.

CHAPTER 18

HIGHSANDPLATEAU

*A soul or two,
or three or four.
You'll never know until
you walk across the Saltpan floor.*

Io heard a rumble in the distance. She stood at the edge of her pond and saw the last of the seven peaks of the Land of Man crumble. Her gut pinched. She saw a glimmer coming down the peak, something reflecting off the light of the seven suns. It was time.

Io sat, her wrists settled on bare knees as she drew on a vortex.

"Cara," she chanted. "Cara, Cara, Cara, Cara, Cara. The Shadowline wants your soul."

The meditation didn't take long; Io could bring the vortex much faster since not much time had passed. She stood and ran into the water, her lithe frame transitioning into that of the crab. As her shell dipped into the water, she saw the vortex. Io hesitated, waiting for just the right time. On the other side of the vortex, she saw Cara as a grown woman now. She was running down the mountain, her eyes black as night. Cara screamed when the giant beast reared up to frighten her. Cara fell.

"Not today, Arrow." Io lurched forward at the last second and pulled Cara through the vortex just before she hit the ground. What Io had done didn't go unseen. The Arrow howled and dashed forward, antlers gleaming with hate. Io gripped Cara's dress with her pinschers, not wanting to injure her flesh, dragging her further from the vortex before it closed.

Dropping from the sky and finding oneself underwater was a strange sensation; mid-scream Cara began choking on water.

Io dragged her to the island, changing forms as she broke the surface.

Cara was crying, her hair dripping pond water, her clothing soaked. "Where is he? Where is he?" she asked.

"Where is who?" Io squeezed water from her hair.

"Gail. The cartman." Cara coughed and wiped water off her face. "I was trying to find him. I... I... I kept him too long. I hurt him. He was blinded."

Io walked to the house of bones and sat. Pond water dripped from her hair.

Cara moved to her knees and looked around. She took in the small island, the large pond, the expanse of sparkling sand. "Where am I?" she asked.

"The Saltpan." Io reached to the side and pulled out two blankets, tossed one to Cara. "You'd better dry off and get up here."

Cara wiped her face and arms before wrapping the blanket around her shoulders. Her feet slipped in the soft sand as she stood and walked forward to sit next to Io. "Who are you?"

"It's a long story."

"I remember falling." She rubbed her eyes. "I couldn't see. My vision was gone."

"Now that you've transversed time, the Arrow's curses are

undone." Io was curt; it had been a very long time since she'd entertained a guest at her home. But Cara was more than a guest.

"Time was different at the top of Highmount. Slower. Dragging. I was sure it would never end."

"It never moves here," Io warned.

"Okay." Cara nodded. "That sounds absolutely terrible."

"I find ways to entertain myself."

Cara waited for more but Io didn't elaborate. She was deep in thought and Cara decided to *look* and see if her vision was just as good as it was before the Arrow had turned her blind.

Io felt the air between them change. She turned to Cara and found her eyes changed. Glossy and milky, she was somewhere else. Io grabbed Cara's narrow shoulders and shook her. "Hey! Come back!"

Cara blinked a few times before focusing on Io. "What?"

The seven suns were setting in the west.

"What did you do just now?"

"I was looking into the future."

"Oh." Io brushed sand off her foot.

"Oh?" Cara sounded offended.

"I can do things too."

"Dark magic?" Cara's voice was low, like she knew better than to utter the words. They were never spoken in the Goldlands.

Io shook her head. "We are more than magic."

The Celestials lit the sky right then. Bursts of pink foamy clouds of dust and lightning cracked between stars.

Cara's eyes gazed up and her voice was troubled when she said, "I've never seen them like this before. They're mad, I think."

"They're bored." Io threw a handful of sand. "They know."

"Know what?" Cara's eyes scanned the night sky.

"There are two of us together now."

Chapter 19

Highrock

The Goldland gates were a massive spectacle. Iron interlaced with thick ropes of glittering gold and feldspar crystals. Noomii leaned away, shading her eyes in the dim of the carriage shadows.

"You look like you could hiss," Drax said. "Your eyes will adjust."

The driver stopped the horses for inspection. Men and women in goldspun uniform approached. They pulled telescoping mirrors from their pockets to look under the carriage and over the roof. They looked inside, poking their mirror sticks in darting fashion, within a millimeter of Drax's nose and under Noomii's bench. Satisfied, they opened the gates and let the driver lead the horses through.

"That was intrusive," Noomii said.

"Have you been to the Goldlands before?" Drax whispered.

"Never." Noomii craned her neck and shielded her eyes so she could look out the window again. The horses climbed the steady incline. The climb was so steep Noomii wished she'd brought her climbing gear in case the horses gave out. If it would even still work. Her gear had sat in a Watchtower closet for all these years. The ropes were probably dry rotted and the pulleys and carabiners rusted solid.

"Do you recognize anything?"

Noomii scowled. "How would I recognize anything on my first visit to the Goldlands? I've never been here before." Noomii motioned to the buildings lining the streets. She tipped forward to try and see where they stopped, but they breached the clouds, turning them ocher and shadowed.

Drax nodded but a small smirk ticked his cheek. "Where would you like to go first?" he asked.

"I'm not sure." When Noomii looked back at him, he was holding the octopus of ocean Jasper. "You still have that?"

"Of course. You spoke of mountains before. Why?" he asked as he toyed with the octopus. The Goldland suns shined through the windows onto the Jasper and glittered the inside of the carriage.

"I used to climb them." Noomii's back straightened proudly. "I've climbed all seven mountains of the Land of Man."

"And now you've climbed the eighth." He moved the carving to his pocket. "I just wanted to see it sparkle, being so close to the sun and all."

"This isn't a true mountain," Noomii scoffed. "They destroyed the others to build this. The Goldlands are nothing more than a charade. They are trying to forget the old Gods. Cover the stories and memories with gold shine and obtrusive rules about how to live."

"Some might say the same for the Watchtower."

"The Creator would never—" Noomii's mouth snapped closed.

Drax's brows rose. "Don't speak of the Creator here," he whispered. "Let's get out and walk." Drax whistled to the boy and when the carriage stopped moving, he opened the door, then turned and held out his hand to assist Noomii.

One of Noomii's hands settled on the window frame, while the other hovered, searching for support as she stepped down.

"Take it," Drax muttered.

She'd only taken the hand of Gail.

"You are not a Darkmoor girl today," he reminded her. "Take my hand. Now."

Noomii settled her hand in his and stepped down. From the corner of her eye she saw movement, a golden-cloaked woman watching her. Noomii turned her head and blinked twice. "Mother?" she whispered and began walking away.

Drax grabbed Noomii's arm, pinching, and pulled her back. "The Goldlands are filled with ghosts of our past," he murmured in her ear. "We bury them in the Darkmoors and they reemerge up here. Remember? Goldlanders don't interact with ghosts. We don't want to stand out. Ignore the wisps."

Goldland-born walked in the streets, paying little attention to Noomii and Drax. They'd dressed for the occasion and didn't look out of place but walking amongst the spirits would make them stand out. She should know this. She vaguely remembered her mother mentioning it; or was it a child's lullaby, or a drunkard's song? Time had dulled her memories. She couldn't remember exactly but she knew Drax's words were the truth. Noomii glanced down at the road; it was paved in varying lengths of ocher-white cords and her shoes made a hollow knock with each step.

"Mud and bone," Drax said. "Streets of white and buildings of gold." He hummed the tune. "Your best-dressed, your skin is cold. Your first love the Goldlands hold." Drax patted his hand over his heart. "I had a lady once, She should be here." He sounded desperate. So suddenly desperate and changed from his usual calm demeanor that a fleck of fear infiltrated Noomii's gut.

"So that's why you came?" Noomii started walking toward the edge that was visible in the distance. She was feeling loomed-over, watched, noted closely under a microscope, and it made her skin crawl. The towering buildings of the Goldlands were stifling. "Will you leave to search for her?"

Drax cleared his throat as he picked up step to follow her. "No need to search in the Goldlands, the spirits will seek us out. She will find me."

Noomii caught a glance of the sea and wove between the Goldland-born on the streets.

"Where are you going?" he asked.

"To the edge." Noomii pointed. "Answers have never come from a stifling crowd." She shivered as her pace increased. "This is too much." They reached the gardens and the bluffs. "I was raised in the stick-built buildings of the Darkmoors. There was distance —"

Drax interrupted, "—and there was mud." He reached into a nearby flowerbed and dug a handful of dark mud, holding it up for her to see. "There is mud here. You are not so far away."

"Are you sure? I had a dream once," Noomii looked away, took the mud in her hand as she remembered. "A dream that I pressed a spec of amethyst into a sand creature, and it came alive."

Drax blinked as she spoke, studying her face with an intensity that showed he believed her. "Show me."

Noomii rolled the ball of mud that was in her hand. She pinched and pulled it until she'd formed a small bird, she flecked it's back with her nail to create feathers. "It's a flickadee." As she spoke, she reached into her pocket and broke off a piece of the amethyst then pressed it into the carving's chest.

Drax was watching her closely.

Nothing happened.

"I guess it was just a dream." She shrugged as she set the mud-bird on the ledge of the flower bed, feeling foolish.

"Noomii," Drax whispered.

She turned to find the bird of mud was alive.

Drax was looking at her wide-eyed. "You know," he paused as his eyes widened, "—that's magic?"

"This could just be a dream." She blinked hard. "Magic isn't real."

"But that is." He pointed at the bird as it fluttered off into the trees. "That's true magic. What are you? What did the Watchtower do to you? Are you left over from the old Gods?"

Noomii wasn't sure what to say. She noticed Drax wasn't afraid, no; he was intrigued. He moved closer to her, his eyes searching her face as though he were remembering something long forgotten. "Tell me, Noomii. It has been a very long time since I've seen power like that. It has been a very long time since I have had a sense of remembrance of the old Gods."

CHAPTER 20

HIGHSANDPLATEAU

A stone, a stone
what a precious stone.
Don't judge it too harshly
this is what made your bones.

Cara's stomach grumbled loudly. "I'm so hungry. I wish I'd brought some pickled shrimps or liver sugars or sea-salt-tea." Cara dug through her bag before pulling out a packet of snacks. "Do you want some?" she offered Io.

Io grabbed the packet, crushed it in her hand before flinging it across the pond.

"Hey, what are you doing?" Cara shouted.

Io stole Cara's bag, she dumped it out on the ground and scattered the belongings, finding the packets of food she'd brought. She threw them across the pond to turn to dust in the harsh sun of the plateau.

"I was going to eat that!"

Io's eyes narrowed. "You must promise me something. Right now." She grabbed Cara's shoulders.

"What?" Cara was annoyed, looking after the snacks that had been tossed away.

"You will never touch another piece of food nor drink to your lips." She shook Cara's shoulders, hard. "Promise me! Or we will never escape this place." Io's eyes were wild. "We will never escape if we are rooted here by our stomachs. Never!"

Cara's face was pale. "Okay," she promised. "Okay. I won't eat a thing."

"Never past the lips." Io grabbed a handful of sand and rubbed it across her mouth until her lips were as brown as her sun-kissed skin. "Not a morsel." She rubbed sand across Cara's lips until they were no longer pink. "Nothing."

Cara nodded as she touched her rough lips and spit away the specs of sand with a tiny breath. She wasn't accustomed to hunger pangs.

❦

Cara's days were much different on the island compared to Highmount. There were no journals to write in, no days spent waiting for interactions with someone else, no watching the Land of Man go on without her and being filled with loneliness. Here Cara had a friend of some kind.

Io lived like a nomad, her pillow was a pile of sand, her bath the pond, her clothes nonexistent. But Io had something Cara had craved for many years: freedom. Living under the Arrow's rule had left Cara feeling empty. She wasn't free to make all her own decisions. At least here, she could try. At least here she had no one else to answer to but a tiny and nearly naked woman. Io was far more engaging and less threatening than the Arrow.

Cara looked beyond the shade of the bone shelter. Io was meditating. She did that a lot.

To pass the time, Cara collected the handful of gemstones she'd brought in her bag.

Ruby Fuchsite was a gemstone of green muscovite mica speckled with little red corundum crystals, which told a captivating story.

"Tell me about that one?" Io asked, her eyes suddenly open and inspecting.

"I met a girl once who was very good at reading the stones. I think I only do a semi-decent job at it." Cara confessed. "I'm sure others have done better."

"Tell me."

"Ruby Fuchsite." Cara held up the gem. "There was a daughter of a god, so beautiful that she fled to the moon for peace and quiet. During this time the trees and plants grew day and night trying to reach her. A cactus finally grew as tall as the moon in the night sky and when the goddess reached out to touch the moon-flower that had sprouted from its stem, she pricked her finger on the cactus spike and droplets of her blood splattered over the Land of Man."

Io's eyes narrowed.

"What?" Cara asked. "I warned you. The worst part is that I wrote my stories down in the journals for the Arrow. I was a Watchtower servant. Chosen to read the histories of the gems." She rolled the piece of ocean jasper that was in her pocket. "I'd rather change them for my old life back."

"Which one?" Io asked.

Cara's brow furrowed.

"Which old life would you like back?"

"I'm not sure what you mean by that."

There was a long silence as the seven suns set behind them. "It was still a good story," Io said. "I liked it. You could have made it a little more dramatic." Io cleared her throat. "Her blood splattered over the Land of Man and all who craved the daughter died in a river of her blood, gurgling her name one last time."

"There's something wrong with you." Cara stared into Io's pale eyes. "The sunlight has damaged you."

Io broke into an outrageous laugh. When she finally caught her breath she said, "Time has damaged me, sister." Io waved her arm toward the Land of Man, changing the subject. "What do you see out there?"

Highsandpleateau was a lower perch than Highmount, but Cara could still see far.

"The seven mountains are gone." She scanned the valleys. "The Goldlands look taller. The sea is shrinking."

"Keep going," Io urged.

"The girl with Darkmoor magic is pacing on the peak of Highrock."

"Further."

"The edge of the world is dark and blunt."

"Keep going."

Cara's vision dropped off the edge, wrapped around the bottom and saw shadowed things on the underside of the Land of Man. "There's something below us. Dark. It's... so black. It's all shadows."

Io touched Cara's arm. "Stop. Do you see a tower? Or a mountain?"

"I'm only used to going forward, not side to side." Cara's brow beaded in tiny jewels of perspiration as she tried this new task. "Everything is so dark. I see trees. Water. Sand. But... it's all black."

"If it were a gemstone, what would it be?" Io asked, leaning closer.

"Onyx." Cara knew instantly. It would be soulless, ominous, worse than looking into the dark abyss of space. There was a shadow to her left. Cara focused, seeing a figure in a suit, detailed dark silk, over its head was an umbrella with tendrils hanging down. They moved slowly, the darkest of shadows. Cara had felt this magic before, malevolence of the Darkmoors. Here it was tenfold. The tendrils explored the air between them, the figure never moving. It stood still as a statue. The tiny hairs on Cara's arms rose, gooseflesh covered her.

"Come back," Io said.

Cara closed her eyes and shook her head. She rubbed her arms and moved out into the harsh sun of the Saltpan, arms outstretched, seeking its warmth. It was hard to escape when you were limited to a tiny island in the middle of a pond, in the depths of a blazing hot desert.

Io followed. "Tell me about the Darkmoor girl."

Cara took a deep breath. "She mans the Watchtower at the edge of the world." Cara pointed to the tiny peak in the distance. "There is something dark in her soul. I felt it the first day I met her. She seemed kind on the outside. I've been watching her all these years. I looked into the future and saw what she'd become."

"The Darkmoors are more than magic. It's primordial magic sifting through the bog-land rot. More sinister than the Celestials on a bad day." Io waved to the sky.

"She was born of it."

Io bit her lip. "We must save her. Before it's too late."

"She was raised by the worst of it," Cara warned. "The people of the Isle could have helped her."

"We aren't all Goldland born. All that shine makes people think differently. But the Darkmoors... the Darkmoors have a *mood*."

"The strange thing is the Darkmoors are mostly empty now." Cara *looked* and saw only a few people among the streets. She came back to Io. "There's barely anyone."

Io stretched her arms. "The moors ate them for dinner. Slurped them in like a glass-noodle." Io took notice of Cara rolling something between her fingertips. "What's that?" She took Cara's arm and plucked away the gemstone.

"Ocean jasper. It reads like this, when you see ocean jasper it means the creatures of the sea are leaving the water and the God of the sea is up to no good."

"Bah." Io shook her head. "That's shit." Then, she popped the tiny piece of Ocean jasper into her mouth and bit down with a firm crunch, bursting the gemstone into tiny pieces. Shards stuck to her lips. She spit the remains out in a spray of saliva then dropped to her knees. "Ah. There you are."

Cara couldn't believe the scene that played out before her.

Io reached forward and touched a tiny spec of black with her fingertip. It stuck as she raised her finger to show Cara. "You see what that is? Tell me."

Cara knew in her gut, she didn't have to think for a second. "Onyx."

CHAPTER 21

THE ETERNAL BARTENDER

Pina started her day at noon with a head full of fog and a gurgling stomach. Drax laughed as she dragged herself into the bar and asked for hot water and breakfast. She winced as she slid onto a bench near the smallest window, the sunlight sliding across her face, illuminating every crease from a heavy sleep on a rumpled pillowcase.

Drax piled eggs, oatmeal, and bacon in a wooden bowl and brought it to her. He was careful not to spill the mug of hot water.

"Rough night?" he asked as he set the bowl down gently, trying not to make much noise.

"It wasn't the night," she opened a small packet of herbs and emptied it into the mug of hot water. She glanced at him quickly. "Rye is the Creator's punishment." She squeezed half a lemon into the mug before she sipped at the water.

"Maybe so." Drax wiped crumbs from the table. He stood at the edge for a heartbeat. He wanted to say more, ask more. Pina could tell, she could feel the energy vibrating off him; an eagerness that she hid much better than Drax. She kept her eyes on the mug, waiting. The scrape of the pub door interrupted them. The moment was broken. "Enjoy your meal," Drax said, a bit gruff, as he turned and made his way to the bar.

Pina watched him go, his shoulders squared, back straight as he met a young man from the docks at the bar. Drax glanced once in her direction. She looked away, steadied her gaze out the window and tried not to daydream about how things could be.

Pina ate, the solid breakfast setting heavy in her stomach and easing its ache. She shouldn't have drunk so much last night. She left money on the table and headed for the door.

Pina spent the day sitting on the beach and staring at the waves, tanning herself in the rays of the seven suns. By the time evening came she was exhausted from the fresh air and her skin was bright pink from the sun. She returned to the Rye House, ordered a drink and food and took it up to her room. She stood by the window and watched the moon, then prayed to the Goddess, to the Creator, to anyone who would listen. She begged for something different.

"There was a prophecy that the sea would freeze over, frozen rain would fall from the sky so thick that man wouldn't be able to see their hand in front of their face."

Drax's face was slack. "I haven't heard that one yet."

"My mother said that it was written by one of the Watchtower servants." Pina took a sip of her drink.

"My guess is they write a lot of the history. Their books have never been brought down from the Watchtowers. How would anyone know?"

Pina swirled her spoon through the food on her plate. "So, you've never seen the sea freeze over with blue ice?"

"Never." Drax folded his arms and leaned on the bar. "I've seen a variety of things that are hard to explain. But that one. Nope, not yet."

He was too close. Pina could see the flecks of gold in his irises, the light-colored stubble growing in across his chin and jaw. She leaned back in her chair and pressed a finger to her sunburned arm.

"There is a BoneCarver shop down on the other end that could give you a salve for the burn."

Pina shook her head. "It could be the last I'll ever feel. I'll pass."

Drax paused, waiting for her to say more but she didn't. He knew he shouldn't pry. "The last you'll ever feel?"

Her eyes flicked toward the window. "There's plenty I won't be seeing again." Pina stood and went to her room.

Drax watched her go, his mind racing with the ominous message.

"Excuse me," an old woman tapped on his arm.

Drax focused. "Apologies. What can I get you?"

The old woman smiled. "A nice, tall glass of your famous rye."

Drax grabbed a glass from under the bar and shined it thoroughly with a clean rag. He filled it to the brim. When he moved to give the old woman her order, she had moved to a booth. He made his way to her, taking in her clothing and stature. Although old she looked well, her clothes aged but frayed stitches of gold thread were noticeable. Drax wondered where she came from.

"Is there anything else I can get you?" Drax asked as he set the mug in front of the woman.

"Not today, dear." She nodded as she slid a gold coin across the table.

CHAPTER 22

HIGHSANDPLATEAU

Io stood, a hand over her eyes as she glared in the distance. "That fool is making his way here again."

Cara stood and walked next to Io. "What fool?" Her Goldland gown had the arms ripped off so she was bare-shouldered, the layers of skirts thinned to only one. She was afraid she'd be as naked at Io soon to survive the heat of the Saltpan.

Io pointed.

"Will he die, walking across the desert like that?" His image wavered in the heat.

"Can't kill what's already dead." Io moved to the shade of the bones. "He's a ghost of some kind. Or at least here he is."

"Like in the Goldlands?" Cara asked. "I miss having spirits around. It made life less lonely."

"Well, that's a ghost who will keep you tethered to this bullshit." Io waved to everything around them. She turned to look into Cara's eyes. "Don't eat any food he brings here."

Cara nodded.

It took most of the day, but the fool finally reached them. He stood at the edge of the pond, hesitant to cross.

"Just do it, you pansy," Io muttered.

When he finally crossed, Cara shot to her feet and ran to greet him. "It's you!" She was smiling side. "I thought the Arrow had killed you. I went to find you that day."

The man tipped his head like he didn't understand.

"At the peak of Highmount." She tipped her head, narrowed her eyes on him. "Do you not remember me, Gail?"

"Ghosts don't have brains," Io shouted.

"I remember you, Cara DiCara of Highmount. You made me late." He rubbed the side of his face. "I couldn't go back."

"We are here now," Cara said.

Gail set his pack down and began pulling packets from it. "I have pickled liver sugars, candied pink shrimp, elderberry licorice."

"Put it back," Cara warned. "We won't take it. Take it back to the Land of Man. Give it to some poor starving soul there."

Gail's fingers trembled over the packets. "This is the one thing I must do. I cannot stop myself. I cannot take it away."

"Tempt us like the Nebula Devils." Io picked up the packets and threw them into the pond. "Not today."

Gail turned to leave but Cara caught him by his tattered sleeve. She paused, breaking all Goldland barriers she'd been raised with. "Gail, have you shown her kindness? The Darkmoor girl, Noomii? You mean something to her."

Gail nodded. "As much as I can in this state. In her state. She is fixated on the stones. You know how they are. An obsession."

Io glanced between the two, judgement clear as the sun on her face.

"We do what we must," Cara said.

Io stepped forward. "I'm searching for someone and I think you can help me."

Gail stared at the small, wild woman. She held her hand out to shake, her free hand grasping her wrist. "I've been thinking about this." She wiggled her fingers. "You know of the old ways. Which means you know of someone I'm trying to find."

"I may." Gail mimicked the handshake. His right hand shot

forward, free hand gripped his right forearm as he rotated her hand in a circle, stopping with his palm open, their fingertips barely touching.

"I'm searching for someone with power. Someone hidden away. Like the powerful daughters sent to the Watchtowers. I've been searching for a very, very long time."

"I have only seen the ones at the Watchtowers."

"Where else do you go?" Io didn't give him much time to expand. "Where else could you go that you don't feel restricted?"

Gail was clearly thinking hard. He glanced to Cara.

"I don't think she's looking for Noomii," Cara said.

"Have you been to the underside of the Land of Man? Have you seen blackened things like this?" Io held out the tiny spec of onyx on her fingertip. She flicked it at Gail and he caught it in one sharp movement. "And here I thought you were of ghastly makings."

"I may still be." Gail inspected the spec of a gem. He closed his eyes, drawing memories from the onyx. He started to hum a child's rhyme:

"At the bottom of the sea
At the bottom of the sea
The God of the sea lies at the bottom of the sea
Cross his ways or piss in his sea
The Celestials will curse and your father will banish you,
to the bottom of the sea."

"I may be a spectacle in the Saltpan, but on the Land of Man I am mostly alive." Gail looked uneasy. "The old Gods punish their children on the Land of Man. It is nothing but a chessboard. A giant made of onyx has risen in the sea. This person you search for hides in its shadow." Gail dropped the tiny gem. "I may not return."

He started to walk toward the pond.

"Wait," Io stopped him. "You saw the floating stones. Do you remember when the Moongate was whole?"

"I remember when the sand fell from the skies to form the seven mountains." He moved his arms, storytelling with his hands. "I remember the Koi and defiant gravity. I remember Kings and Queens, and times when magic flowed freely. But a whole Moongate, not in my lifetimes. Not that I can remember. But much has been lost." Gail tapped the side of his head before he waved goodbye and waded across the pond. On the other side he shouted. "A whole Moongate may bring more chaos than answers. It will let forth the underside of the Land of Man."

Io and Cara stood side-by-side and watched him walk away, across the glaring heat of the Saltpan and return to the Land of Man.

"He used to drag a cart up the mountain," Cara said. "It's strange seeing him without it. I only knew him as the cartman for such a long time."

Io grunted. "I guess I could refer to him as the bagman."

Cara pointed. "Noomii knows him as the helmsman."

"I like idiot better." Io crossed her legs as she sat.

Chapter 23

LandbeforeitwasGold

Divine and Cira stayed in the valley for years. The people of the valley came to trust the demigod, or at least, not hide from him. There was no gold here, no jewels. Just a simple life like how Cira had been raised. They had lazy mornings, slow-paced afternoons with small chores and long walks. Quiet evenings with simple dinners and valley grown wine. Divine was gentle each night when he undressed Cira and laid her on the bed and worshipped the body that had been sacrificed to him. Cira's feelings had changed, she looked forward to his awkwardness and she learned to close her eyes when he seemed more beast than man. Through it all there was never a child born and the emptiness haunted Cira.

Divine would help her tend the garden or hunt for meat or shop in the market, but he told her that he needed time in the forest, time to seek his beastly nature. Each afternoon he walked off into the tree line only to return in a few hours. But as time drifted on, Divine was out longer and longer. Cira set the table later and later for dinner. An ache grew in her center, not just from the absence of a child but from the absence of her husband.

The night carried an icy breeze and a second shawl couldn't

warm Cira's bones. Divine could, warmth seemed to fill the room when he was near. Cira waited until the moon was directly overhead before giving up on him. Her fingertips throbbed with angst, her heart heavy with disappointment. She checked the windows and doors, and went to bed alone. There was no help undressing this night.

In the morning she woke to a warm body next to her. Divine was laying on his stomach. There were dirt streaks across his back and salty rivulets dried to his shoulders. He looked so innocent in sleep, so strong, his face flexed and relaxed. She wanted to touch him, to replace the memory of loneliness. He smelled like damp soil, not the usual pine needles and smoke. Instead of waking him, she got out of bed, her feet crunching on balls of hard dirt and little rocks.

Cira found clumps of moss and sod tracked through the house leading from the back door to the bedroom. The door was open, and ants and a few spiders had found their way in. Anger welled deep inside. Cira gave Divine his space like he asked, but this mess was out of control. Cira set water to boil then went to grab the broom and dustpan. She swept the bugs out to the yard, slammed the door closed and began sweeping up the dark soil and grass. Divine came out of the bedroom in the middle of it.

"You could have wiped your feet before coming in." It wasn't a nice comment; Cira was fed up. It didn't matter that he was the son of the Arrow. She was not his maid, her mother at least had taught her that. "You could have closed the damn door as well."

Divine snorted. "I could have, but then I wouldn't get this view." He slapped her ass.

Cira tried to stand from her bent-over position but Divine lifted her and carried her back to the bed. This time, he was more animal than man, he smelled more of dirt than he did of summer fire. There was no gentleness of their early times together. Something had changed. Cira pulled the blanket over her body when he was done. He stood and snorted; confusion flexed his face. Divine made his way to the bathroom and as the shower started, Cira wiped tears from her eyes.

"Would you like some of these sweet potatoes for dinner?" Cira asked Divine as they walked through the valley market.

Divine nodded, his hands tucked in his pockets.

He'd been off since this morning. Cira had tried to ignore what happened between them by inviting him to go shopping.

He stood a few steps from Cira as she chose the sweet potatoes. The lady at the farm stand smiled warmly at Cira and startled when she noticed Divine standing there. The woman leaned forward to catch Cira's eye. "There's a venison sale today," she warned.

Cira's hand hovered over the largest sweet potato in the basket. "Where?" she whispered.

"Around the back of the clothing shop," the woman warned. "Best keep him away."

"It would be better if you'd all stop selling venison so openly." Cira tipped her head just enough to catch a glance at Divine. He'd walked further away, toward the flower stand.

The woman tskd. "If the deer population weren't so plentiful this season." She nodded in Divine's direction. "Do you think they came to this region because he's here?"

"No," Cira answered immediately. "No, he has nothing to do with it."

The woman's eyes widened as if to ask, "Are you sure?"

Cira set the potatoes in her shopping bag. "Thank you for the produce," she said before turning away. She slowed as she walked up to Divine. He was touching the gentle, yellow petals of buttercup clusters at the flower stand. She sidled up next to him. "Do you want to get some for the house?" she asked.

"Yes." Divine grabbed three large clusters of buttercups and left payment for the girl selling them.

"Let's go home," Cira offered.

They walked the long path to the valley house. Horse-drawn carts went by every so often. People waved from their gardens and front porches. Cira thought it was much different from the first day they arrived. The valley was somber and fear stricken back then. Now they were happy and had been prosperous in food and family. Cira wondered if Divine had something to do with it. If his Demigodness brought the good seasons to the valley. She didn't ask. Maybe the woman was right?

A mood had enveloped Divine and Cira wasn't sure how to help him. He was fighting something internal. The change made her miss their early days together even more. Yes, he was awkward and overconfident, but he was sweet to her. These days he was distant and gone, his mind elsewhere. She figured being sacrificed to a demigod wouldn't be easy, it could have been a lot worse. She was lucky that he'd been gentle all this time. With each step the ache in her hips reminded her of the morning. Emotion swelled, her eyes watered. Cira didn't want it to be like this.

"Where have you been going at night?" Cira finally asked.

Divine stiffened. "Not far. I stay within the valley." He gave her a lopsided smirk.

"You spend more time in the forest than you do at home."

"Not really." Divine shook his head.

"But you do." Cira was trying to suppress her emotions. "You leave in the afternoon. You don't come back until the middle of the night. We were so close and now I barely see you." She stopped and touched his arm.

Divine stepped away from her, his eyes red and focused. "You have no idea how hard this is for me. You have no idea how I struggle to keep balance. I could control it in the Goldlands, but here," he waved his arm toward the dense forest where small birds chirped, "here it is different. There's no boundary."

"Can't you try to—"

Divine interrupted. "I did this for you. For us. For this," he waved his hands between the two of them, "union to work. I had to accept the sacrifice and I did. I accepted you. I have done everything I can to make you comfortable."

Cira pressed her palms down her skirt to dry them. "And I thank you for that."

"You could thank me in other ways," he snapped. "It's been long enough. You could bear me a child."

Cira's jaw dropped. "I..." She couldn't control that they hadn't made a child, for the Creator's sake they tried.

"You could fill that void." Divine's voice was gruff. He lifted the cluster of buttercups in his hand and shoved a whole cluster in his mouth, chewing slowly and watching her.

Cira's eyes stung with tears. She looked away, disgusted, trying to collect her thoughts and when she could control her voice she finally said, "Maybe if you spent more nights in our bed instead of the forest, I might have blessed you with a child." Her voice started to rise. "Maybe it has nothing to do with me and everything to do with you and your mutated seed."

She regretted the words as soon as they left her mouth.

Divine shook his head, the weight of his antlers threatening. His eyes clouded, turning black.

Cira stepped back.

"I am what I am." He threw the rest of the flowers on the ground and ripped his shirt off. He stomped and the ground shook. "You shouldn't forget that I am a demigod. I too have power." He stomped another foot, moving closer. His body wavered; muscles tensed.

Cira was backed up to a tree trunk. His face began to change. He leaned forward until she could feel his breath on her cheek. Cira turned her head and closed her eyes.

"You didn't have a problem with my mutated seed when you were screaming my name," he growled in her hear.

Cira held her breath.

Divine let out a high-pitched whinny and then the heat of his body was gone.

Cira opened her eyes and saw his dark figure leap across the pasture.

The moon was full and breath fogged in the chill of forthcoming winter. Divine didn't come home. Cira sat on the back stoop, the same spot where she watched him walk into the treeline on the far edge of the field for so many nights. Cira never moved; she waited until the suns set and the moon rose. She waited until the evening fog thickened and the valley turned to a sea of white cloud. She waited until she saw movement in the forest. A group of deer had come out to graze in the pasture. She knew which one was Divine; the tallest, the darkest fur like a swath of black hair, the thickest legs that seemed totally undeerlike. That was him down on all fours. He sniffed a doe, a frail lithe thing. He sniffed and nudged and then he mounted.

Cira shrieked in horror, her heart breaking instantly. She leapt off the stoop and ran across the field barefoot. She screamed as his hot breath rose in mist, as his strong hips thrust into the doe, as his antlers absorbed the milky moonlight.

How could he do this? She'd given her entire life. He'd live for ages, and she'd only have this once chance at life. She'd lost everything and he'd burned her like this. The woman at the market must have known this was happening. Everyone from the valley, they must have seen him and never told her. It all came together and Cira knew she'd never be the same after this betrayal.

As she witnessed the horror before her, the emptiness that haunted Cira transformed into true rage. "All this time you've been fucking deer!" she screamed as she neared Divine. "You are a beast! An animal! There is nothing human about you!"

He snorted as he dismounted the doe and came after her. Half transformed. His wild dick swinging long and hard. Cira wanted to vomit. She threw her hands up and... black smoke poured from her palms. It languished through the air, circled Divine. It dove down his throat with vengeance; it squeezed him until he no longer took a breath. And when his heart took its last beat and he dropped to the ground boneless and pale, the murky vapor retracted into her palms.

CHAPTER 24

HIGHSANDPLATEAU

"Ah, there you are." Io shot up to her feet and started for the pond.

"Wait." Cara grabbed her hand. "Where are you going?"

"I've found another one of us. Stay here." As the water touched Io's toes, she transformed into the crab and dipped under the surface.

The vortex was opening and water from the other side spilled into her pond. Io ambled through, she found the iron cage and the corpse within it. She grabbed the face bars with her pinscher and tugged the cage until it fell into her pond, then closed the vortex to stop the spillage of seawater.

Io dragged the heavy cage to the island. She changed into her human form as she broke the surface. "Help me!" She shouted to Cara.

"What is this?" Cara asked as she grabbed onto a hinge and pulled. Her skirt caught under the heavy thing and tore up the side.

They dragged it mostly out of the water, until Io could look into the face cutout. It was a pale, dead woman.

"Oh no. Oh no!" Cara started panicking. "What did you do?"

"Shut up." Io threw sand at Cara. "She'll come back to life. That's what she does. That's what we all do. We just have to wait."

Io sat in the warm sand and inspected the coffin. It was decorated with whirls and whorls as ancient as the handshake she presented Gail. She scraped a fingernail against the rusted iron and worried that soon the contraption would be nothing more than an oven in the heat of the Saltpan.

"Where was she?" Cara asked as she inspected the corpse inside.

"The bottom of the sea. Just like that child's rhyme said. It's morbid really, the Gods teaching children rhymes like that." Io pushed sand over her feet, burying them. "While we wait, you could try something for me. Have you ever looked to the past?"

"I've never looked to the past, only the future."

Io stood, grabbed Cara's shoulders and turned her around. "Try it this way. In reverse... Now, Cara, I need you to go all the way back. To the beginning. Can you do that?"

"I can try." Cara nodded as she took a deep breath and dried her palms on what was left of her skirt. She closed her eyes. Focused.

Cara was *looking* in reverse. Back, back, back, back, to a time of amber skies and sand, when one couldn't tell where the land broke from the sky. She kept going to a time when the Moongate was whole. She passed a shadow, paused, moved back. It was the figure in the suit, dark tendrils escaping from under an umbrella. Reaching for her.

Cara blinked and returned to her present. She shivered.

"What did you see?" Io asked.

The woman in the iron coffin woke with a sharp intake of breath, and then she screamed at the top of her lungs.

Cara's focus broke.

"Hey. Hey," Io ran to the opening and looked in. "It's okay. It's okay. We'll help you."

The woman stopped screaming and began to cry, gasping and muttering so badly she couldn't form words.

"I need you to stop and tell me how to open this." Io tapped on the cage.

The woman started shaking her head and screaming once more. Her face twisted in fear, wet hair matted to her head. She tugged at her clothing, rumpling the feathers and fine twine. She slammed her fists on the bed of moss underneath her. She gripped the bars of the face-window, pulled herself up and screamed out.

Something was very wrong with the woman. Io covered her ears and retreated to the ribcage. Cara tried talking to the woman but she wouldn't stop screaming to hear a single word of it.

Eventually Io joined Cara in the shelter of bones.

"She's too damaged." Io shook her head and shouted over the screaming. "A thousand years of death have broken her."

"What will you do?" Cara winced as the screaming mingled with wild animalistic cries.

Io's shoulders slumped. "I have to put her back."

"But... she'll die." It came out as a weak shout. Cara didn't want the woman to hear.

"Yes."

"How do you save her?"

"I must go find her before the coffin. I must find her at a better time. Another time. Not this one."

Io walked out from the shelter of the skeleton and began pushing the cage back into the water. Cara helped her. The woman inside screamed louder. Her eyes widening as she realized she was going back into the water.

"I'm so sorry," Cara repeated over and over again, knowing well that the woman couldn't hear her.

Io changed her form and tugged the coffin under water with a giant claw. She opened the vortex and floated the coffin back to the sea. While she couldn't hear the woman's screams, she could see the look on her face; eyes wide, tears mingling with saltwater, the knowledge that death would come in just a few moments, her mouth open wide and screaming. The last few bubbles of air drifted out and floated to the top of the sea. Io closed the vortex and returned to the island.

Cara was pale. Io was pissed.

"What are we?" Cara finally asked.

A long time passed before Io replied with, "Different. Split."

CHAPTER 25

DARKMOOR

Noomi stood on the bluffs. Out of habit she pulled her telescoping mirror from her pocket and suspended it over the side. She blinked and her head spun for a moment as her eyes focused.

There was a ledge, the ocean far off in the distance, and the Watchtower stood—clear as day. She tilted the mirror just right and saw something more. Under the ledge were the shore and the dirt trails that led to the Darkmoors. There was an open crevice, a nook of darkness. She looked closer and saw something underneath the Land of Man. A dark reflection of everything she'd known, everything she'd ever seen. It was all there; inverted, twisted—whatever you want to call it. It was blackened and burnt, reminded her of Darkmoor mud that had bubbled in the gaze of the seven suns for too long. Noomii's stomach churned and tension zipped down her arms.

She slammed the mirror closed and shoved it in her pocket. "This whole world is just mud and bone and lies." The Celestials lit the sky with firelight as Noomii's thoughts swirled. There was a searing pain in her chest.

"Did you see it?" she asked Drax.

"I see many things," he replied, calmly. "I see that you have magic. I see that you saw something. I see that the Celestials in the skies, who have been dead for ages, are now active." Drax stepped closer. "What comes next, Darkmoor?"

Something like a mirage skipped behind Drax. A woman with flowing red hair and porcelain skin. Her image flickered, her white dress still even though there was a breeze on the peak. Her fingertip scraped across his shoulders. Drax went still.

"Your lady is here," Noomii warned and she wished Drax would go away and leave her with her thoughts. But first, she held out her hand and without saying a word Drax reached in his pocket and set the ocean jasper octopus in her hand.

Drax turned. "Pina?" he whispered as he walked toward the mirage, following the woman's form into the shadows of the nearby towers, mesmerized by her transparent beauty.

The Goldland-born who walked the streets paused as Drax followed the spirit. Their amber eyes flamed dark.

"He doesn't belong," one of the Goldland men hissed.

Drax followed Pina's ghost to an alley between two buildings whose peaks could not be seen.

The Goldland men followed.

Noomii had watched as Gail was killed on the beach and now she watched as Drax joined Pina's soul. Perhaps that was what he wanted; love makes people do strange things. It can bring happiness, it can bring death.

Noomii pulled the carvings from her cloak; she set them on the ledge of the golden-bricked garden then took out the piece of amethyst. She broke the amethyst into as many pieces as she had carvings, pressed them into the creatures. She blew out a steady stream of breath until they grew larger, crushing the garden ledge under their weight.

The octopus was a spectacle as it grew. Feldspar crystal turned to giant tentacle suckers. The bird of yellow-feather jasper grew a wicked beak that divided men in two with a single tap. Goldland-born surged the creatures, brazen and bold.

Noomii stood on the ledge, the breeze blowing her cloak as the sun set and the Celestials lit the night sky. Goldland streets ran red with the blood of man.

The dragon of unakite took to the skies, its breath of flame lit the skyscrapers as though they were candles. The tree of herringbone sequoia grew tall and wide, its branches swept dozens of Goldland born off the ledge to the water below. More Goldland-born came. They emptied out from the buildings; lines miles long, men endlessly running toward the creatures Noomii had brought to life. Gold was a flimsy metal. Armor bent and melted, chainmail tore. The metal glittered and shone as it liquefied and coated the streets in rivulets.

Some caught sight of Noomii on the ledge and somehow, they knew.

"She's got magic!" one yelled and dozens swarmed toward her. "Kill her!"

A memory flashed before her eyes. Not one of this lifetime, but histories were beginning to blur.

Noomii didn't scare easily. She'd been born in the moors, she'd seen the worst of men in the pubs and by the docks; they'd tried to stone her to death before. Though Goldland-born were tall and well-built, they did not scare her. She'd climbed the seven mountains of the Land of Man, she'd looked into the cold abyss of space, she'd forced Gail to row her to the edge that never ended.

Noomii held out her hand, palm extended. A feeling built in her chest, burning and bloated, and she pushed it down her arm, through her hand and out her palm as a forceful pulse. It pushed the Goldland-born into the tentacles of the giant octopus where the men were quickly relieved of their life force. More men came and Noomii repeated it over and over until she was exhausted and alone. Her creatures slowed, paused, turned back into carvings. Noomii ran to collect them all and tuck them into her cloak.

She left on foot as the suns set and the moon rose. Noomii ran toward the Goldland gates. The wisps collected behind her, growing in numbers as the dead Goldland-born souls became trapped. The gates were unmanned so she forced them open and ran down the mountainside. After all this time, she had magic. She paused, looked at her open palms, dried them on her cape, and began running again. She reached the base of the mountain and turned toward the docks. When she reached the docks and the boat, there was no one around to throw stones at her. Noomii kicked off the fancy Goldland shoes and ran across the sand to the boat. She rowed away, navigating easily due to the fireworks in the night sky. She rowed the boat into the rocks and jumped out, running up the steps she'd chiseled into Highrock until she reached the peak. Out of breath, she dropped to her knees backlit by a dark sky. It seems she surprised the Celestials with her actions.

The tower grew, the new band was black flecked with red. Bloodstone. Noomii felt it. She'd hoped the growth of High-mount would fill the emptiness inside, but it did not. The void was a cavern filled with shadows. She had a sudden ache for the mud of the Darkmoors. She wanted to sink into the cool mud, she wanted to lay down until it covered her, consumed her, until she sank to the bottom and was spit out on the other side.

The time of bloodstone was here, because of her.

CHAPTER 26

HIGHSANDPLATEAU

Cara was sleeping under the portion of ribcage without a canopy. Burrowed in a nest of sand, her arm bent to cradle her head, and a thin sheet of threadbare fabric covering her. The stars overhead shined down on her relaxed form. Io was curled in the corner, her small body consumed by the shadow of the last few feet of skin that remained. Io knew better than to sleep in the full light of the moon. But here there wasn't much option. There was only a small corner that still offered a shadow to hide in. The night sky felt like a reflection in a mirror, it went on forever and ever and ever between the starlight and the gloss of the Saltpan. It was hard to see where one would end, but in that sameness, the floating rocks of the Moongate shifted and came together in its original arc. It seems the Land of Man had come into alignment with something.

Cara woke first, her eyes blurry with sleep. Io moved like a serpent, slithering out of the bone-shelter next to Cara in near-silence.

"What was that?" Io whispered.

"I'm not sure." Cara rubbed her eyes.

"Look." Io pointed in the direction of star-shine. "Look right there."

Cara went, her eyes turned to milk and her focus went straight for a minute before she came back. "The Moongate is whole. Something is coming through." She looked further to the Goldlands; they lay coated in blood. "Oh no." She kept going to find Noomii on her knees atop Highrock. "What did you do?"

The air became dense with power. Both women could feel it in their bones. The sky lit with fire as the Celestials burst forward reds and bright orange of stardust.

The black suit was embroidered just as Cara had seen on the man in the underside of the Land of Man. The umbrella was open and tentacles writhed down. It was walking toward them, whistling like the Darkmoor drone winds.

"Ah, my children." It spread arms wide. "I've been searching for you."

"Who is that?" Cara asked Io.

"Our father. Some call him the Creator. Some pray. Some wish on his word. We always do, until we learn better. I've learned better."

"He is darkness." Cara shivered. "I've felt this before. The shadow magic of the Darkmoors gives the same feeling." Goose-flesh rose on Cara's skin as she stood. Io followed.

The man was standing on the other side of the pond. The sky was dark as jet but the power in the man glowed. Tentacles waved in the air like arms searching for purchase, for something to grasp, for something to grip and pull toward. "There should only be one of you," he said. Fingers tapped together letting off small sparks. "There should always only be one of you right here." Pond water lapped at his toes. "Pieces that should not be together. You are splintered." One finger pointed at Io. "Forever."

"I know much about forever," Io said. "They are mine. They are pieces of me." Io gave a possessive glance at Cara.

"No." The man shook his head. "I separated you."

"Perhaps I did not want to be separated. We did not want to be separated."

Fingers of both his hands tapped together now and the tentacles wove away from the sparks that flew. "You need to be separated. It's the only way for you to keep on living."

He was ready to move closer, but Io grabbed Cara's arm and dove into the pond. She summoned a vortex, any vortex to anywhere, she hadn't had much time to dwell on it. She hoped Cara was holding her breath as her pinschers cut into Cara's arm and dragged her through. She felt soft flesh give way to solid bone under her grasp. Cara's mouth opened but no scream came out, it couldn't as they transversed time.

The sky around them was ocher. Sand dripped from the heavens in the distance. But here, tiny stars funneled into a steady stream and coated the ground. The children of the Goldlands would be told that the star shaped grains of sand of Highsandplateau were nothing more than the skeletons of marine protozoa from the ocean floor, but now Io and Cara knew the truth.

Io sat and pulled Cara's limp body close. Cara's arm was bloody, it stained the sand below. She held on to the serrated wound, trying to provide pressure to stop the blood. "Io," she whispered.

Io plucked a fish bone from her sarong and plucked two hairs from her head. "This will hurt." Io looked deep into Cara's eyes. "I'm sure you don't ever remember dying before. But you might today." Io went to work, sewing Cara's arm back together. Pulling tissue to tissue. The pressure slowed the bleeding. "I'm sorry about this," Io muttered as she leaned closer and bit the hair to cut it. The stitches were better than crude. Io was sure the golden threads of life would have done a better job, but she worked with what she was given. She always had.

Cara was pale and unconscious. Io sat by her side, her fingers sticky with blood. There was a puddle draining into the pond where she rinsed her hands. Hours had passed and Cara still hadn't come back to life. Io was starting to worry. She watched the pond closely, afraid her father would jump out and pull her under. This game had gone on for lifetimes. And it had taken her lifetimes to find these pieces of herself. Pieces of her soul split into three, reborn after each death. And there was always magic, no matter how far it had been banished. No matter which of the old Gods had found it and forbidden it on the Land of Man, it never stifled or snuffed out. Io just had to find it over and over again. Once together they could save Noomii, they could save each other.

Io took this time to meditate and find the woman in the iron coffin again. Maybe this time she could find her alive. Before glancing at Cara, she thought, maybe they could all be alive at the same time, and fix this. They would be whole. They could stop the bloodstone from coming.

Chapter 27

LANDBEFOREITWASGOLD

Divine lay under the full glow of the moon, his face pale and an antler broken during his fall.

Cira dropped to her knees. "What have I done?" she whispered. She was hollow and confused. All she had known was Divine since leaving childhood. Her fingers brushed over his mouth, his eyes, over heavy black locks, solid antlers. She remembered the first time she'd grown brave enough to touch them, grasping with both hands as sweat glazed her brow and Divine made love to her. Her fingers drifted over the now broken piece. She collected the shard in her hand and stood, sliding it into her pocket.

"You've killed my son." Arrow appeared.

Cira had never laid her eyes upon an old God in the flesh until now. He stood before her, all horns and bone and ghastly. She froze, afraid to move, afraid to breathe in his presence. The night wind that usually hushed the valley stopped. All became still. As still as Divine's corpse.

"He was the only son who ever survived birth." Arrow knelt and touched his son's broken antler.

"There was something wrong with the way he was," Cira

finally said. "He was more beast than man, every day he got worse. You had to have seen what he was doing!"

"What a sacrifice he made for your happiness." Arrow sneered. "You made him leave the Goldlands. You brought him to the valley. You put the beast in the woods. You took his humanity away the moment you took him out of the city." He stood and waltzed around her in the moonlight.

"I didn't know," Cira said.

"And what of you?" Arrow sniffed the air around her. "You're not so innocent. There is something here, a spark that has yet to take flame. What are you born of?"

Cira's back straightened. "I am a bastard of the valley. Nothing more."

Arrow laughed. "You are definitely not a bastard. Not with that spark inside your soul." He tipped his head in question, his eyes narrowed. "Can you not feel it?"

"I don't know what you're talking about." Cira lied, because the old woman had mentioned it to her years ago when she was sacrificed to Divine. But Cira had never felt anything. She'd never seen the smoke come out of her hands before, she wasn't sure what had just happened. She only knew the heartbreak, the rage, the cavernous void that now filled her chest.

"So you say. Still, you must be punished for killing my only son." Arrow ran at her, he tipped his horns down and the tips stabbed into the fabric of her clothes and the heavy moss cloak. He lifted her atop his antlers.

Cira screamed. She screamed as he galloped off her land and down the winding road that led into town. She screamed as he ran so fast that the people of the valley weren't sure what they'd seen or heard. They only knew that the moon darkened, and the night sky went still while each and every one of them were filled with existential dread. The valley would never be the same after this night. Something would always be missing from the valley.

Arrow galloped out of the valley and to the gulf. The old God moved faster than any creature she'd met. He strode to the end of a dock. Floating in the water was an iron coffin, waiting. Arrow flicked his antlers and Cira fell.

Except, she didn't fall into the coffin, no, she fell through it. She kept going, arms and legs cycling as she fell right through the iron coffin and into the cool water below.

Hands gripped her shoulders and pulled.

"Hold your breath," a small voice whispered.

Chapter 28

Highsandplateau

There was no iron coffin to drag across the sand and Cira came out of the water screaming. Arms and legs were flailing as Io dragged her out of the water. But, this time she stopped screaming when she saw Cara. Her eyes widened with awe as Io transformed from a kidnapping crab into a slight and nearly naked girl. Her pinschers tapped together joyously as her hands changed to skin and bone.

Io pointed to each of them with a pale finger. "Io, Cara, Cira. There," she nodded, "we are finally together." Io grinned with the accomplishment that had taken her so long to complete. Lightning crashed through the heavens at the proclamation.

Cira shed her cloak of moss, leaving it to dry in the sand as she wrung out her short dress of mottled-brown turkey feathers.

"She's better than last time," Cara said, inspecting the girl.

"Definitely less damaged," Io agreed.

"What do you mean?" Cira asked as water ran down her hands and dripped off her elbows. She set the feathers of the dress straight again with the palm of her hand.

Io and Cara's gaze met. Secretly, they decided not to tell her what fate held, what Io had saved her from. No one needs to know that they'd spent a thousand years dying over and over again at the bottom of the sea.

"Let's just say, the last time I found you, you weren't healthy," Io said.

Cira took in the ocher sky, the sand dripping from the heavens in the distance as an eternal hourglass. She moved her foot in the sand, reached down to pick up a handful of it. "I've never seen sand before. Nothing like this." The substance filtered through her fingers and dropped to the ground once more.

The three women felt at peace for the first time in their ever-repeating lives. It didn't matter that they were secluded in a strange time, that they barely recognized the Land of Man before there was true land and sea and mountains. They were finally together and all that time they'd felt the void, it was finally filled.

Cara's fingers drifted over the stiches on her arm. Crusted blood flaked off on her fingertips. "Do you remember the other time?," she asked Cira.

Cira was confused.

"She doesn't know," Io interrupted. "She hasn't died yet."

Cara's lips pressed together. "You found her before."

Io nodded. "And now I need to find one more. Before our father returns."

"Where are we?" Cira asked as she rolled the last few bits of sand between her fingertips.

"A time before," Io said. "I'm not exactly sure. I had to move fast to escape our father."

"I don't have a father," Cira said as she rubbed her arms.

"I don't think we remember," Cara said. "We've forgotten."

"It's the splitting," Io said. She moved closer to the other two. "Let me show you." She gripped their hands and formed a circle. Closing her eyes to meditate, Cara and Cira did the same.

Their bodies shook with electric current, with dark smoke, with power. They saw into the past. They saw the cycle that had kept them apart for millennia. They saw themselves whole, as one. A tall girl with dark hair, highlighted with golden threads and tiny flowers. Eager eyes, a welcoming smile. They saw a father, the Creator, with open arms, a heart full of love. They saw a war amongst the old Gods, an onyx spear that pierced her chest. Blood-tinged lips, ghastly pale skin. The Creator roared in agony as he pulled his dead daughter to his chest and wept. The tentacles of his face stroked her hair lovingly. Black clouds thundered around him, electricity crackled and snapped. He laid her down and pressed his hands over her. Sweat beaded his brow. Muscles tensed. The girls' body blurred. It resonated like a plucked string on a violin. As the Creator worked to bring her back to life, he broke her further. Lightning cracked as her body distorted, further and further, until she split into three. Three empty souls, each a fraction of what his daughter once was.

The Creator cried in agony. He clapped his hands together. He swore and spit at the Celestials in the sky watching. He turned to his daughter, broken, never the same and then at his hands. He wasn't sure if this was better than death, but he couldn't live with himself knowing how badly he'd failed. He sent them away, trapped their souls in the Land of Man for safekeeping. And in his disgust, in his self-pity, he retreated to the shadows, to the darkness of the underside of the Land of Man through the Moongate.

He would never be the Creator they'd intended him to be. He was a carver of worlds, a chess maker of minds. This Creator was meant to fill the universe with worlds of life. Instead he was stuck, banished. The longer he was there the more his mind twisted. The darkness of creation leached out of him the further he descended into misery. It leaked into the mud of the moors. It leaked into the hearts of the people of the Land of Man. It threatened the God of the sea. It tainted the old Gods with twisted minds. The Creator was beyond saving. He'd paid them back though. He'd broken the Goddess of the moon. A daughter for a daughter. It was only fair.

The women came back to their present.

"It's too late for him," Cara whispered, her eyes glossy.

Io nodded. "Too late for him. But it might not be too late for her."

Cira looked confused.

Cara tried to explain what the Land of Man had become, she tried to explain the Watchtowers, the gemstones, the girl who would grow to man the Watchtower at the edge of the world.

"She couldn't see any of that from under the sea," Io reminded her.

Cara took Cira's hand, reached for Io's. "I have to show her."

Cara sent their minds into fast-forward. She showed Cira what would become of the mountains and men.

"What a mess," Cira said when they were done.

"Now what do we do?" Cara asked.

Io sat and crossed her legs. "I must find Gail."

"The idiot?"

"That one precisely."

Cira's hand gripped the antler shard in her pocket.

"What's that?" Io asked.

Cira pulled the antler out. In the ocher light it looked aged. So much more aged than the demigod she'd taken it from. The green parts had turned brown without sunlight and the center as hollowed as her heart. "It's mine," Cira said. She gripped the open base and could feel that there was power.

"Save that for later," Io warned.

CHAPTER 29

HIGHROCK

"You've ruined everything!" Noomii screamed at the night sky.

She closed her eyes and imagined... when it was all gone—man and Goldland and Darkmoor—Noomii turned her creatures on each other. Tentacles snapped and crushed, fire burned and cindered. The dragon was last. Maybe it was because Gail might have been afraid of dragons. Maybe it was because something so great should always die last. The pink and green beast consumed itself tail first.

And now it was much smaller. The land was neat and tidy. There were no slopes, no sandy beaches or muddy Darkmoors, no Goldland, no dark lands of confusion and lies. There was simply the Watchtower and a small expanse of water. Highrock stood in the middle of the ocean, surrounded by water lapping at the blackness of space. Noomii stood alone; the wind whipping her hair, the sea-salt air bristling away the last of her humanity, her skirts molding to her legs as the vacuum of space echoed in her ears. The silence was better than the consumption of the Land of Man. The crumbling chomps, the screams, the slick sucking sound of creatures taking gulping bites of mud. Noomii had ordered her leviathans to consume it all, and they did, and then they consumed each other. There was nothing left. The onyx man was gone and the water had risen to the base of the Watchtower. Her magic was darkness and death.

She could have ended them all. She could have ended everything on the Land of Man.

Noomii's eyes flicked open, unsure of what to do next.

She'd manned the Watchtower, learned things her mother had never told her, she stood atop the steeple that stitched together time and destroyed it all. She would never understand why the Creator never answered her light in the Watchtower, or why Gail never stayed, or why Drax had to show her the upside-down. There was a stairway that stretched from the bottom to the top and a row of ornate carvings were all that was left of her work.

The Celestials set off plumes of stardust to burst in purples and sparkles of white. They urged her on. And for a moment, Noomii understood there was a certain depth to the layers of Highrock that she'd never noticed before. There were darkness and death, a cyclical lesson to be learned. The same story over and over again, and Noomii was present for every one of them. This was a trap and she'd been running in a circle for eons.

Noomii curled her toes around the edge, tempted to fall back, tuck and roll and keep going until she submerged herself in the pond at the center of Highrock, emerging anew, bathed and fresh. But the ground shook under her foot. Highrock grew with a deep rumble. Noomii knew what this layer would hold. It would be gray with confusion, speckled with amethyst, there would be creatures of eons past reemerging to engulf the Land of Man and destroying everything the Creator had made. And when Noomii arrived at Highrock again, she'd chisel a new step into the rockface without remembering every layer atop was a stratum of her life.

Noomii didn't run and leap, like the previous Watchtower servant, she simply took one step and fell like a droplet of rain embracing gravity whole.

Until her fall came to an abrupt halt.

Someone gripped her, forearm to forearm, a hand wrapped securely around her elbow, lifting her from death and onto the peak as though she were hollow. "On the occasion that you drop into the sea from exhaustion or doom or regret, I will wait here to collect you and return you from where you came," the voice said.

CHAPTER 30

THE ETERNAL BARTENDER

It had been three days and Pina had been nothing more than a ghost in the tavern. She ate and drank, disappeared for the day, and returned to the bustling tavern for the night. A shadow followed her; gloom hovered over her head as though something unbearable were looming closely. That didn't stop the pull of Drax's eyes, the upturn of his lips when he saw her, or the feeling that someone was pushing him in her direction. On this night, Pina kept her head down as she made her way across the tavern to the stairwell in the back. She climbed, the noise and music at her back. Drax watched until a man from the docks slammed his palm down on the bar top.

Pina called down and ordered breakfast to her room and Drax went to deliver. She opened the door. Her hair was twisted up in a knot and she was dressed in a dark blue gown.

Drax cleared his throat. "You look… very nice." He tried not to stare.

Pina stepped aside so he could enter the room and set the breakfast tray down.

The door closed.

Drax turned.

"This will be my last night here," Pina said. "Thank you for helping me."

Drax nodded.

"There is one last thing I'd like you to help me with." Pina moved closer.

Drax noticed the slit in her dress that revealed a considerable length of bare leg and hip.

Pina touched the chest pleats as she moved closer, pulled the vee at her cleavage a bit to reveal more.

"This is a dangerous game you're playing."

Pina smiled sweetly. "It's nothing." She stood in front of him, breast to chest. Her hands hovered over his shoulders. "I'd very much like to touch you."

"Once you do, there's no going back." Drax's voice was thick as his hands closed into fists at his sides.

Pina settled her hands on his shoulders, feeling firm muscle beneath, her hands rubbed down his chest, across the hard plane of his stomach, and to his belt.

Drax was quick to move, gripping her wrist and holding her hands in place. He leaned forward, his mouth hovering over lips. Only a moment passed and Pina welcomed the heat radiating off his body. Drax pressed his lips to hers.

Pina trembled.

Drax stepped back. "You've never—"

"It doesn't matter," she interrupted. "I want to. Now." Her fingers curled around his belt and she pulled him closer.

"I don't want to return to the tavern," Drax said as he looped a leg around hers and leaned down to suck on her nipple.

Pina's back arched and her hands went to his hair.

Drax's hand made lazy circles across her stomach, down each

of her thighs, before moving between her legs. His finger parted her cleft, still damp from their recent lovemaking.

Pina moaned and arched more. "Please," she whispered. "Yes, please. Don't stop."

Drax moved from her nipple, tasting and kissing a trail to the vee of her legs. He used his mouth to pleasure her.

Pina shivered as Drax moved over her. When he was deep inside, she wrapped her legs around his waist and tightened.

"I would like to stay this way forever," she said.

"It is my only wish to pleasure you over and over again." He dropped his hands to the mattress, caging her with his body.

"I leave in the morning." Pina pulled the blanket to her chin.

Drax frowned. "Reconsider."

"It's not my choice."

"We all have choices."

"This was my last." She tipped her chin at him. "Tomorrow I am to be sacrificed to a demigod."

Drax froze mid shirt-buttoning.

"Spend the day with me," Pina asked.

Drax laughed. "I had been looking forward to taking you to bed since the moment you walked through the doors of the Rye House. Now you tell me that this is nothing but a last fling." He pulled up his pants and tucked his shirt in. "Are you trying to break my heart, woman?"

"Not intentionally." She let the sheet drop, revealing her pale, naked skin. "I've heard men don't have hearts. And bartenders are especially heartless."

"Fairytales," Drax scoffed. He made as though he were headed for the door.

Pina made a whimpering sound.

He turned, took four long strides and dove onto the bed. "You play a hard bargain. I'll stay. Broken heart and all."

Drax took Pina to lunch on the beach. They ate steamed gulf shrimp glazed in butter and candied oysters. They drank pink cardamom tea topped with spirits that left them giddy and careless. Drax kissed her hard under the docks at low tide, his hand sneaking up her skirt since they were alone. Water lapped at their toes.

Pina made a soft noise of pleasure.

"Perhaps the God of the sea will bless you with freedom," Drax whispered against her lips as his fingers pressed into her. "He could give us more time."

Pina bit his shoulder rather than cry out.

"Stay with me," Pina begged.

Drax stripped naked in record time. He didn't care if the other renters in nearby rooms heard them, Drax had one goal this night and it was to try and change her mind.

It was cold when Drax woke. The seven suns had not taken over the sky.

Drax reached out, touching Pina, rubbing her back and her bottom. She felt cool. He moved closer. "Are you cold, love?" He kissed her bare shoulder. He noticed the black bottle on her nightstand.

She'd gone to the BoneCarver.

Drax scrambled upright and rolled Pina to face him. She was like an angel, sleeping forever. Her eyes closed. Her lips parted. Her chest did not rise with breath.

"No!" Drax shouted. "Gods, no!"

He shook her lifeless body. "Pina, why?" He pulled her close. "Why did you break both our hearts?"

Chapter 31

Highsandplateau

The ocher sky never got lighter or darker and the constant dripping of sand from the heavens was unnerving. Io was familiar with the lack of passing of time.

Io picked up a moon rock and handed it to Cara. "Tell me what you see."

There was a time when man lived on the moon. Giants roamed the Land of Man, great beasts taller than trees. They crushed man under their giant feet. Ate them as snacks while lounging under the shade of mountains. The Creator sent the few remaining men to the moon until he defeated the giants and made the Isle safe again.

Io takes the moon rock from Cara and sets it in Cira's hand. "What story do you see?"

Cira squeezes the rock. "I'm not sure what you mean. But I don't think this is a rock. This is cheese." She licks the rock. As she does, she is reminded of the time Divine bought a salt lick. Tears formed in the corners of her eyes.

"Where do demigods go when they die?" she asks the other two.

Cara was silent.

"They turn into stars," Io said.

The Celestials send streaks of falling stars. Io pointed. "You see. They are watching us."

Cira looked up. She threw the moon rock as far as she could and screamed, "You're a disgusting pig! I hate you!" She kept screaming as Io and Cara watched, surprised at the outburst.

When Cira is done she turns. "I was married to the son of the Arrow. He kept sneaking off into the woods to fuck the does. I don't think I'll ever forgive him."

"That's great and all, but demigods don't become Celestials," Io said.

"Well at least they know I'm disgusted with this place."

Io nodded in agreement. "Also, that's not cheese. You're demented."

Cira shrugged before throwing the moon rock across the sand.

Cara went still. Io sensed it.

"When are we?" Cara asked.

"Very early," Io answered. "Or very very late. But I'm going to bet on early."

Cara suddenly sat on the ground and her eyes turned to milk.

"What is she doing?" Cira asked.

"She has the sight." Io pointed to her eyes. "She can see through time."

"And you?" Cira asked.

"I can travel through time."

"And me?"

"We'll find out soon enough."

Cara hushed the two as she went forward, her vision wrapping around and around and around the Land of Man until she saw what had happened. She saw Noomii lose control, the death she'd caused, the creatures she'd created. "No," Cara whispered.

Bloodstone was coming at the palm of Noomii. Her face was twisted in confusion and angst. Tears dripped down her cheeks.

"We have to stop her," Cara said.

Io warns. "He will try to stop us. The Creator. We will be running from him at every turn once we leave this place."

"What are you trying to stop?" Cira asks.

"We." Io circled her finger. "All of us."

CHAPTER 32

TimeBeforeMoonstone

Sons of Gods and daughters of monsters,
Fight your war and nothing more,
Sons of monsters and daughters of Gods,
Fight for your memories and nothing more.

"Do you think we'll find peace?" Noomii asked, gazing at the full moon above the valley.

Gail stepped out of the cool brook, water dripped from his body and drew his short hair into spikes. "This is quite peaceful. But if you ever lose your peace, I will find you and return you to where you belong." He lowered himself to his knees and elbows and crawled closer to her, predatory, like a large cat. "Right by my side. You are actually the most peaceful creature I've ever seen in the valley." He tugged on the strap of her top, revealing summer dark skin. "The most beautiful creature I've ever seen." He kissed her stomach.

Noomii laughed, gripping the fabric of her shirt and rolling away. "Not so easy." She moved to her feet and ran toward the stream. Splashing as she went, the water soaked the soft fabric of her skirt. "It's so cold." She laughed as Gail followed.

"Not to me." He jogged toward her. "I'll warm it for you." As his toes touched the water it began to warm. He moved closer, closing his eyes as the tiny rapids of the brook rose to his knees.

Noomii splashed him. "It's like bathwater."

"The people of the valley might enjoy it." He tipped his head downstream.

Noomii hushed her voice. "They'll write stories about the night the old God of the sea warmed the brook so they could all bathe before winter with warm water."

"I am not the old God of the sea." Gail reminded her.

"They don't know." She advanced on him. "They don't even know you exist."

"Must you rub it in?" He grabbed her by the waist. "We can't all be as celebrated as the Goddess of the Moon." His hands drifted over her bottom, gripped, and pulled her up.

Noomii wrapped her legs around him and held on to his shoulders. "If they knew what the prince of the sea had in his pants." She stuck out her tongue and reached a hand between them. She traveled further down his front, between his waistband, and gripped his manhood.

Gail jerked. The water around them heated further, releasing a mist to the cool air. "Gods, woman." He leaned forward and licked her neck. "Out in the open like this? Someone could see. The God of the moon could see." Gail's eyes were half-lidded as she stroked him. He dropped to his knees and pulled Noomii down onto his lap.

"The old God of the sea could see," she reminded him. "You know how our parents war secretly. This will cause chaos for eons." She smiled and kissed him.

Gail's hips thrust up. He kissed her hard, his tongue probing, hot and demanding. He held the back of her head steady. The water around them steamed, the fog swirled in torrents. Noomii twisted her fingers in his hair, holding in her moans of pleasure so as not to disturb the nearby village.

Clouds moved over the full moon and it seemed the Land of Man was giving them their time, whether their parents approved or not. The ground shook with their climaxing.

Gail held her still. "There is nothing more I could want in this world but you."

Noomii opened her mouth to reply but she was interrupted by the ground shaking again, this time more violently. "What was that?" she asked.

There were screams coming from the village. Fires lit the sky.

"Oh no. The people of the valley." Gail lifted Noomii to her feet. They straightened their clothes and began running in the direction of the village.

The brook cooled and the fog dissipated. A large figure was running toward them. Gail recognized Divine, the half-man half-stag demigod.

"What are you doing in the valley?" Gail shouted.

Divine slowed as he approached them. "Collecting weapons." He tossed a spear to Noomii, swords to Gail. "Follow me."

Gail and Noomii changed direction and began running with Divine.

A shadow above the trees paced them, the old God of the Eastern Mountain had taken to the sky.

The ground shook again. Noomii lost her footing and fell. She moved to her feet again before Gail could help. "Go. Just go," she shouted.

"What is happening?" Gail yelled over the screams descending upon the valley. He skipped sideways, ready to run back, making sure he was able to help Noomii to her feet if she didn't catch up.

"It's a war." Divine whooped laughter. "You know how petty and bored our parents get."

The clouds cleared the glowing full moon, giving them more light to run by.

"This is ridiculous." Noomii shouted.

"It's been a long time coming," Divine said.

"Who are we defending?" Noomii asked. "Whose side are we on?"

Divine replied, "The side of your fathers. We don't get a choice. I promise not to maim you." Divine whinnied at his joking.

Noomii and Gail's gazes met.

"Where is this war located?"

"The Saltpan." Even though he ran on two legs, Divine looked to be galloping, and moving faster.

Large shadows left the mountaintops; the old Gods had taken flight.

"At least they gave us flat ground to war on."

The three ran.

The shadows of the old Gods arrived well in advance of them. As they neared the Shadowline they could hear the slamming of metal, the screams of the humans they'd brought to war.

Arriving late, Divine, Noomii, and Gail stood on the Shadowline.

"See you on the flipside, friends," Divine shouted as he ran to fight by his father's side. The two of them were a sight, the ghastly God of the Eastern Mountain and his half-breed son.

Gail gripped Noomii's hand. Neither wanted to move forward.

The Saltpan was covered in blood, the mirrored ground glistening. Each God's army fought to the death. They fought for the God they'd worshipped for ages; it didn't matter the reason why. The men fought and killed and shouted for what they'd believed in.

The God of the Eastern Mountain rode a giant beast resembling a mammoth.

The God of the Northern Mountain, a giant spider.

Weapons clashed. The shadowline was so dark between the Saltpan and the Land that it hid the warring Gods from the humans.

Celestials lit the nights sky; eruptions of every color covered the galaxy.

"Look," Gail pointed out the Creator.

The Creator was attending to injured humans. His daughter too. He shouted at the warring Gods. Demanded they stop. He shouted to the night sky and swore to the Celestials who'd tasked him with carving this land. "Why isn't he fighting?"

"He's trying to save his creations," Noomii said.

"He can make more. He could make more on another land. Another planet."

The humans that the Creator and his daughter had brought back to life ran back to the fight as though they'd never died. There was no fear of dying for the old Gods they worshipped, they had no allegiance to the Creator, barely acknowledged that he existed.

The Creator shouted across the battlefield to his daughter. "Cario, save as many as you can!"

She signaled to him that she understood. As she began moving to the next injured human, a black arrow flew through the sky.

"No!" Noomii shouted from the shadows. She bent to heal a young man, then a boy, then a horse. Cario stood oblivious to the war, only focused on healing the wounded. She stepped forward. "Cario!" She shouted to her friend. But it was too late.

The black arrow impaled Cario through the chest.

"Nooooo!" the Creator screamed so loud that all movement ceased.

Creator ran to his daughter's side.

"Cario!" he shouted as he pulled her body straight and lay her on the ground. His hands hovered over her wound; one pulled the black arrow as another worked to heal the wound.

Noomii ran forward, dropped to her knees, held Cario's head in her lap, stroked her cheek, and whispered, "Cario, come back. Please, please come back."

Magic spiraled out of the Creators palms and into his daughter's body. Threads of life stitched and stitched and stitched her heart and spine. Blood poured out, more blood than he could replace. It took much more effort to bring a God back to life, especially one with Cario's power.

Tears ran down Noomii's cheeks. She thrust her arm forward. "Give her mine. Give her my blood!" She shouted. "You have to save her."

Blood soaked into the Creator's pants. His hands turned to fists and he slammed them on the ground. The Saltpan patina shattered.

"Keep trying!" Noomii screamed. She lifted his arms and placed his fists on Cario's chest. "Bring her back! She can't... she can't be gone."

Tendrils of black and white seeped from the Creator's hands.

Noomii pulled the spear from where it was secured on her back and sliced her forearm. Blood seeped out. "Use mine."

A tendril of magic reached for the blood dripping down Noomii's arm, it brought the stream to Cario's heart. Threads of life worked harder, stitching and replacing but it wasn't working. The Creator choked as he felt her soul begin to fracture. Her soul was splitting the harder he worked.

The Divine Arrow stepped forward, resting one hand on the Creator's shoulder. "It's too late."

Noomii was about to shout at him to go away but one look from the ghastly Divine Arrow and she stayed quiet.

The Creator's powers weren't going to fix her. He began to realize that this lifetime was over for Cario. He could bring her back, but it would have to be as something else. He could recycle her soul, but she would never be as she was.

The Creator stood. He picked the black arrow up off the ground and held it high. "Which of you shot this arrow?" he asked to the Gods surrounding him. "Which of you killed my daughter?"

None spoke up.

Noomii stroked Cario's hair and cried silently.

"Speak up!" The Creator shouted. "We are Gods. Are we not?" He turned and scanned every one of their faces. God, demigod, human. "Who did it?"

Silence.

The Creator snapped the onyx arrow over his knee. He threw the arrowhead end into the heart of the Eastern Mountain God's beast. "Answer me!" The beast dropped with a thud. He pointed to the Gods surrounding him with the tail end of the arrow. "Which one of you did it?"

When there was still no answer, he dropped the end of the arrow. The Creator clapped his hands together and Cario's body disappeared. "A child for a child." The Creator tugged Noomii up by her hair.

Noomii struggled, and she turned to find Gail but he was gone, vanished into thin air. Drained of blood, she was too weak to fight back.

The Creator reached out and drew the demigods closer. "And so we will all suffer together. Your children will suffer like mine has. A never-ending loop for eternity will be their fate." The demigods disappeared from the Saltpan.

The Creator flashed. He was halfway across the desert. He flashed again and walked through the Moongate. It tumbled as he disappeared into darkness on the other side.

The Divine Arrow scanned his six brother and sister Gods. "Y'all fucked up real bad," he said with a snort before turning and galloping toward his mountain.

CHAPTER 33

TimeBeforeBloodstone

Stars erupt and souls break,
the Shadowline takes,
Souls erupt and stars go dark,
the Goldlands are stark.

Cara came back to the present, her milky eyes turning clear. "It's not good." She shook her head. "Nothing has changed. No matter how many times I look."

"We need to find Gail," Cara says to Io. "He can stop her."

Io stopped meditating. Annoyed. "I haven't been able to find him as his original version." She shifted as she sat on the sand. "Let me know when you find the right version of him."

Cira stared at her fingers. "I'm hungry."

"Too bad!" Io and Cara shouted at her.

Io laughed.

Cira looked at the two women as though they were crazy.

"This was a hard lesson to learn," Cara said. "The food

anchors us in time and place. An empty stomach is freedom to roam."

"I see," Cira said.

"You've spent a thousand years on the sea floor. You'll get used to it." Io exhaled and shook her head, cleansing her energy. "I need water," Io said. "It's my conduit." She waved her arms. "I can't work with air and sand."

Time passed as they walked the plains of a world before its Creator and old Gods were set upon the soil to taint it. The women practiced their skills. They found a small pond filled with murky water.

Io made a face. "Primordial slime. Perfect."

❧

"I've found him!" Cara jumped to her feet. "I've found him. Gail. I had to go really far back but I think I've found the perfect time to pull him from."

Io gripped Cara's hand. "Show us."

They formed a circle and looked through time. Cara took them in rewind as fast as she could. Before all the stories of the gemstones. Before the women were banished to the Watchtowers and the Land of Man turned sour. She showed them the war. Moved forward to Gail standing in the Shadowline alone, his left leg moving back as he was about to leap forward, his face twisting in agony, his mouth open to shout.

Their eyes opened.

"That's what we need." Io said as she sat on the edge of the pond.

"What are you doing?" Cira asked.

"Going to get him," Io and Cara replied at the same time.

Io pointed to the two women. "Stay close. There's no telling what could follow us through."

Io crossed her legs and settled her hands on her knees. She

meditated for hours, drawing the energy and placing her mind in the correct time. The thick pond water wavered as she rotated her hand and drew a vortex. Io stood, walked to the water and transformed. She snapped her pinschers and went under. Cara and Cira watched from above.

Io reached through the vortex, gripped onto Gail before his mind was fractured, and tugged.

Cara and Cira reached for each other at the sound of a cry filled with agony, a roar of pain. The water shuddered. Io and Gail slid forward on a wave.

Gail's face paled as he scrambled to his feet. "What the hell just happened?" He moved to grab his swords but Io moved faster, kicking him swiftly in the groin. Gail dropped to the ground.

"How dare you!" Io shouted at the man who was three times her size. "How dare you grab for a weapon when we are helping you?"

Gail groaned and dropped to his side. "Who are you, puny devil woman?"

Cira laughed.

Cara's hands threw to her throat to stifle both laughter and cries. She had never seen Gail like this. Whole of mind and body and spirit. It made a difference. His golden eyes were sharp, movements quick and controlled.

"I always knew you were a fool," Io said as she kicked sand at him. "Even whole you are a fool." She tapped the side of her head and glared at him.

Gail stared at Io. "You speak like you know me."

"Of course we know you." She waved her hand to the other women. "We've been dealing with your foolishness for eons."

"Stop calling me a fool." Gail moved to his knees with a groan of pain.

"Stop giving me reasons to." As Io plopped down in the sand, she motioned for Cara and Cira to do the same.

Gail took note and sat with them rather than deal with her antics any longer.

"Will you tell me what just happened?" Gail asked. "One moment I'm watching the old Gods war, the next I'm," he waved his hands, "here. What is this dreadful place?"

Cara cleared her throat. "It's the time before the Gods and the Creator."

"And who are you three?" he asked.

"You might recognize us. Or, pieces of us," Cara replied. "It's hard to explain. You have the memories, you just need to access them."

"Where is Noomii?" he asked. "What did you do with her?"

"She's not here," Io said.

"Clearly." Gail was tensing. "You made me leave her in the middle of a war. She needs me. I can't be here." The more he thought about Noomii the more agitated he became.

Io held out a hand to pause him. "You will see her soon. We will save her together." She shifted, settling her hands on her knees, palms up, fingertips touching. "We just need to determine the perfect time and place."

The waiting grated on Gail's nerves. He kept asking Cara, "Have you found her yet?" He kept asking Io, "When will we leave this forsaken place? I can't stand it much longer. That sound of the sand falling is horrendous."

Io replied, "One day you may be tasked with a new world. You should learn to enjoy the lack of chaos in your life."

Gail made a face. "There will always be chaos. I need to get back to her." He patted his chest over his heart.

"Give us time," Cara suggested.

Gail tugged at his hair which had grown ragged during their time, his cheeks hallowed, the planes of his body sharper. "Can't you just get her from the same time you collected me? Why all this meditation and thinking?"

Cara touched his knee as they sat in a circle together. "We cannot disrupt her growth or your growth. There is more at play. More than simply the Goddess of the Moon and the Son of the sea. Bloodstone will come if we aren't careful."

Gail rubbed his face. The three women had taught him how to access the memories of his life after the Saltpan War. He remembered bringing Noomii to the Watchtower at Highrock. He'd watched her grow old for lifetimes, never remembering. He remembered Cara and Io. He remembered trying to fill the endless task the Creator had given him. Always feeding them so they'd anchor. They knew and it seemed they'd finally forgiven him.

It could have been days or it could have been weeks before Io and Cara finally determined a handful of opportunities to intersect Noomii. The group discussed it together and decided to try intercepting her at the Goldlands, before she ended the Goldland with her creatures.

"We will all go through the vortex," Io warned them, drawing in the sand with her finger. "I've never brought so many through before. It could go badly. I'll do my best to find you all again and bring you here."

Gail was silent but energy radiated off him.

"Be calm, demigod of the sea," Cira warned.

Cara nodded. "She will be on a precipice. Don't scare her."

Io made her way to the small pond and began calling the vortex. Cara, Cira and Gail waited behind her.

"Will you be in this form on the other side?" Cira asked. "Or will you remain a crab?"

"I have no idea," Io replied.

"Your crab form is a little strange," Cira said.

Gail chuckled. "This form isn't much better. The Goldlands will not take kindly to a naked heathen."

Io flashed a side-eye before her foot kicked back and struck Gail's shin.

Cara warned, "Shut up, you two."

Gail gripped his swords and nodded in agreement.

The pond water wavered as the vortex below took shape. Io moved closer, transforming and tapping her chitinous claws as she went underwater. The others followed, gasping in giant breaths before their heads went under.

The Vortex glowed, reflecting the Goldland sheen. Io waved them on. She snapped at them to move through before her. Cara went, spilling onto the Goldland streets. Cira followed. Then Gail. Finally, Io stepped through. She left the vortex in its place, shrinking the hole.

Cara paused. "There is no water here," she warned.

Io's eyes were strained, "We must hurry."

"She's on the bluffs," Cara told the group. She ran around the corner, her feet making familiar hallow taps on the Goldland streets. Her heart swelled. All the time at Highmount she had wanted to return. Now that she was here and knew the truth, her return was melancholy. "Don't look at the wisps," she warned the others.

"We might have a problem," Cira warned. "Last time I was here they followed me like a herd of cattle." Cira shivered.

"Let's go," Gail took the lead, eager to find Noomii.

He paused, recognizing a familiar face amongst the wisps. Drax, the son of the old God of the Western Mountain walked by him, following a spirit.

"Drax!" Gail reached out to stop him.

Drax fell out of his trance to turn and focus on Gail. "You're dead. I watched you die on the docks."

Gail smirked. "But here we are." He grabbed at Drax's shirt. "Come with me." He pointed to Io in the distance. "Come with us and help."

Io's pinschers maneuvered into a very unladylike gesture. "We did not agree to stragglers," she shouted back.

"Ignore her." He shook Drax. "Come with us."

"What are you doing here?" Drax asked.

"I've come for Noomii," Gail said. "To fix this."

Drax was entirely too calm. "Yes, someone must." He looked toward the pale wisp with long red hair. "Just not me."

"No. Don't. You'll die here. Come with us and live. Help us fix what our parents destroyed."

"Even if what you say is true. Pina was mortal." He motioned to the wisp. "She won't be there she won't be here. There is only one way we can be together forever." Drax slapped Gail hard on the shoulder. "Good luck, man. May we meet in another life."

Drax strode away, oblivious to the warring and attention he'd brought himself. He walked to death with open arms.

The fighting had intensified. Noomii's creatures were giants. The dragon of unakite clouded the skies, its breath of flame lit the skyscrapers and melted them to embers. Cira screamed as the giant tree of herringbone sequoia's branches swept dozens of Goldland born off the ledge to the sea below. More Goldland-born came from the streets leading to the bluffs. They emptied out from the buildings; lines miles long, men endlessly running toward Noomii and her creatures. Gail was brought back to the Saltpan War and the way man fought without good reason. Gold glittered and shone as it liquefied and coated the streets in rivulets.

"Hurry," Io shouted from where she stood, holding the vortex. "I have to go back to the water soon!"

Wisps caught notice of Cira. She ran by Cara's side, not far behind Gail's long stride.

"Noomii!" Gail shouted. She couldn't hear him. The sounds of the creatures and the wails of Goldland-born as they fought and died drowned out his voice.

Goldland-born shouted, "She's got magic!" And dozens swarmed toward her. "Kill her!"

"No!" Gail answered their cries. He gripped his swords and fought his way to Noomii.

Wisps fluttered and clustered around Cara and Cira.

Cara recognized the scene playing out before them. There wasn't much time. The Darkmoor girl was going to the shadows, drawing magic from their father's darkness. Movement caught her eye. "Mother," Cara whispered.

Gail leapt across the bodies that littered the ground. He shouted for Noomii. And, for a heartbeat, he thought she'd heard him. Her eyes focused on his figure only to be torn away as the Goldland mob descended upon her.

"We are getting to the point of no return," Io shouted from across the streets.

"Leave me," Cira told Cara as the wisps surrounded her, eyes wide as the wisps grew in number.

"Never." Cara grabbed Cira's hand. "My mother is here too." She nodded in the direction but didn't make eye contact. She knew this place too well. She couldn't risk the Goldland-born noticing and making their task harder. "They want you to bring them back to life, Cira." Cara swung a long spear that she'd taken off a dead man. It dissected the wisps and they disappeared for a few moments.

At the bluffs, Noomii held out her hand, palm extended. Gail recognized the dark tendrils of power circling her. "Noomii!" he shouted. "Nooooo!"

Cira and Cara did their best to keep up with him but between the slippery streets and the unforgiving wisps, they were too far behind.

The dark force pushed the Goldland-born into the tentacles of the giant octopus where the men were quickly relieved of their life force. More came and Noomii repeated it over and over. Gail leapt over piles of bodies. He slipped on the blood of the Goldland-born, and it stained his palms, his clothing, the soles of his shoes.

Noomii's eyes had gone dark, she barely focused as she killed.

Gail would never reach her in time, he realized this.

"Come back!" Io shouted from the vortex. "It's too late."

Cara and Cira turned and made their way back, wisps following. Cara swiped at them with the spear, backing down the alley toward Io and their escape. Io shoved them through the vortex. The spirits wavered before turning away, their last chance at a second life gone.

"Gail!" Io yelled. "Get back here you fool! It's too late."

Gail was hesitating, watching Noomii from a crouch in the distance.

Whatever was going through her head on those bluffs, she was too far gone to bring her back. Gail's heart sank. He'd never wanted to see her like this. His Moon Goddess was pure and light. The Creator had turned her into death unrelenting. Gail turned and made his way back to Io. He did his best to remain hidden so as not to be killed by Noomii in her rage. He crawled amongst the bodies that littered the streets, hid behind food carts and carriages until he'd made it safely to Io.

"Another time," she said, her eye stalks twitching. "Hurry."

Gail dove through the vortex. Io followed.

The four of them swam out of the primordial pond and collapsed on the shore.

Cara's hands dug into the ocher sand, happy to not be surrounded by blood and dead bodies.

"She was really bad off," Cira said, walking in a circle, making sure none of the wisps had followed her.

Io snapped her fingers in disgust. "I was too late. We should have been a few moments earlier."

Gail wiped water from his face. "I don't think it would have helped."

"Can you be sure?" Io asked.

"That was not the Noomii we wanted." He shook his head. "Wherever her mind was in that moment, even if we'd gotten there earlier, she was too dark. She's never been able to create before."

"It was the mixing of our blood on the battlefield," Cira said.

"Oh," Gail replied as he flopped onto the sand on his back, looking up at the dark abyss of space. Footsteps caused Gail to look to his left. Io was advancing on him. She kicked him hard in the ribs before he could move out of the way.

"You're a goddamned fool." She snarled. "We didn't agree to pick up stragglers."

"He wasn't a stranger. He could have helped." Gail gripped his side and rolled away, up onto his knees, ready to defend himself from the small, nearly naked woman.

"We didn't agree on it." She repeated. "No surprises. We can't be causing more chaos to the timeline."

Gail rubbed his side. "It was the son of the God of the Western Mountain."

"We didn't need him," Io argued. "We don't need him. We only need Noomii."

"That's great," Gail shouted back. "He'd rather walk to his death than come with us anyway." Gail rose to his feet and walked away from the three women.

Cara and Cira glanced at each other before looking at Io.

"What?" Io snapped.

More time passed on the ocher land. The four of them sorted through memories and timelines to find the perfect instance to save Noomii.

"Why not before the Saltpan War?" Gail argued.

Cara shook her head. "We need her to learn."

"She needs to help us defeat the Creator. Can't do that with a naïve child of the moon." Cira was the most patient of them all.

Gail nodded in understanding.

Cara's eyes cleared as she came back to them. "Why not after she demolishes the Goldlands?" Cara touched the other three and *looked* to the time she was referencing. Noomii stood alone on the peak of Highrock contemplating all she'd done, what she could have done. The result of Cario and Noomii's blood mixing, giving her powers of creation, the confusion it caused.

Cara brought them back. "You see?"

There was silence as each of the four thought deeply about what was about to happen next.

"There's a pond, at least," Cira said. "You could change forms and close the vortex."

"That's good." Io nodded in agreement.

"There's a finite amount of time before we're too late for her," Cara warned. "Once she jumps..." Cara's face was pinched in apprehension. "I don't know what happens if we are too late. It's all gray. Undecided. She hasn't been reborn yet. I'm not sure where to find her."

The three women were staring at Gail, waiting on his response. His forehead was creased in concern. "Okay," he finally said. "Don't be too late," he warned Io.

Io sat by the pond and meditated, drawing her powers to the correct time and place. A bit earlier than last time, she'd decided. Better to be early than late. The other three waited behind her. When the pond rippled with the formation of the vortex, they all moved closer. Io transformed. She waited for them under the water, motioning for them to be quiet as they came out the other side. She stopped Gail before he could go through. Her antenna-eyes focused on him. Her human form shuddered in the clear cara-pace. "You are not the fool," she said to Gail. "You are much more."

Gail nodded, assumed that was Io's best attempt at an apology, and she sent him through.

Io crossed last. The vortex closed behind her and they broke the surface of the pond in the center of Highrock. Gail motioned for them all to be quiet. They slunk out of the water like serpents sent to spy by the God of the sea.

Noomii stood alone; the wind whipping her hair, her skirts molding to her legs as the vacuum of space soaked up the last rays of the seven suns. The silence was deafening.

The Celestials set off plumes of stardust to burst in purples and sparkles of white. Cara and Cira's eyes were drawn to the spectacle. Noomii sighed loud enough for them all to hear. The three women looked to Gail. Io waved him forward. He crawled across the dense grass that grew on Highrock, silent as a serpent, determined as a man aching to save the love of all his lifetimes.

Noomii curled her toes around the edge, her arms spread wide.

Gail knew what would happen if he were off by one beat of his heart.

Noomii took one step and plunged like a fallen star.

Gail was close enough. He lurched forward, nearly sliding over the edge of Highrock. He gripped Noomii forearm to forearm, his strong hand wrapped securely around her elbow as he would have done if she'd fallen during the Saltpan Wars. "On the occasion that you drop into the sea from exhaustion or doom or regret, I will wait here to collect you and return you from where you came," Gail said.

Noomii looked up, startled by the voice of who'd saved her.

"Gail?" she whispered.

He lifted her from death and onto the peak as though she were a wisp. Light as a feather and hollow boned. All that had happened emptied her body and soul.

Noomii's eyes were wide, her mouth hung open in shock. "How?" she asked. She reached forward to touch him. Her hand hovered over his shoulder, remembering the caste rules. She was a bastard of the Darkmoors, he was... something. Something more than a traveler who'd been to the Goldlands. Something more than a helmsman. This Gail was different. Solid. Energy and strength radiated from him. His clothes were no longer tattered from years at sea. He looked just like when she'd carved him from moonstone in that dream.

Gail took her into his arms before she could think on it any further. He hugged her so tightly that she could barely breathe.

Noomii stiffened, unfamiliar with the touch.

Gail released her. "In another lifetime you would have melted into my embrace." He searched her eyes. "You would have asked me to kiss you."

She looked at his lips. She'd wanted this for so long. "Then kiss me."

Gail pressed his lips to hers before another breath passed between them. He pulled her back into his arms.

"You are dead," Noomii said between kisses. "I watched you die." Her hands moved to his neck, stretched to tangle in his hair.

"I've a secret." He wiped her tears away with his hands and held her face. "We never truly die."

Noomii nodded, her eyes closing and head tipping down. "I've been trying to figure that out. I'm so confused." She turned her face toward the stroke of his thumb. "What are you?" she asked.

Before Gail could answer, there was movement behind them. Noomii shifted quickly, her hands out, finger splayed, dark tendrils ready to destroy circled her hands.

Io, Cara and Cira froze in place.

"They're with me." Gail touched Noomii's arms. "Put this away. They're here to help."

Noomii's head tipped in confusion. "How did you all get here?"

"We'll show you," Gail said. "We'll leave the same way."

Io stepped closer.

"Why are you naked?" Noomii asked as the dark tendrils of magic receded into her palms.

Io smiled. "I've no need for simple pleasures like clothes."

"Or manners," Cira said with a chuckle.

It was enough to break the tension and Gail introduced the women. "Io, Cara and Cira," Noomii repeated. She paused. "Do I know you? There's something familiar..."

Io nodded and took Noomii's hand. "You've known us at some point, but, maybe as one and not three."

The explanation confused Noomii but there wasn't time for Io to explain at this moment.

"We must leave and get to a safer time. We'll explain more once we get out of here," Cara said. "Is there anything you'd like to bring?"

Noomii looked to Gail for guidance. He nodded in agreement with Cara. "We must leave as soon as possible."

"Let me just go grab a few things." Noomii ran to the Watchtower house, collected her carvings and the last of the amethyst. She settled it all in the pockets of the long thick cloak lined with beaver hide given to her by Drax. She stopped in the kitchen and looked around. She grabbed the black chocolates Gail had brought her when he was nothing more than a helmsman. She shoved them in her pocket and ran out the door.

"I'm ready," Noomii said as the others were looking at something in the distance, something close to the edge of the world. "The abyss of space will suck you in if you don't look away," she warned.

The others turned. "Come on," Io motioned toward the water. Gail took Noomii's hand.

Io stood at the edge of the pond. Drawing the vortex to return was quicker. She knew where they were going, felt it in her bones. The bond strengthened as the vortex took shape.

Noomii made a noise as Io shifted into the crab and went under water. Cara and Cira followed. Gail started walking but Noomii dug her heels in.

"Come on," he said to Noomii. "This is how we travel through time and space."

"Is it safe?" Noomii asked.

"Is it safe?" Gail laughed. "So asks the girl who climbed the seven mountains of the Land of Man, who rowed to the edge of the earth, who pummeled the Goldlands. Traveling through the vortex is the safest thing you'll do in this lifetime." Gail prayed that she'd move her feet and get the heck out of here before the Creator found them.

Highrock rumbled and shook.

"What was that?" Noomii asked, eyes wide.

Io snapped her pinschers. "The Creator is coming. Let's go!"

Gail picked up Noomii and ran for the water. He dove underneath without warning. Noomii kicked and punched. Io swung her pinscher and hit Noomii in the back of the head, sending her unconscious. Gail glared at Io. Io shrugged with both pinschers in the air. They dove through the vortex and it closed swiftly behind them.

The women broke through the surface and settled on the sand. Gail carried Noomii, stripping her of the heavy coat and laying it out to dry.

"That was a bit much," he scolded Io. "You could have damaged her."

Io kicked the sand. "We can't all be heroes," she griped.

Noomii woke with a startle. She sat upright, spit out a mouthful of water and gasped. Gail was there with her, taking her hand and rubbing her back. "It's okay," Gail said. "Everything is fine."

"Why?" Noomii moved her head to look at Io, stopping short and rubbing her sore neck.

"Sorry about that," Io said. She was tapping thumbs to fingers in succession on both hands. "We couldn't risk you delaying us any longer."

Noomii blinked twice. "The Creator was coming."

"Sure was." Io stopped with the tapping and scooted closer to Noomii. Gail put a protective arm around her.

"I won't hurt her," Io said. "She could probably hurt us more." Io looked to Cara and Cira. If she were whole, she'd be stronger than all of them combined. But that was not the way things were right now. Even if she went back in time and prevented Cario's death, it would just happen again at another time in history. It was meant to be. The old Gods would have never learned. Eons of transversing through time had taught Io this. The path they were on was the only way to make a difference.

Io held out her hands to take Noomii's. Noomii hesitated. "You are the Goddess of the Moon," Io reminded her. "Rid yourself of those Darkmoor caste idealities. The Land of Man was never meant to grow into that."

"I am the Goddess of the Moon?" Noomii asked. She looked to Gail. "How hard did she hit my head?" Noomii looked to the three women, none of them offered a different story. "So, all this time I've been praying to myself?"

"It's good," Cara said. "Worshipping yourself builds character." Cara offered Noomii a soft smile and nodded toward her hands. "We have something to show you."

Noomii settled her hands in Io's. Cara touched Io's arm. She went in reverse, around and around the Land of Man, stopping at important points in time to show Noomii what she wasn't remembering. Lifetimes she'd forgotten. They showed her the truth behind the stories of the gemstones, they sped past the Saltpan War to show her the times with Gail.

"This will be hard," Io whispered, knowing what was coming next.

Cara brought them back to the Saltpan War. Noomii saw herself running to Cario and she now knew that Cario was her closest friend, her best friend. They'd grown up together, learned to wield their powers together.

"Save her!" Noomii heard her voice scream. She felt the power of the Creator and the power surging from the threads of life as they stitched Cario's heart and spine.

Noomii felt the sharp ache from the tip of the spear as she sliced her forearm. Warm blood trickled down her arm. Her voice said, "Use mine."

A tendril of magic reached for the blood dripping down

Noomii's arm, it tugged at vein, pumping more away from Noomii's body. Her head swayed with dizziness. The threads weren't working. The Creator choked on grief. Noomii knew in her gut that her friend was never coming back. Their blood mixed and creation magic flowed into Noomii.

The Divine Arrow stepped forward, resting one hand on the Creator's shoulder. "It's too late." His voice was deep with an odd timbre.

Noomii felt hate for the Divine Arrow, disgust at him for interrupting such a sacred moment.

Noomii's eyes followed the Creator as he stood and picked the onyx arrow off the ground, holding it high. "Which of you shot this arrow?" he asked to the old Gods surrounding them. "Which of you killed my daughter?"

None spoke up.

Noomii stroked Cario's hair, grief settled in her throat and threatened to release, but somehow she cried silently, swallowing it down.

"Speak up!" The Creator shouted. "We are Gods. Are we not? Who did it?"

Silence.

The Creator snapped the onyx arrow over his knee. He threw the arrowhead end into the heart of the Eastern Mountain God's beast. "Answer me!" The beast dropped with a thud. He pointed to the God's surrounding him with the tail end of the arrow. "Which one of you did it?"

The Creator clapped his hands together, Cario's body left the Saltpan as Noomii's hands were mid stroke across Cario's hair. Tears dripped down Noomii's face as she relived the moment her friend died, the moment the Creator failed to stitch her back together, the moment she was fractured into three and banished from Noomii's life.

"A child for a child." The Creator's voice was unusual.

Fear now filled Noomii. He tugged Noomii up by her hair.

The Creator, whom she'd trusted her entire life, who'd formed some of her fondest memories, who was as close to a father to her as the God of the Moon.

Gail, Noomii thought. Noomii struggled, she turned to find Gail was there one moment, running toward her and another he was gone, vanished into thin air. There was a flicker of a dark space that didn't belong. The telltale snapping sound of a pinscher echoing in the darkness of the Shadowline.

Bile rose in Noomii's throat.

"And so, we will all suffer together. Your children will suffer like mine has. A never-ending loop for eternity will be their fate."

The demigods disappeared from the Saltpan. All of them. From the Eastern, Northern, Southern Mountains. She knew the demigod of the sea had vanished during the original timeline, destined to a fate like her own.

"I'm so sorry to have to do this," the Creator whispered, he pet her hair like Noomii had done to Cario. His heavy palm smoothed over her skull, his warm thumb brushed her cheek. The weight of his hand was worse than gravity. Blackness filled Noomii's vision.

Cara brought them back. Io released Noomii's hands.

Noomii moved to the side and threw up. "Sorry." She held up a hand. "I need a minute."

She stood, unsteady on her feet. Gail tried to help but Noomii slapped at his hands and pushed him away. "Give me a minute. Just, give me a minute. Please." Noomii walked off, a million tiny stars crunching under her feet. She paused, bent and picked up a handful and threw them into the sky.

A considerable amount of time had passed.

Gail paced around the primordial pond. "Is she going to come back?"

"When she's ready," Cira said. "Give her time to process it all."

"What if she leaves?" Gail itched his cheek then ran his hands through his hair. "She could go back to the moon."

"No." Cara said, pointing up. "There are no moons or suns yet."

Gail breathed out a long sigh before turning to stare at Noomii's small figure in the distance.

"What about those?" Cira pointed to the random stars that she'd thrown. "What are we going to do about that?"

Io waved them away. "I'm sure they'll fall back down."

"You hope," Cara said.

Noomii walked back to the group. She rubbed her face dry and took in a deep breath. Io, Cara, and Cira were standing together, waiting for her. Noomii stretched out her arms and took the three women in an embrace. "You're alive," she said, crying once again. "I thought I'd never see you again. I was so sick. What happened during the Saltpan War, it changed me before the Creator did. I lost you."

Gail was watching from nearby.

"Well," Cara said, "you have three of us now instead of one."

Noomii was nodding as she released her friends. "I do." She held her hands up. "Just, please, don't ever die in front of me like that again."

Io chuckled. "We'll do our best."

"That's positive thinking," Cara said.

"We still have to defeat the Creator," Cira reminded them. "We can't stay in this place forever, hiding. We must stop him."

"Will you help us?" Gail asked Noomii.

She nodded. "Yes. Yes, I will help you."

CHAPTER 34

SALTPAN WAR

"We have one chance at this. My pond will be behind him." Io warned. "I won't be able to get us out of there quickly." She moved to the primordial pond and drew on a vortex. "I will say that I won't miss this bland land, nor the sound of the Celestials creating the Land of Man from stars."

Holding their breath, they watched through the Vortex for the right time to move through.

Cara shivered, remembering this night. It seemed like ages ago. The nocturnal sky was like a reflection in a mirror, going on forever and ever and ever between the starlight and the gloss of the Saltpan. It was hard to see where one would end, but in that sameness, the floating rocks of the Moongate shifted and came together in its original arc.

There was movement on the island where Io and Cara slept.

Cara woke first, rolling to the side to see what was happening. Io slithered out of the bone-shelter, stopping next to Cara. The two spoke but none of them could hear from this side of the Vortex.

Io pointed in the direction of star-shine. The direction of the Moongate.

Cara watched her past self as her eyes turned to milk and her focus went straight.

The air became dense with power. Both women could feel it in their bones. The group could feel it from the primordial pond a hundred timelines away. The sky lit with fire as the Celestials burst reds and bright orange.

The Creator stepped through. His black suit was so unlike what he wore during creation of the Land of Man. He carried an open umbrella to hide himself from the Celestials. Tentacles of dark power writhed down. Once limited to his face and chin, they took over his head and draped far below his shoulders now. He was whistling like the Darkmoor drone winds. Noomii tipped her head to the side, remembering the sound that drew her to the moors as a child.

"Ah, my children." The Creator spread his arms wide. "I've been searching for you."

The Creator stood opposite the pond of Io and Cara, his back to where Io was about to fully open the Vortex.

"There should only be one of you," he said. His fingers tapped together, letting off small sparks. "There should always only be one of you right here." Pond water lapped at his toes. "Pieces that should not be together. You are splintered." One finger pointed at Io. "Forever."

Io spoke back.

"No." The man shook his head. "I separated you."

"Perhaps I did not want to be separated. We did not want to be separated."

Fingers of both hands tapped together now, and the tentacles wove away from the sparks that flew. "You needed to be separated. It was the only way."

He was ready to move closer, but Io grabbed Cara's arm and dove into the pond. She summoned a vortex and jumped through.

"Now," Io warned as she circled her claw, and the vortex grew wider.

They exited the ocher land and stepped into the mirrored Saltpan.

The Creator's back went straight.

He turned to find the five of them watching him.

Io transformed into her human form.

"That was a nice trick," the Creator said as he took one step forward. His index finger stretched out and he counted. "Once again. There should only be one of you. Definitely not all three." He took one more step. Pieces that should not be together."

Noomii advanced. "How could you?" she shouted. "How could you do this to us?" Gail gripped her arm to stop her from getting too close too early.

"Children, did your parents send you all to clean up their mess?" the Creator asked.

"They can't remember their parents," Io reminded him. "You took that from them. From us."

Sparks zipped from the Creator's fingertips. "A child for a child. They would have never learned." He tapped his thumb and middle finger together. "Now. I must send you all back to where you came."

Noomii's arms raised, her palms out flat, darkness curled.

Cira did the same.

"You don't know where we came from," Io challenged him.

The Creator's eyes narrowed. "You all smell like the spark of creation." He looked to Io.

She smirked and nodded. "Are you not proud, father?"

Sparks flew from the Creator's fingertips. Black smoke poured from Noomii and Cira's palms. They met and intertwined, smoke and sparks battled with force.

The group moved together across the Saltpan as they fought the Creator. Cara's eyes went white as she told Noomii and Cira what move the Creator would be making next. Gail stood guard next to Cara, grabbing her shoulders to move her out of the way, missing wayward sparks and smoke from the Creator.

"You're cheating," the Creator snapped. He shook his fingers free before sending out a zap to Cara's stomach.

Cara slid across the icy Saltpan floor. Gail ran to collect her.

Noomii reached into her pockets and pulled out the carvings from Highrock. "I worshipped you all those years you banished me to that mountain in the sea." She rolled the octopus of ocean jasper across the Saltpan floor. It burst to life under the stars.

"Impressive, Goddess," the Creator paced, contemplating his next move. He waved his arms, digging into the sand, specs flying in a tornado as he formed then released his own octopus of sand and inky smoke. Giant tentacles flopped onto the Saltpan and the ground shook under their weight. Suckers undulated, stirring sand and air, searching for kill.

Noomii kept digging in her pockets. She rolled her carvings closer and closer to the Creator. Each burst to life.

The Creator matched her beasts with his own. The Saltpan was filled with monsters that tore up the reflective ground, made it rumble and made sand fly. They stomped in the pond, splashing water out. They crushed the beast's ribcage where Io had slept for centuries.

The Creator laughed. "Is that all you have, Goddess?"

Noomii dug in her pocket for the chip of amethyst. She tossed it to Gail. "There is a giant of onyx outside my Watchtower. Press this into his chest and he will come alive. Bring it here." She pulled the coat off and tossed it aside.

Gail ran faster than he'd ever run in his life. Faster than when they'd ran to the Saltpan War together. Faster than the moment Io plucked him out of the air and he couldn't save Noomii the first time. His feet barely made a noise as he crossed the Saltpan and the Shadowline. A surge built within him, power he'd never called upon. One leg after another, his knees went higher, his steps became longer until he stepped into the air as though he were dreaming. He channeled a father he couldn't remember and transformed into something fast and dark. Gail flew like the old Gods over the Land of Man. Shadow and hollowed bone. He was a dark wisp in the night, something he'd seen the old Gods do as they left their mountains to fight in the Saltpan War, and others. One day soon he'd remember all the wars the old Gods soared to. Gail sped forward, his focus on the onyx giant in the sea.

The creator grew more monsters out of the Saltpan, his fingers danced in strange formation as he brought the koi fish back to the skies. The man-eating giants and the colossal, bloodied sultan of the time of rhodonite. The ground shook with their footsteps.

But this time, Noomii and Cara knew the weaknesses of these beasts; they'd spent eternity studying them, writing about them, watching them in the eternal gemstones that pushed the mountains up. And Noomii had her own version.

The beasts fought. The Creator shot bolts of electricity past his creatures. Noomii, Io, and Cira moved out of the way. Sand took to the air and obstructed their vision. They learned to dance apart in this war so they weren't an easy target together. Cara hid by the Moongate, shouting out weakness in the Creator's battling for her sister and Noomii.

A bolt of electricity wrapped in ink shot out and hit Cara in the arm. She screamed and rolled behind the Moongate.

"You let her be," Io yelled to the Creator.

He laughed and did it again, this time his blast shattered the Moongate, sending the rocks into the atmosphere. They shot far into the heavens, into the universe, blasted through the plumes of colored space dust.

Cara's pale, limp body stood out amongst the rocks that remained.

"No!" Io shouted. All that power in one place did something

to Io. She channeled it. She transformed into the crab without needing to touch water, she grew and grew and grew until she was as large as the koi that swam through the air, flicking at the beasts with their fins. Io had giant pinschers and chitinous legs like swords. She snapped her pinschers, jabbed them out and cut off the head of the disgusting bleeding sultan. It rolled across the Saltpan, blinking as it came to a stop in the distance. The fat body of the Sultan dropped with a thud powerful enough to topple the Eastern Mountain.

The Creator swore and sent his octopus of sand and darkness after Io.

Cira ran to Cara's side. She shoved away the heavy rocks, revealing a barely breathing Cara. "Don't do this," Cira warned.

"Is she okay?" Noomii shouted from a distance, trying not to take too much focus off her power.

"I don't know," Cira replied. "She doesn't look good."

Heavy footsteps coming from the Land of Man interrupted them. Noomii and Io looked up to see the onyx giant from the sea headed their way, a shadow flying at its shoulder.

The Creator flashed, moving several feet at a time and surprised Noomii with a blast from a new direction. His tentacles writhing in the electric shine. Noomii dropped to the ground and rolled under one of the giant koi, its lips smacking and ready to eat her but too slow to catch her. Noomii ran a distance away, magic flowing out of her hands in stuttered streams.

Tentacles of the sand octopus flopped onto the ground as Io clipped them off before finally stabbing the body through and through with her legs.

The giant of onyx arrived, crushing the tentacles under its heavy feet.

Io scuttled out of the way.

The shadow in the sky zoomed to the ground and changed into Gail, and he ran to Cara's body. "Go," he told Cira. "I'll take care of her." He grabbed Noomii's discarded coat from nearby and covered Cara with it.

Cira stood, her heart heavy. She reached in her pocket and pulled out the antler she'd taken from Divine's dead body.

"What's that?" Gail asked.

Cira told him.

As Gail was settling the coat on Cara, his hands came across a lump in the pocket. He reached in and pulled out the bag of black chocolates.

"I have an idea," he whispered to Cira.

The Creator had found a new trick that worked quite well at avoiding Noomii's blasts and Io's pinschers. He jumped ahead in time, a second here, two there, moving his location by a few feet to a few hundred. Io and Noomii focused on the Creator, leaving the creatures to battle each other. Without Cara to tell them where the Creator would be, there were a lot of surprises.

Gail ran up to the Creator, palms out. "I have something to tell you," Gail shouted above the sound of the monsters fighting. "You can fix this."

The Creator paused. "Are you stupid, boy? There is no fixing this. There is no fixing what the old Gods did."

The Creator's mouth was open and ready to spur more hate. Gail acted fast, as he turned into shadow and flew across the space between them, slamming the black chocolate into the Creator's mouth. Gail's form wrapped around the Creator's head, forcing him to swallow.

The Creator clawed at Gail, tore his shadow form.

Cira was next. Running, avoiding being stepped on by the giant creatures, she wove across the battlefield. She dove around a slapping tentacle, rolled under a giant crushing foot, moved to her feet, and ran faster.

The Creator saw her and clawed harder.

Gail wrapped himself tighter.

Cira stabbed the Creator in the heart as hard as she could with Divine's antler.

Gail turned back into a man. His bloody body fell heavy on the ground. Cira grabbed his hand and dragged him away while the heavy footsteps of the onyx giant came closer.

The Creator stilled, his hand wrapping around the antler, pulling. But he was too late; the onyx giant slammed one heavy foot down and the Creator became an ink spot on the Saltpan.

Cira dropped to her knees, grabbed the antler and scooped up the inky slime that was all that was left of the Creator. She held her hand over the top. A solid chunk of onyx fell off the giant and rolled against her foot. Cira picked it up and capped the antler.

The onyx giant disappeared. One moment it was there, the next there was simply the blinking stars in the night.

The Creator's creatures fell and crumbled. Noomii's stilled before shrinking down to nothing but carved figurines again.

Noomii ran closer, dropping to her knees at Gail's side, out of breath.

Io scuttled to them, shrinking down to her normal size.

Cara was sitting up, wrapped in Noomii's coat. She stood, steadied herself, and walked to Gail's body.

The women stood over Gail. Blood seeped from his wounds. Skin was torn back, revealing bone and muscle. His clothing was shredded. There was no breath.

"No." Noomii shook her head. "Not now. Not this." She looked up to Io, her eyes red.

"He will come back, he always has," Io said as she transformed into her human form.

They waited. There was still no breath.

The Celestials in the heavens knew better than to send one plume of dust in celebration or angst.

"Cira," Cara said, leaning on Io's shoulder. "You have to try."

Cira nodded knowingly. Her palms opened and hovered over Gail's bloody body. She closed her eyes and drew on the power she'd used to end Divine's life, to fight the Creator. She drew on that power and pushed it to Gail's body. *Thread the bone*, echoed a childhood memory of when the Creator was more than just an angry father, more than just a resentful creator of life.

Tears streamed down Noomii's face as stroked Gail's hair, the strong angle of his nose, the sharp cheekbones, the lips she'd hoped she'd kiss again and remember.

"Look," Io said as she pointed. She whispered, "It won't be the first time he's died. Probably won't be the last. Stay, and he won't spend so much of his next life searching for you."

Noomii's eyes flashed over Gail and she recognized the golden threads of life as they stitched his broken body. Bone connected to bone with golden slivers. Muscle moved back into place, skin began to grow and adhere to fascia.

Gail took a breath.

Noomii bent to his ear and whispered, "On the occasion that you drop into the sea from exhaustion or doom or regret, I will wait here to collect you and return you from where you came."

Her hand reached out for Gail's, squeezed hard. He squeezed back.

Io and Cira stood at the inky spot that had been the Creator. Memories flowed between them.

"We remake him," Io suggested.

Cira tensed. "At what risk?"

Io held up a palmstone, the same one that had been given to them during the Saltpan War. "We do it better."

Cira nodded remembering the childhood urge to mix the gemstones with creation. He never let her. He'd forbade the idea and she'd buried it in the recesses of her mind. Now was a time for change. Now was a time to do something different, something Cario had always wanted to try. She knew it would work. It had to. Now Io, Cira and Cara, agreed with the memory with a single nod. They gripped hands. Io set the palmstone next to the inky blackness that was seeping into the saltpan sand.

Energy flowed from their fingertips and enveloped the murky mess on the ground. It bubbled to tar. The threads of life glowed and heated the ick until it bubbled and smoked and turned white. Bones formed first. A skeleton began to be built, grain by grain, spec by spec. It had taken Cario days to build her mountain rodent as a child, remaking her father was going much faster.

"There's not enough left," Cara worried as the puddle that was the Creator thinned.

"We must thread the bone," Io said as she smashed the palmstone with her heel. Small shards littered the Saltpan floor before moving into place.

"We need more," Cira said, worry wrinkling her brow.

Noomii collected her carvings from the battlefield. She stood next to Cira, crouched, and smashed the carvings to bits. Noomii had worked so hard to carve them from the layers of the Watchtower, but she had no hesitation to donate her work to the cause.

The threads of life selected shards of quartz, specs of feldspar crystals, fuschite and onyx, bloodstone and lapis lazuli. Lastly, Noomii threw down the final piece of amethyst. All had meaning and metaphysical power of their own. All held memories of the Land of Man.

The bits of gemstones were threaded into the Creators bones. His marrow would always remember their history, the mistakes that were made, the judgements that were dealt. His skeleton was a patchwork of history of the Land of Man; the old Gods, the demigods, the Saltpan War, and himself. The Creator was remade to be better than he was.

The women wove sinew and vessels, organs and skin, facial features, and hair. He looked like the father of their childhood. A father both gentle and terrifying. A father so devoted to his daughter that he could never see a future path without her by his side.

When they were done, the skies erupted in burst of color and electricity. Lightning struck the edges of the Saltpan and sand vibrated under their feet. Eyes blinked, fingers twitched. The Creator sat up, looked around him and paused. His gaze rested on Io, Cira, and Cara.

Eons played in repeat during the time that gaze was held. The air grew thick and heavy to breathe as the women worried they'd made a mistake. They were new to this, after all. They hadn't created much in their time, only a mountain rodent and now a God of creation. It was a jump greater than a chasm wide, greater than a universe wide. Gods had been created by Celestials. And here the women were, dabbling with unmatched power.

"I can try to fix you again," he suggested. "I can make you whole." His eyes were filled with hope, hope that he could finally piece her back together. The problem was, Cario had died so long ago, and distrust was still there from eons of hurt.

The three looked at each other. "Not now," Io said.

Two figures appeared in the distance, one glowing like a star and draped in a layered cloak of gold. The other appeared to be a child, nothing but a shadowed figure in the night.

The group readied themselves for another fight.

Noomii edged her knees under Gail's shoulders and wrapped her arm protectively around him. She prayed that the figure would leave them.

"Who are you?" Io shouted.

"I mean no harm," an aged voice shouted back.

Cira tipped her head in recognition. "I've heard that voice before," she told the group.

The old woman got closer, pulled her hood down and Cira recognized her.

"You were at my wedding," Cira said. "You were my servant." Cira's brow creased in confusion.

"Was I now?" The old woman smiled sly as a fox.

"That was forever ago," Cira said.

"Isn't it always?" The old woman stopped and wrapped an arm around the boy. "I have a new friend for you all. I've been watching him, as I've been watching you."

Noomii recognized the boy who Drax had hired to take her to the Darkmoors. A dark tendril snaked out from under his cape sleeve. The old woman slapped him on the back. "Stop that, right now," she warned him. She pushed the boy closer to the group. "He is one of you. Although, he has a lot to learn since the Darkmoors took him. He wasn't much more than a baby during the Saltpan War." She paused and let the hint sink in. "Don't leave him alone."

The boy looked at the group apprehensively. Io reached out and took his hand.

The Creator nodded in agreement with the old woman, his tentacles calm and relaxed around his shoulders, finally. The boy was someone's son. One of the old Gods who'd gone missing or laid seed to the wind uncaringly. It wasn't uncommon for something so careless.

"This is your fresh start, without the sins of your fathers." The old woman began to walk past them.

"Wait," Gail raised his arm. "What about Drax?"

"What about him?" the old woman asked.

"He is lost. Forever chasing the soul of a woman he loves."

"And?" The old woman's face was calm, her eyes still, her mouth a fine line, unwavering without a twitch or a pull of muscle that might lead the conversation to its next phase.

Gail lowered his arm and glanced at Noomii. "Can't we go get him? Can't we release him from the loop of despair he's destined to be stuck in?"

"When it is time."

"We can't leave him there."

"Why not?" the old woman asked. "You were stuck, chasing the Moon Goddess for eons. You both lived a hundred lives. You had a hundred chances to fall in love. A hundred chances to savor that original drop of desire. A million years to explore every first. And look how you turned out." She nodded. "Why limit the time of Drax and Pina?"

The old woman walked past them, in the opposite direction of the Land of Man, toward the far edge of the Saltpan where none of them had ever ventured.

Noomii looked down at Gail, her eyes wide with questions.

"Before you make me take you out there, can you give me a moment to fully heal?" he groaned.

Noomii bent and kissed his lips. "As you wish, my helmsman."

"I can't row a boat across the sand," Gail protested.

Cara raised her hand, "He's very good at pulling a cart." She motioned to her beltloops. "He has these strange pants with holders for the cart handles."

Io and Cira remembered the conversations they'd had with the Creator as a child. He was convinced the demigods would be no better than their parents. But they had been. They will be.

The End.

Praise and Preview of 'Veil of Shadows' Dark Fantasy Series

Love and Destiny Collide in a World Where Darkness Knows No Rest.

"Veil of Shadows" delivers a riveting blend of Supernatural & Constantine with the pulse-pounding tension of The Walking Dead, unveiling an unrelenting battle between good and evil. Delve into a realm of fated mates entwined in a deadly dance, where bad omens are a harbinger of darkness. As lovers turn to foes and friendships are tested, join the struggle against Angels, Demons, and the living dead. Brace yourself for an action-packed, paranormal dark romantic fantasy you won't be able to put down.

Some people are cursed. Or in Meg's case, damned. She's on the run, harboring a deadly secret. Sparrow, an unexpected travel companion, knows she's hiding something more profound. Unimpressed by tales of her sinful past, he hungers for the truth, especially about the day she killed those seven men.

Meg finds the Seven Kingdoms of Heaven are far from wonderful. Meg's promise to never leave is tested as Sparrow's behavior grows strange, yet again. As the daughter of an Archangel and the Devil's own spawn, Meg knows paradise comes with complications. Love, however, has the power to change even a world-weary country girl, even if it means losing her mind.

There is no rest for the wicked. Meg's determination to forge her own path leads her to the Earthen plane, where she battles personal demons and seeks a new life. But the absence of Sparrow is a heavy burden, and Nightingale haunts her dreams. To make matters worse, an unknown hand keeps unleashing zombies nearby, forcing Meg to confront her heritage.

Haunted by Sparrow's shocking betrayal, Meg faces a breaking point. Caring for an amputee Angel and two refugees from the Earthen plane adds to her mounting pressure. With King Gabriel imprisoned and a kidnapped baby Thrush in her care, time is running out to prevent Thrush from sharing the Nightjar's fate.

Revenge and redemption collide, forcing Meg to confront her inner demons and desires. Will her quest for vengeance consume her, or can she find the strength to protect those she holds dear? In a race against time and her own turbulent emotions, Meg's choices will determine the fate of those she loves.

As Meg grapples with the heartbeat in her womb and the constant threat to her friends, she decides it's best to disappear. Fleeing to the Earthen plane to hide and plan her next move, she encounters mysterious help amid thunderstorms and insatiable hungers. Will Meg destroy the one man who would follow her through hell and high water?

Discover a world where love battles darkness, destinies entwine, and wickedness knows no rest.

"I was hooked from the get-go..." -ABNA Expert Reviewer

"It's unfortunate that one can't predict or be a part of aiding which books go viral, as Sparrow Man by M.R. Pritchard is certainly worthy of such reward ... this novel took me by complete surprise. What I thought was a simple zombie story morphed into something wild and completely unforeseen. Yet it fit perfectly within the world Pritchard has created, mysteries unfolding into fantastical developments. The eclectic characters were a joy to follow and the romance unfolded without being forced."- TheBehrg, KindleScout winning author of Housebroken

"Whoever thought a trip to Hell could be so interesting! Pritchard does a good job balancing humor and thrills— hell, it's mostly funny—and delivering the reader a cast of characters so unbelievable that you can't help but love them." - Charles, Vine Voice

"Another great fantasy ... with humor, edginess, childlike joy, and the frailty of love. Pritchard reminds us to nurture those we hold dear as we root for her characters to have a happily ever after." - Muddy Rose Reviews

"This is the story of being there for someone who is going through a tough time, of love and trauma with strong characters that you can't help but like. Meg, and Sparrow, stand out in a well told tale. I am not normally into fantasy but this one grabbed me as it is so much more." -Misfits Reviewer

Preview Chapters from 'Veil of Shadows'

FAULTS AND FEATHERS

"Tell us what happened," the man from the center of the desk-of-questioning says to me.

"It's in the report," I reply. "I wrote it down already."

My eyes flick from left to right. There are three of them sitting across the room from me; wearing dark robes, their aged faces placid and expectant, waiting to hear my story.

"We need to hear it from you," the man to the left says.

"Do you remember what happened?" the one on the right asks.

Like it was yesterday. You don't forget that shit.

"You said I could go," I remind them, pushing my sweaty palms across the legs of the maroon scrubs they gave me to wear, my Newcomer uniform. It seems I always wind up wearing these things, formless scrubs or jumpsuits.

"We've put out a notice," the one in the middle says, weaving his fingers together. "We can't let you free into the general population until someone comes to collect you."

I look away from the three men toward the corner, the wall, the floor, anything but them. I'm tired of looking at them. And yet, they are my last hope to find the one thing I want. Jim.

"When did it start?" the one on the left asks.

I let out a breath of air that I didn't realize I was holding. "When they came looking for guns."

"Who?" the one in the middle asks.

"Whoever the Governor hired." I look back at them. "All I know is it wasn't the local law enforcement."

"You knew them?" the one on the right asks, his thick white eyebrows migrating to the top of his forehead. Furry icebergs, that's what they look like.

"Yeah." I cross my arms over my stomach and sit up straighter. Everyone knew the local law enforcement, that's what you get in hickville.

"Go on," the one in the middle offers, waving an aged hand with his index finger extended. "Tell us the rest," he beckons.

"I was alone. Waiting for my fiancé to get home—"

"His name is Jim?" the one on the left asks. "Correct?"

I narrow my gaze at him. "Yeah, Jim Sullivan. If you know this already then why are you asking me?"

The one in the middle clears his throat and I swear I hear him kick the one on the left under the table. "Go on," he urges.

"I was waiting for my fiancé, Jim, to get home from work, and the doorbell rang."

"Did you answer it?" the one on the right asks.

"No."

"Why not?"

"I could see them through the window." I shake my head a tiny bit. "They weren't good men."

"You could tell this just by looking at them?" the one on the left asks.

"Yes." They keep asking questions from each end of the table, back and forth. The one in the middle is starting to look as annoyed as I feel.

"So you didn't let them in because they looked bad?" the one on the right asks.

"Because I was alone and pregnant." I look at the corner again. "There were seven of them. One of me."

"So you were outnumbered?"

I glare at the one on the right. "Men like that; you can see it written all over their faces. They were all hyped up from confiscating guns all day. Their trucks were blocking the street. None of the neighbors were outside." I shrug, tired of wondering why no one else came to help me. "Too afraid I guess. I told them to come back when Jim got home. I told them that I didn't know where the guns were."

"But you had to know," the one in the middle says.

"It doesn't matter. They weren't good men to begin with," I repeat. "I tried to stall them. Offered them sodas on the porch, but they wanted to search the house."

"But you knew where the guns were," the one on the left says.

"Of course I did!"

"Please, Meg, don't yell." The one in the center raises his palms toward me, placating-like. "These walls aren't soundproof. We don't want to disrupt the others."

There is a moment of awkward silence as the three men wait for me to continue.

"They broke down the door. I guess it was best that Jim wasn't there after what happened, after what they did to me. It's best he didn't see that." I shake my head, pick at my nails. The one in the middle squirms in his seat. Yeah, they read my report.

"Why didn't Jim stay when he found you?" The one on the right asks.

"I told him to go. When he found me and what I did... I told him that I would find him later when it all blew over. We had a place set up to meet in case of an emergency. Jim was always prepared for an emergency."

"So he left you?"

"He had to. After what I did I knew there'd be trouble. The guns were illegal. Hell, it wasn't just the guns. Those were twenty-five round magazines. State law says you can only load a max of five rounds per magazine. And there were more of them. Those were felonies, each magazine, and there were a lot."

"So he left you there with all those injuries?" The man in the center asks with a frown.

"I told him to," I reply. "Argued that the state would show leniency to me after what those men did. They would have locked Jim up forever if he had taken the blame."

"How much time did you get?"

I roll my eyes. "Here, let me tally up the charges for you. For seven men breaking into my house and raping me, tossing me down the stairs, killing my unborn child and threatening to kill my fiancé, I got seven months in the county jail, which includes the hysterectomy and three blood transfusions."

The man's face pales to a stark white.

"You think I got what I deserved?" I ask.

"Well..." The one on the left clears his throat. "You did kill them all."

I glare at him. "Wouldn't you?"

"What happened next?" the one on the left asks.

"Went to the Hospital. Then county lockup."

"But you didn't serve all of your time. You escaped?" the one on the left asks. "How?"

"Have you ever seen Shawshank Redemption?"

"That's how you got out? With a spoon?" the one in the middle asks.

I guess Canada has a slight affiliation with great American movies. I nod yes to him.

"What did you eat? You were there for months."

"Rats from the walls." I control a shudder, remembering that. I could handle the walking dead. I could handle the shuffling and the moaning. It was the biting into the flesh of a warm rodent that made my skin crawl.

The men look at each other.

"We find it hard to believe you made it out alone," the one in the center says.

I shrug. "Call it an act of God then. There was no one left but me. The rest had all turned."

"So you believe in God?" the one on the left asks. His eyes rise in an almost hopeful expression.

This is what they're looking for here, believers. Well, they won't find one in me. "No," I tell them firmly.

"But you just said–"

"It's a phrase." I lean forward, pressing my elbows into my thighs. "That's all."

"So when you got out, where did you go?" the one in the middle asks.

"Where I knew I'd find guns to protect myself," I reply. "The local drug dealers."

"So you used to do drugs?" the one on the right asks. His expression turns into one of concern.

"No, Chuckles," I say out of extreme annoyance. "I went to high school with them. We all grew up together. Tiny town. Remember?"

They shuffle papers and murmur to each other.

The man from the center of the desk-of-questioning looks at me. "You still haven't cleared up our questions. Why did those men target you and Jim?"

"I don't know." I shrug my shoulders.

"Look, Meg, we want to let you in. We think you would make an excellent addition to the community. You could help us here. But if you want to see your fiancé, answer the questions."

"I have." The reply comes out with a sigh. I'm tired of this.

"Why did you come all the way here?" he continues. "Why didn't you just give up and find one of the Safe Houses near where you were?"

"Jim had a plan. We were to meet in Kingston. I just want my home, with him. I wanted to get home again. That's why I'm here now. I just want Jim back."

"But you can't truly go home. You came here," the one on the left points out.

"I'll be home when I find Jim. Home is where he is." And as the words leave my lips, for a split second I wonder where Sparrow is and what he's doing.

"Isn't that what the army men used to say?"

"I don't know," I reply.

"Can't you see," the one on the right starts, "you're just like them? We need someone like that here, especially a woman. That would be great for recruitment."

"No, I'm not army." I shake my head and straighten in my uncomfortable chair.

"I think so," the man on the right argues.

"I don't care what you think." Agitated and tense, I'm ready to launch from this stupid chair. "I'm not military. Just a country girl from a small town."

"You sure? You talk like them, like those men. You have that look in your eyes," the one on the left says.

"What look is that?" I ask.

"Like you've almost lost all hope."

Never have six words ever hit me so hard. Not even all the crap daddy used to say to me. I sit up a little straighter. "Like I said. I'm not military." I glare at them, all three of them. "I never went away to war. I never saw the travesties of third world countries. I only witnessed what happened here." I point at the floor.

"Shouldn't..." the man in the middle rubs the stubble on his chin, "shouldn't you be more... emotional?"

"You want me to cry or something?" I shout. "Fuck off!"

"Ms. Clark!" he stands, his robes swaying. "The others will hear you."

"I don't care." I stand, tipping over the lone chair that they gave me to sit in and head for the door. "I'm done with this."

"We did not dismiss you."

I bang on the door with my fist. "You don't need to. My free will tells me that we're done here. I can dismiss myself."

"You're in a Safe House now, Meg," he continues. "Your free will is something you're going to have to get used to giving up."

"Bullshit," I mutter as the door opens.

"This will impact our final decision," he warns.

"I hope it does," I reply, just out of earshot.

"Third day is always the hardest," my Parole Officer, Deacon, says as he escorts me to my cell.

Parole officers used to be the ones to watch over criminals, keep track of them and where they are. Now they're used to help assimilate Newcomers to the Safe Houses. They are our guides; they help in the research and the admission process. If there is a family member or friend who might be in the community or another one nearby, the Parole Officer is responsible for finding them and helping them claim us. People like me who aren't a walking corpse... yet.

"Lots of emotion rolling around for the last overnight in the cell," Deacon continues.

"The last night in the cell?" I ask, my steps echoing on the metal platform we walk across.

"Yeah."

"Doesn't everyone spend the night in a cell here? The only difference is if they are with someone that they love, family or friends."

He doesn't answer, just moves one thick hand to his collar and adjusts the white band there before stopping and opening the door.

"Did you find Jim?" I ask as I step into my cell.

"You know I can't tell you that," Deacon says as he reaches for the door and slides it closed, locking me inside. "If we find him, he'll claim you. Until then you should use this time to reflect on what you've done with your life." Deacon tips his head and gives me a stern nod before walking down the elevated platform, hopefully to find Jim.

Needing to cool down from the questioning, I head for the shower. That's the one nice thing about these Safe Houses; they may be jails and prisons used to lock the survivors inside, but there's fresh water, food and safety and something that my last jail cell never had: a shower.

Stripping off the maroon scrubs they gave me to wear, I turn the water on hot. I scrub my skin and wash my hair. Stepping out of the shower, I take the small towel off the sink and dry myself. I reach for my clothes, the ones I wore here and cleaned in the sink, a pair of worn jeans and a light blue top with a wide neck. They don't like this shirt here. It shows my tattoos. Deacon already told me to stop wearing it three times. He said the people here don't like women with tattoos.

Turning to the mirror, I comb my hair with my fingers, thankful it's just above my shoulders and easy to take care of. It's straight and black and a few days without a shower don't show so easy. After almost a week with my hair like this, I don't even miss my old hair. Long hair got me nothing but trouble. Men like long hair and it's easy to grab onto. Sparrow Man helped me cut it. I don't think I'll ever have long hair again.

The summer tan that once darkened my skin is already fading, leaving behind a spattering of freckles over my nose and under my eyes. I'll be back to pale as a ghost in no time being indoors like this, and all it took was a few days. I adjust my shirt across my shoulders. I like this shirt. Makes my eyes look a brighter blue, and yes, the tattoo shows. It's a black quill across my right collarbone. Maybe that's why Sparrow Man helped me so much–he has a thing for feathers.

I should tell them that there are more tattoos under the shirt, a spattering of tiny stars across my left shoulder, a heart on my right hip, and an anchor on my ribcage. They would probably kick me out if they knew all that.

"Dinner!" a voice shouts from outside the cell door.

I leave the bathroom.

"Nothing funny," the chick with my plate of food warns as she twists a key, opening my cell. She tosses the tray on my bed, tipping over the glass of milk and wetting the bedspread with it. She smirks as she locks the cell door before leaving.

"You're an ass," I tell her.

"And you're not supposed to be wearing that shirt." She smirks again. "Makes you look like the sinner you are."

"I hope you wake up with a third eye." I mime an unkind gesture in her direction.

"Third eye'd be nothing compared to what your third day's gonna be like." She laughs and walks away.

That delivery chick is a bitch. If I have to stay here much longer, I might kill her. All she had to do was set the tray down. She didn't even have to step into the cell. I pick up the tray, placing in on the table that's next to the door, and pull the bedspread off the bed. If the milk soaks through this place will stink all night. I don't know what it is about unpasteurized milk, but it smells terrible after a few hours of being soaked into the linens.

I was hoping Deacon would say something to her, if we all complained enough, but no one else in containment wants to risk being thrown out. I guess I shouldn't risk it either, since this is my last hope of finding Jim.

I eat the stew. At least, I think it's a stew. I can see what looks like tiny chunks of potato and carrot, but the meat... yeah, the meat. I try not to think about it.

When I'm done eating, I pull on my clean pair of socks and my shoes, tying them in double knots. Reaching for my bag, I pack my other things inside of it; the scrubs they gave me and a package of crackers that came with the stew. I set the bag next to my bed. Just in case. You always have to be ready to run these days.

Lying on the bed, I stretch out, hands behind my head, feet crossed. Tomorrow, I tell myself. Tomorrow this will be done. Jim will come to collect me and then I can live out the rest of this life with him, just as we planned. And I will finally be home.

Get the complete 6 book series.

About the Author

M. R. Pritchard delves into the profound clash between good and evil, the mystical realms of gods and monsters, and the intricate transformations of ordinary people into beings of immense power. Her gripping narratives often unfold within the haunting backdrop of apocalyptic or post-apocalyptic landscapes, offering a unique blend of suspense and wonder.

M. R. Pritchard is a two-time Kindle Scout winning author, her short story "Glitch" has been featured in the 2017 winter edition of THE FIRST LINE literary journal. Her short story "Moon Lord" has been featured in Chronicle Worlds: Half Way Home (Part of the Future Chronicles) and will be time capsuled on the moon on the Lunar Codex in 2024.

Visit her website MRPritchard.com and Subscribe. You'll get subscriber only content, deleted scenes, updates, special previews of new projects, and book deals.

Also by M. R. Pritchard

Other Books by M. R. Pritchard

Science Fiction/post-apocalyptic:

The Phoenix Project

The Reformation

Revelation

Inception

Origins

Resurrection

The Phoenix Project Compendium Edition

The Safest City on Earth

The Man Who Fell to Earth

Heartbeat

Asteroid Riders Series

Moon Lord

Collector of Space Junk and Rebellious Dreams

Steampunk:

Tick of a Clockwork Heart

Dark Fantasy:

Veil of Shadows Series:

Sparrow Man

Nightingale Girl

Scarecrow

Raven King

Nightjar

Night Owl

Etched in Darkness

Embrace the Night

Shadows of Destiny

Midnight Serenade

Echoes of Treachery

Temptations of Fate

Omens of Darkness

Temptations of Fate

Veil of Shadows Omnibus 1

Veil of Shadows Omnibus 2

Veil of Shadows Omnibus 3

Veil of Shadows Omnibus 4

The Sky is Starless

The Night is Endless (2025)

Standalone Fantasy

Thread the Bone

Fantasy/Fairy Tale Love Story/Romance:

Muse

Forgotten Princess Duology

Midsummer Night's Dream: A Game of Thrones

<u>Poetry/Short Stories</u>

Consequence of Gravity